THE
UNSEEN
SERIES

BOOK ONE: THE FIRE UNSEEN

The Fire Unseen

THE FIRE UNSEEN

Book One of the Unseen

by Andrew C. Jaxson

To Jase and Ollie, my true superheroes.

ONE

The accident was the first time I saw someone die.

The blast knocked me from my feet, and flames licked at my arms. My skull cracked as it hit the glass. Searing heat. Blood clouding my eyes. A child screaming.

A young boy lay next to me with his face half-burned. He reached for me, pleading, and then he was gone.

My vision blurred, and I blacked out.

The world was gone. Everyone I knew, everyone I loved. I stood on a desert plain under a dark sky. The stars were red, and aside from them, there was no light. The sand stretched as far as I could see. It was dead flat; I could run for weeks and never reach the horizon. This was not my world.

The wind picked up, and it smelled of death. I had been here forever. I would be here forever.

Nearby, a figure perched on four limbs. It was human, or it used to be. Wrinkled grey skin rippled as it moved. It had no interest in me.

A face emerged in the sky above, a colossal, obsidian face that blacked out the stars. Its eyes were dark, lightless, hungry. I was drawn to them; they called for me like magnets. The desert shifted under my feet, rolling like an earthquake, and a field grew around me, but not one made of grass. I stooped to get a closer look. The field was black, and slimy. It moved against the wind, of its own accord. It was alive. I touched it, and my hand came away red with blood.

The figure nearby noticed my presence and crawled towards me with backward joints. The face in the sky opened its mouth, ready to swallow the world.

I was conscious again. Voices swam through the blood in my ears. The boy lay next to me, and he wasn't moving. I raised my arm to try and feel out my surroundings.

"The Unseen are getting stronger," said a voice.

"Here, of all places," another replied.

How long was I knocked out? Sirens screamed in the distance. A fire, maybe? The nearest station was almost twenty minutes away. I must have been lying here for at least that long.

"Did you see the reverb on the girl?"

"I did. Weird resonance. Can't see her now though, and those sirens are getting closer."

My mind was on fire.

The world went blank.

Red and blue lights, subdued only by the blood still clouding my eyes.

"Got another one. No way—she's alive! Help me move this!"

"Looks like she was sheltered by the barricade. Miracles do happen."

Faces, asking my name. A muffled engine through ambulance walls. Needles in my arm. Still, somewhere, a child screaming.

Nothing. Nothing for a long, long time.

"You're lucky."

My brain swam to the surface. Disinfectant stank through the fog of concussion.

"If you hadn't been shielded by that barricade … well, let's just say you wouldn't be in recovery." A blinding light. I recoiled, slapping the torch away. "Sorry. Should have warned you. I'm still pretty new at this."

My eyes adjusted to the light. He was in his early twenties; his brown-eyed baby face was out of place atop a doctor's coat.

He must have seen my own face drop. "Sorry again. I shouldn't have said that. But you might as well know, I'm just an intern. All the senior staff are attending to the more serious cases. We've never had an accident on this scale before. Not out here." That meant I wasn't a serious case. Or at least not as serious as others. He kept talking. "Can I try again? I need to check your vitals."

I nodded, not yet sure if I wanted to attempt a verbal response. The intern checked that I could feel all my limbs and

3

performed a few other tests I didn't understand. He tried to get me talking, probably to make sure my concussion wasn't too serious. "Can you tell me your name?"

I swallowed. "Ari. Ari Carpenter." My full name's Maria. But I never really liked it much. My parents were huge fans of *The Sound of Music* or something. I think it makes me sound like I'm eighty instead of sixteen.

"Nice to meet you, Ari. I'm Nathan. Do you remember what happened?"

I croaked, trying to respond. My name seemed to be all my throat could muster.

Passing me a glass of water, he said, "Just small sips for now. Do you remember where you were?"

"Founders Road. The café."

"Which café?"

"The only one we have," I shot back. It was a dumb question to ask. A country town like Ettney doesn't normally have more than a church, post office, and a pub. We were lucky to have the café. Still, I was probably in the regional hospital in Cawley, now, so how was he to know? I apologised.

"That's fine. You must have a nasty headache. I'd be cranky, too. Do you remember what happened?"

Things were still a little hazy, but a few key memories came floating to the surface. There was a teacher's strike, so we had the whole morning off school. I was hanging out at home with Josh and Caitlyn, and they sent me up to Founders Road to grab lunch before we headed into class. They probably had no idea where I was now or what had happened.

I'd been waiting outside the café. Technically, it wasn't a café. More of a takeaway—fish and chips, milk, bread, that sort of thing. But the owner had decided "Bill's Café" sounded fancier than "Bill's Takeaway," so a café it was. Everyone said it in a sort of ironic way, one of those small-town in-jokes no one else got. I'd been waiting for my order, holding the little ticket they give you with your number on it—which seemed pointless since there were never more than three people waiting for their orders at one time. Part of the fancy café image, perhaps. Anyway, my number was 34. No idea why I remember that. Some things just stick in your memory. But as I stood there, it got so cold, just for a moment, and then—

"There was an explosion."

Nathan nodded. "An oil tanker hit a power line just up the street from you. The police think there must have been a short in the tanker's insulation, because as soon as the live wires touched it, the whole thing went up. Never seen anything this bad out here before. Not like this. No reason for the tanker to swerve like it did, either, from what I've heard. Freak accident."

I suddenly remembered being thrown through the glass shopfront and raised my hand to my face. Only a few scratches, but the back of my head had started to throb. "Why doesn't it hurt more?"

"Well, for starters, like I said, you got lucky. The ambo's said you were protected by the metal café barricade. It must have been blown in after you. It shielded you from most of the blast. Plus, I've pumped you full of painkillers. They'll wear off in a couple of hours, then you'll probably feel it a bit more." He checked the drip running into my arm. "We can always give you a second dose if you need it. Keep me updated. The good news is you shouldn't need to stay in here too long. You were concussed, but we've done some tests, and everything looks okay up there."

"So my brain's not going to explode or anything?"

He smiled. "Not that I can tell. There's a first time for everything, though." He saw the panic on my face. "Sorry, I'm kidding. You'll be fine. Anyway, you seem to be making a fast recovery. I'd like to keep you under observation for a few days to be safe, but if nothing changes, you'll be free to go home. Just keep an eye on those stitches on the back of your head. Don't want them coming loose. I'll be back later with an attending to check up on you. Can you give me contact details for your family? There was no phone or ID on you. I think they'll be very relieved to find out you're okay."

Great. I would have to get a new phone and bank card. They were probably melted under a bunch of metal. I gave him my mum's number, and then I was alone.

The boy's face floated back into my mind. His eyes. His desperate eyes. How could I care about something stupid like my phone after what I'd seen? After what had happened to him?

My mind was wandering down a dark path, and I tried to distract myself by moving. As I propped myself up in bed a little, the coloured stars that filled the edges of my vision warned that sitting up any farther would be a mistake, so I had to try and twist around a bit to see the whole room. I was surprisingly flexible, considering. That was a good sign.

I took in my surroundings. The room was that ugly shade of mud-yellow that was big in the eighties. Mustard, but with a little pink thrown in. It was comforting, in a weird way, as my room was the same colour when I was young. Beeping came from elsewhere in the room, but the curtain was drawn so I couldn't see any of the other patients. They made no noise, so they were likely still unconscious.

Outside the windows was a busy street. Well, busy by my standards. At the end of it was a squat brown building bearing the town name. Cawley was more than an hour from home, at least driving the speed limit. Driving like my mum, it would take half that. Australia's a big place, especially inland, and the space between towns can be enormous. Still, that's nothing a lead-foot can't solve.

Mum was probably at her single mothers' support group in the city, toting my sister along. It had likely been a few hours since they'd left, but it was a long drive back. My parents split a while ago, so she was going to this club thing to make friends and talk about how bad their ex-husbands were. Not that Mum and Dad were even divorced yet. It was, to quote their lawyer, a "trial separation," which sounds a bit like a weird medical procedure: *"We're going to attempt a trial separation of this man's pancreas."* Besides, they'd been on a trial separation for three years, which practically made it permanent anyway. Hopefully they wouldn't worry about me when Nathan called.

At some point, I drifted back to sleep. Dreams mixed with morphine and memories to create a disturbing, blurry cocktail.

Standing on the street, my father leaped in front of the truck, his face covered in blood and ash. The truck exploded, and the flames twisted into the fiery hair of my mother, wrapping around my chest, burning my heart. The boy became my sister, eyes bleached white with fear before she shattered like the shopfront glass. A figure stood nearby, watching. He had no face.

I woke in a cold sweat.

"Rough day?"

I jumped and looked towards the voice. The stabbing pain in my neck meant I'd turned my head too fast. A man sat in the visitors' chair. He was older, a fatherly type. Flecks of grey dotted sparse hair, and his eyebrows raked toward the ceiling, giving the impression he was permanently deep in thought. His mouth smirked upwards at the sides, the smile reflected in the corners of his eyes. I tried to match his detached tone. "Yeah. I never got my burger from the café. I'm really freaking hungry."

He laughed at my pathetic attempt at humour, probably more out of sympathy than genuine amusement. I appreciated the sentiment. At least he was trying. "You're lucky," he said and smiled again.

"People keep saying that."

"With twenty-three dead and nineteen injured, you could be a lot worse off."

The numbers took a moment to sink in. In a town of ten thousand or so, accidents on that scale just didn't happen. I probably knew some of them. What if they were my friends? My family?

My smiley new roommate noticed the look on my face. "I'm sorry. I didn't mean to upset you."

The pity in his voice annoyed me. I don't like to be patronised. "Who are you, anyway?"

"For now, just a friend."

What was this, the start of a bad stalker film? I frowned. Smiley guy was starting to creep me out, and I was feeling more and more trapped in here. He met my eyes, and I tried to look defiant.

His voice darkened as he leaned forward. "We saw you, just before you went through the glass." His breath was musty.

"Who's 'we'? Who let you in here?" My throat dried out, undermining the tough voice I was trying to put on.

The man sighed and sat back in his chair, folding his arms across his torso. "My apologies again. Sometimes I'm too enigmatic for my own good. Suffice to say, your world is going to change soon. There is a calling on your life, my dear, and it will soon become clear to you."

I snickered. This guy was nuts, or a super-religious weirdo, or both, but I was too tired to interrupt as he moved in close to me, his eyes glinting.

"Underneath the surface, in the shadows, in the unseen moments, in the spaces between now and not yet, between past and future, there is destiny."

The awkward length of his pause meant he was expecting some sort of response.

I'd tried to stay nice, but my grinning visitor was beginning to bug me. "I've had a long day, and I'm not interested in whatever crazy religious thing you're trying to convert me to. I'm in a hospital bed, my head is aching, and I – I just saw someone die." I took a breath to compose myself. "So get to your point or please just go away."

"All right. I'll move straight to the point. But you won't understand."

I rolled my eyes. My head was starting to throb even harder. I tried to turn over, toward the window. Hopefully, he would take the hint.

He didn't. "Just before the blast hit, we saw you. You have a kind of resonance."

Resonance. That's what the voices had said, back in the café. The strangers I heard in the dark. The memory triggered a shiver down my back. I turned and looked back at the man. "They said that. After the accident. They said something was getting stronger. They said it was the Unseen."

He swore under his breath, surprised by the word. Standing, he composed himself. "You're different, Ari. You have a calling. You're one of us."

How did he know my name? I looked around, straining to see the chart above my bed. But the doctor hadn't written it there yet.

Before I had time to ask, he opened the door to leave. Flashing me one last grin, he glanced over his shoulder. "It's coming, Ari. When it does, you'll know. And you'll find us."

A memory played at the edges of my mind, a dream of a dark sky and a field of blood, and something worse, an unspeakable face …

Something else had happened in the accident.

TWO

It was easier to forget down here. Forget the accident. Forget those who died. The boy was visiting from out of town with his family, his name was Adam, I knew that much. When things settled I'd try and find his family, to tell them … something. Anything really. I wasn't even sure what I would say, but it felt important that I meet them.

The truck driver was the father of Indira, a girl from my school. I didn't know her well, but I heard she was a wreck afterwards. A family of four were killed too. They were driving on the other side of the road and got hit by the blast from the explosion.

My lungs burned, and I had to resurface. I took a breath in the cool air and then sank back down. The porcelain bathtub in my bedroom's en suite had become a sort of sanctuary since I'd returned home.

I tried to think about something else, but it was pointless. The stories drowned my brain like the water around me now.

Mrs. Annalund, the primary-school teacher speared through by metal debris …

George, who retired to our town from the city to pursue painting, crushed by the truck as it spiralled onto the sidewalk …

Aside from Adam, the hardest to think about was Shaylee. She was in the year above me at school. In a sort of sick irony, she'd once told me she wanted to be an emergency room doctor when she grew up. She died on the operating table.

So much death, but somehow, in some weird twist of fate, I was still here. That didn't seem fair. A forum post I read said survivors' guilt was common. But knowing what it was didn't make it any less real or make the others any less dead.

My lungs burned again. The water was cold now. I'd been in here a while, and I didn't feel much better. Time to get out.

It'd been about forty-eight hours since I was discharged. Before that were three blurry days of tests, pain, and medication. It was strange being forced to stay in one place for so long. I should have had more time to think about my weird smiley visitor, but amongst the haze of painkillers, exhaustion, and Mum fussing over my injuries, there wasn't much time to think about anything except how badly I wanted sleep. I was more struck by how unusually caring Mum had been. Dad couldn't get out of work in the city, but Mum, for once, had actually made an effort.

Since returning home, I'd had nothing but time. School was cancelled for the week, as most of the town was affected by the accident, either directly or through someone they knew. The blessing and curse of small communities is that everyone knows everyone. I was going crazy at home, though. I almost preferred the hospital, because in there, I'd had no time to think.

I stood up, grabbed a towel, and let the plug out. I hurried to dry myself before the water started making that growling noise as it went down the drain. I'd always found it scary when I was little, and every night, I used to try to get dressed and escape the bathroom before the water drained too far. The noise no longer terrified me, but old habits die hard.

At the moment, I was avoiding mirrors. The blackish-purple bruises on my face weren't something I wanted to see. But tonight, I caught sight of myself as I dried my hair. The marks seemed to be healing. I paused and looked closer. It was probably time to inspect the damage anyway.

Slapping both hands on the counter, I took stock of my recovery. The fluorescent light wasn't exactly flattering, but at least the marks on my neck were fading. The stitches on top of my head weren't noticeable at all anymore. A benefit of having black hair, I guess. I wasn't supposed to get the stitches wet, but I didn't much care.

Sighing, I stared right into my eyes. I looked different since the accident, and not just because of the bruises. I seemed darker inside, or maybe just older. Sometimes it's hard to tell which is which.

My eyes are unusual, anyway. One is bright aqua blue, and the other is brown. I've read that having different-coloured eyes isn't uncommon, but it's definitely not normal. That kind of sums up my life, to be honest.

I've always felt a bit out of place. I'm the girl who hangs back from the crowd. Some days, I just feel disconnected, like everyone else is having fun and I'm just watching. Like I'm standing outside in the cold, looking through the window at someone else's family. I have a few close friends, but I don't make new ones easily. I know a lot of people, and I hang out with a group, but when it comes to being close with someone, it takes a while for me to trust them.

Trust was even harder after Dad walked out. That does something to you. It's sort of like part of you shuts down, at least for a while. That survival mechanism kicks in, and your defenses go up. Everyone tells you to be strong, and everyone tells you he isn't worth your tears, and everyone tells you that you should hate him, but at the end of the day, you still want him to be there and he's not. It's easy to get cynical, but I have to remind myself sometimes that not everyone is like him. I have to remind myself that there is good in the world. I think we all need to now and then.

I threw my pyjamas on and headed out to the back room. It was a hot night, so I was wearing a pink nightshirt I got when I was twelve. It didn't exactly fit the best anymore, but it was comfy, and it was only my mum and sister around, so I didn't really care.

Mum was lying on the lounge, asleep. The TV was blasting some awful reality show, but Mum's slight snore meant she'd obviously lost interest in it some time ago. The only light in the room was ever-changing, provided by the cheesy romance playing out on-screen. An empty wine bottle sat next to the cabinet. She'd been drinking again. I could smell it from here.

Mum wasn't a violent drinker, but since the split, it'd been the only way she could get to sleep. Most nights, I was the one who ended up making dinner for me and my sister. Tonight, I stopped for a moment and looked at her, my mother, unconscious, still in her work clothes, oblivious to the world and the needs around her. The needs of her family. The few days of attention she'd given me in the hospital were about all she could muster. She was burned out now. When I was a child, she'd been this amazing, fiery, red-headed force of nature. Now, she just looked very, very small.

"Ari!" My sister came bounding in, full of nervous energy. When Skye decided something was important, everything else had to be dropped immediately so the world could revolve around her. I motioned for her to be quiet so she wouldn't wake Mum. Skye had dark hair like mine, but her eyes were such a deep shade of brown they were almost black. In the blue light of the television, she looked otherworldly.

"Sorry," she hissed in the forced and incredibly loud whisper of a six-year-old. "I can't find Stewie; he's not in the yard."

I sighed. Stewie, our weird little pug, had a habit of digging under the fence and escaping. He normally came back, but Skye wouldn't settle until she knew he was okay. I was going to have to head out and find him. Great. I loved my sister to bits, but I was still in a fair amount of pain and the humid summer heat had made my pyjamas stick to my skin. It was gross. Heading outside was the last thing I felt like doing.

"At least come with me," I huffed.

Skye nodded, and I grabbed my dressing gown and went outside. The sun was setting, so we didn't have much time to find Stewie before we lost the light.

My bare feet warmed by the still-hot pavement, I trod the route I had covered so many times before. Inventive as he was, Stewie was a predictable creature. He would be down by the park, on the edge of the creek, desperately trying to catch a beetle. Any time he escaped, that's where we found him.

Skye's porcelain fingers interlocked with mine. She was so small, so fragile, but she was also my whole world. It's amazing how something so tiny can take up so much space in your heart. With Mum mostly off in space, I had become a kind of surrogate parent, and I threw myself into the role with as much energy as I could manage. It was hard, being both big sister and mum, but without me, Skye would be lost. As if she knew what I was thinking, she locked her gaze with mine and smiled. "Love you."

"Love you too." I could never stay mad at her for long.

"Piggyback?"

"Sure."

She climbed a fence and jumped on my back, legs and arms wrapped around me like a backpack. It hurt a bit, as I was still sore from the accident, but it was nothing I couldn't handle. I breathed in the hot summer air, which was thick with leftover humidity from the afternoon storm. On the horizon, just below the quietly emerging stars, clouds flashed as the storm passed over the lake, lightning shimmering like fireworks in the inky sky.

I'd always loved summer. With windows and doors propped open, everything felt a little more connected. You could hear dishes clink as families had dinner, faint snatches of conversation drifting through their open windows, and so even Skye and I, walking outside, somehow became a part of other families' routines, their bedtime rituals, laughter, even their fights. It was nice to get a glimpse into other lives, even if only for a moment.

Reaching the edge of the park, I focused on the task at hand. Time to find this idiot pug. The sun had fully set now, and the streetlights cast a green glow over the playground. I'd never liked this park at night. It backed onto a reserve that was split in two by a dark creek, one that began somewhere up in the mountains and trickled all the way down. The forest here was connected by a thin thread of trees right up to the Ettney National Park.

Looking out into the reserve felt like looking into a chasm where wilderness took over and humanity wasn't welcome. There was an urban legend about a ghost in those mountains, sparked by the occasional missing hiker or tour group stray that never turned up. The ghost stories were ridiculous, of course; people get lost in national parks all the time, especially one as wild and huge as this. Still, staring at the dark tree line, my mind got away from me, and the forest became an ominous blanket of charcoal trunks and murky shadows.

Somewhere in the darkness there was a flutter of wings and the scream of a rodent. Skye jumped, and I shuddered. We needed to find Stewie as soon as possible. I peered into the twilight, trying to make out the stumpy tan figure of our dog. But nothing moved.

"Stewie, where are you?" I muttered, my gaze roaming across the park. The place was still and silent, the only movement the grass swirling in the wind. I took a step forward, and froze.

There was a figure amongst the trunks. Black against black. Silhouette against shadow.

Despite the hot night, my spine chilled. But the figure didn't move. A trick of the dusk? I shook my head and glanced away. The last shreds of blue were disappearing in the sky above, and thunder still cracked in the distance. When I looked back, the figure was closer. Stationary, but closer. He was watching us.

Somehow, the crickets stopped. The wind stopped. There was silence. The streetlamps faded, the light draining out of them like blood from a vein. For a moment, the whole world went dark, but the shadow man was darker still.

I wanted to hold Skye tight and run, but I couldn't move.

The figure felt dangerous. Deadly. We were both going to die if I didn't run.

I didn't run.

"Stewie!" Skye called, and his loud bark broke my trance. I snapped back to the world like a rubber band, and the streetlamps once again flooded the park with anaemic light. Snatches of a commercial drifted from the television in the house across the road, and Stewie bounded across the grass as if nothing had happened. Skye didn't seem to have noticed either, neither seeing or fearing the figure in the trees.

But I had. So I grabbed our dog and ran, Skye still perched on my back. I didn't dare look behind me to see if the figure was still there. My foot hit the gutter, and I stumbled, sure I could feel him closing in behind us. Our front porch light gleamed like a lighthouse through the sticky air, and when we reached the threshold, I fell inside, slamming the door shut and locking it behind me.

"That was fun! Thanks!" Skye jumped down and hugged Stewie, unaware of my terror.

I turned to reply but gasped instead when I saw her face. Her chin was covered in blood. "Skye! Are you hurt?"

"No … Why?"

I washed her face off, but she had no cuts anywhere. There was a throbbing in the back of my head, pulsing in time with my heartbeat. I placed my hand on my stitches, and it came away wet. I took a deep breath. The cut in my head was weeping again, probably from the increased blood pressure. Skye's chin had hit it as I ran. It was *my* blood on her face.

I didn't want to freak her out, so I tucked her into bed before retreating to my room.

The blinds were open, and the windows were black squares now night had truly fallen. Closing the blinds, I turned on the TV in my room to make some background noise. I'd been imagining things, surely, just creeping myself out like I always did down near the reserve.

A red drop fell onto my cheek. I went to the bathroom and looked at myself in the cabinet mirror. My head was bleeding badly now. I undressed and got in the shower, red streaks running down my body and staining the white ceramic tiles, spinning into pinwheels as they twisted round the vortex in the drain. I washed my hair until the water ran clear and then placed a towel on my pillow in case my wound leaked any more.

Then I went to bed, but left the light on.

THREE

"Investigations continue into the truck accident that claimed twenty-three lives in Ettney. Blackwood Logistics, the tanker's parent company, is claiming human error, providing investigators with a full-service history earlier —"

I punched my alarm clock, and the voices stopped. It was a harsh awakening and an unwelcome reminder. I forced my eyes open and blinked, adjusting to the light that filtered through the crack in my curtains. The TV chattered dimly in the back room. I did *not* want to be awake. My hazy brain pieced together the reason for my alarm.

Monday morning.

School.

I sat up, and pain behind my eyes shocked me further awake. I fumbled for the painkillers on my bedside table and downed them. Then I looked back at my pillow. A red stain soaked the towel where my stitches had leaked overnight.

In the warm morning light, my encounter from the night before seemed distant and unreal, the memories unfamiliar but somehow still present, like déjà vu. Had it even happened? Perhaps my long walk to find our potato face of a dog had relapsed my concussion or something. I probably should've gone to the doctor, but I'd had enough of scans and wanted to see my friends. If I was still feeling strange after school, I would make an appointment.

Internal conflict semi-resolved, I got dressed, skipped breakfast, and began the slow walk to school. Mum was still asleep when I left – she was on the late shift today – and there were no buses to speak of in our town. You either drove, biked, or walked. I didn't trust my brain enough to get back on my bike just yet. It's a weird place to be, not trusting your own mind, knowing it might give out on you at any moment. Trusting myself was something I had taken for granted for a long time. No longer. I couldn't trust my own perceptions, my own judgement. I was feeling all right, but last night had thrown me. Now I wasn't sure what to think.

A group of guys from school walked a block ahead of me. Some were in my year, and others the year below. Hoping they wouldn't notice me, I dragged my feet. I didn't want to be the center of attention, and they'd only want to ask me questions about the accident. These guys would never normally talk to me, but they would feign concern when what they really wanted were gruesome details. I wasn't up for that.

I pulled out my new phone as I walked and tried searching online for shadow related hallucinations, but got a bunch of results about people on drugs. Maybe the painkillers were getting to my head, making me see things that weren't there. On a whim, I searched the word "unseen", but just got a bunch of dictionary definitions and not much else, even after ten pages of results. I locked my phone and put it in my back pocket as I made it to the highway that ran through our part of town.

A passing truck blew its horn, and I jumped. My shoulders and fists clenched tight, sending a ripple of pain down my back. I turned to the noise, expecting the worst, but the driver was just warning a dog off the road. Nothing to be concerned about.

The doctors had warned me this might happen. My body was having an automatic, sympathetic response, triggered by something connected to my experience of the accident. Very common, but still unpleasant. I closed my eyes, took deep breaths, and resumed my walk to school.

Stepping onto campus was weird. Nothing had really changed; there were the same squat, red-brick buildings, the same musty smell, the same oak trees blushing green in the heat of summer. Somehow, though, it was different. Quiet. Bad quiet. The oppressive silence that happens after tragedy. After all, this was the first time many of us had seen each other since our friends or family had died.

The bell sounded as I made it to the quad. I was only just on time but ambled slowly to roll call. I hadn't seen my friends yet, and now I wouldn't see anyone until second period.

I wasn't very close with anyone in my first class, but I was okay with that. It meant I didn't have to force conversation. Though I did catch people looking at me, trying to casually glance in my direction so they could gawk at the bruises on my face. Nobody was subtle, but at least they didn't ask me outright. Besides, the focus was really on Kelly, the sister of one of the girls who died. I was surprised to see her back at school so soon. I think maybe her parents needed the space, and she needed the routine.

It was hypocritical, but I couldn't help but stare at her. She looked so normal but still somehow different. People are drawn to tragedy. It's a sick fascination we have. We want to understand the pain of others because it makes our own seem less severe. We want to hear stories worse than our own because it reminds us that we, for the most part, are doing okay.

Then again, maybe it's more than that. Maybe somewhere deep inside we're drawn to death. Like a dog to a water bowl, we lap up reminders of our own mortality. Something inside us really wants to be reminded that one day, it's going to be us lying there in a wooden box. The most powerful stories are the ones where people die. Romeo and Juliet, Icarus, Macbeth. Joan of Arc, Braveheart. Maybe those are the only kinds of stories that feel truly real to us because something deep within us doesn't trust a happy ending.

Kelly held it together through the whole of first period. Honestly, though, I didn't really know what I was expecting her to do. I guess when someone you know experiences something that traumatic, you feel like something big should change. Some huge, drastic, sweeping transformation. There was still an emptiness in her though. There was less of her, somehow. She was slower. Absent.

Kelly glanced my way, and I jumped, pretending I wasn't staring at her. She looked away. I glared at the board, cheeks burning. She probably felt like a goldfish in a glass bowl—looked at, talked about … but never talked *to*.

The bell whined, and I shuffled off to my next class. That bell would continue to ring on time, every time, regardless of what happened in our lives. If our town were wiped out by an asteroid, rescuers would be baffled by the sound of a bell deep in the rubble, still ringing every forty-eight minutes.

While letting the crowd herd me to my next class, I caught sight of the new kid who'd started today. Among the other whispers in my first class, I'd heard rumours of a new guy in the year above mine, but now I knew they were true. And I'd somehow caught his eye.

He grinned at me, and for the second time in a week, I was painfully aware of my bruised appearance. By the time I had composed myself, his eyes no longer met mine and it was too late to smile back. I mentally kicked myself for being so awkward.

"Ari, you're here!" Caitlyn's voice bubbled over the background noise.

Caitlyn and I met in second grade, when we'd bonded while pretending to be fairies at recess. Embarrassing, maybe, but when you're seven, that's what you need in a friend. We weren't always super close; like any long-term friendship, we went through our share of phases, but I had no trouble looking like a complete mess in front of her. She passed the track-pants test—that invisible line you cross when you realise you're comfortable wearing your absolute worst when they sleep over. Like any great friendship, we racked up hundreds of hours dancing like idiots, singing badly as loud as we could, and daring each other to try and hit my grumpy neighbour in the head with a paper aeroplane while he wasn't looking. We got him more than once.

I smiled at her. She danced as she ran towards me, eyes sparkling, and slammed into me with a bear hug. It hurt, and my wince gave that away.

"I hurt you! Sorry! Can't believe I did that. I guess I thought, well, you're here now, so—is everything okay?" Caitlyn is a fast talker. Especially when she's excited. "Like,

I didn't think you'd be here, and nobody said anything, but they didn't know anyway and —"

"Slow down!" I laughed. "One thing at a time."

She took a deep breath. "Are you okay?"

"I'm fine. I missed you guys, though."

"We missed you too." A different voice. Deeper.

Josh had come into the picture at the start of high school. He was a quiet boy who normally sat right at the back, away from the spotlight. He was sweet, but because he'd spent most of junior high flying under the radar, we didn't grow close until last year—when I tripped and broke my ankle at lunch, and he carried me to the office and sat with me until Mum arrived to drive me to the hospital. If you ever need an icebreaker to kick-start a friendship, there's nothing quite like being carried piggyback while sobbing uncontrollably. It pretty much demolishes any awkward girl-boy dynamics that might have been there before.

After that, Josh and I spent countless hours talking about literally everything. It wasn't a romantic thing; we were just really close. I mostly talked about my parents' split, and he told me about his little brother, who died in a car accident a few years before. It wasn't that we really even said anything to each other that helped, but the fact that someone was listening and not jumping in every ten seconds with useless advice made a big difference for both of us. With Caitlyn, I'd bonded over fairies, and with Josh, it was pain. They both meant the world to me, and I would have been hopeless without them.

Josh threw his arms around my shoulders. I hadn't been away long, but he seemed taller.

"You *better* have missed me," I said, but the huge grin on my face let him know I was just playing.

He stared at me for a moment, inspecting the damage, his familiar brown eyes connecting with mine. "You've looked better," he said.

"Speak for yourself! I might have been hit by a metal sheet, but at least I can brush my hair in the morning." I flicked his messy brown hair, and it flew across his face.

Caitlyn bounded back in front. "You hardly answered your phone, and your mum said we couldn't see you 'cause you had to rest."

"It's fine, guys. Really." I hadn't wanted to see them, which was why I didn't answer calls or texts, except to tell them I was alright. Mum told them not to come because I asked her to. All I wanted the last few days was to be alone.

Still, it was good to have a distraction now. I wanted to tell them about my encounter the previous night, and about my conversation with the smiley guy at the hospital, but I wasn't sure how to bring it up.

"We're glad you're okay," said Josh. "We were both pretty worried."

"Aw!" I teased, "You're such a softie."

He grinned and shrugged, "Caitlyn's a lot to handle on my own. I needed you here to help water her down."

"Hey!" said Caitlyn, but then she paused. "Actually, no, that's true. I *am* pretty high maintenance. What can I say," she put on a fake posh voice, "no *one* man can meet my needs."

"Are you saying I'm a man, or that Josh is?" I teased. "Either way, you're wrong."

"Oi!" said Josh. "I'm twice the man you are."

I punched him in the shoulder, and laughed. "Enough about me, anyway. Let's talk about something else."

Caitlyn caught me up on the latest gossip, occasionally forgetting to breathe between rapid-fire sentences. Josh jumped in with details, and none of us heard the bell for the next class. We were incredibly late to math but managed to sneak in while Mrs. Walkley's back was turned. She was not the most observant lady, so we managed to continue our conversation in hushed whispers.

As we filed outside for our morning break, I saw the new boy across the quad. He looked uncomfortable. It must have been difficult to try to fit in on a day when people were huddled in groups, oblivious to anything but their own discussions of those who had been lost and the inevitable conspiracy theories that followed a huge accident like this.

It might have been pity, my lingering concussion, or both, but I left my friends and walked over to say hello. It was a long walk—our quad is pretty wide—and on the way over, I had time to observe him in more detail. His dark, short hair somehow managed to look messy, even though there wasn't much to mess with. His eyes were iridescent green, which I had never seen before.

As I walked, I flicked my hair—I'd once read in a magazine that it was flirty. But all I managed to do was hurt my still-tender neck. "Hi," I said brightly, ignoring the pain. "I'm Ari."

"Noah." He held his hand up in a little wave.

"Tough day to start at a new school."

He shrugged it off and leaned against the wall. "No kidding. I can't really complain, though. I mean, today's worse for you guys."

I joined him on the wall. "What brought you here? No one moves to Ettney if they can help it."

"My dad's the new police chief. Transferred here three days ago."

Tough gig. The old chief had been lost in the accident when he'd run in to the crash scene to try and help put out the flames. The fire spread to the fuel tank and caused a secondary explosion, and he was killed when part of the axle blew through his chest. The cops are close in a town like ours, so it would be hard coming in as an outsider, let alone having to run a department still grieving the loss of their previous leader.

Noah must have seen the look on my face. "It's not the first time he's been transferred. He can handle it."

A young boy, Isaac, glared bullets at Noah as he walked past us. The old chief's nephew. Some people cope with grief through anger, and I supposed the son of the replacement was as good a target as any. I tried my best to pretend I hadn't seen Isaac walk past. "Doesn't make it easy for you," I murmured to Noah.

"I've done it before; I'll do it again. We move a lot for Dad's work, so I'm used to starting over." He smiled, so he wasn't being cynical, which was surprising. If I ever had to move, I'd have no idea where to start making friends or anything.

"Well, I hope you stick around. This town needs as many single guys as possible." I went bright red as I heard my own words. What on earth had possessed me to say that?

He smiled and said nothing as I quietly died inside.

After a longer than comfortable pause, I decided it was time to cut my losses and run, telling him I had to get back to my friends. As I walked away, his voice stopped me. "Want to hang out after school?"

The invitation hung in the air, waiting for my response. Before I knew what was happening, I heard myself agree.

"Great," he said, "I just got my licence. There's something I really want to show you." He stopped himself. "I just heard that back—it wasn't meant to be as creepy as it sounded."

I laughed. So I wasn't the only awkward one. "See you after school then." As I walked away, I glanced over my shoulder and smiled.

I couldn't believe it. Who was this new girl and what was she doing in my body? Did I really just agree to hang out with a strange boy after school in his car? This was not like me at all. At the same time, I didn't really care. This new me was *fun*.

The wind stirred for a moment, and there was a new smell in the air, something rank and old. The janitor walked past carrying a dead rat, probably extracted from the gutters of the admin block. They were always running around up there.

He left, but the scent stayed behind, death lingering around me like a fog.

I shuddered but shrugged it off, trying to ignore the weird feeling in the bottom of my gut.

FOUR

I made my way back across the quad, and Caitlyn practically ran to meet me.

"Who is he? What's he like? He's cute! Did you talk? Where's he from?"

The onslaught of questions continued, and I did my best to answer them all, occasionally glancing back in his direction. He kept looking at me, but not in a creepy way. It was more like he was watching over me. It felt … *nice.*

Josh joined in the conversation, asking question after question, and I shyly mentioned that I could answer a lot more of their questions tomorrow.

"Tomorrow?" Josh asked with a mix of curiosity and concern.

"We're hanging out this afternoon."

Caitlyn swore. "Who are you, and what have you done with Ari?"

"I know, right?" I grinned, and Caitlyn let out a squeal. "Maybe the whole near-death experience thing changed me more than I know."

Josh said nothing and looked down at his feet.

"What?" I asked.

"Just be careful," he replied, his eyes meeting mine.

I'd only seen that expression on his face once before. Sadness mixed with … something else.

"What's going on?" I pressed him.

He didn't reply but glanced at Caitlyn for a moment. She returned his look with a knowing look of her own. There was an awkward pause before the bell broke the tension, marking the end of our break.

As I crossed the quad back towards my next class, our principal, Mr. Stewarts, intercepted me. I'd always liked him, even though most of the other students called him a psycho. Regardless, he seemed down today. "Maria Carpenter, good to see you're recovering well."

"Thanks, sir. I got lucky."

"Perhaps. But it's nice to have some good news. We lost some wonderful students and staff in …" His voice cracked, and the tear at the corner of his eye made me like him even more. He coughed to clear his throat. "You have a visitor in the office. Would you mind heading there before you go to your next class? We'll sort it out with your teacher."

Caitlyn was waiting for me, but I waved her on.

"Why?" she mouthed at me, but I only shrugged and pointed towards the office.

The admin building smelled like old ladies and photocopiers, and I always felt uncomfortable there. As I creaked open the front door, a familiar face made me stop dead.

The man from the hospital.

The smiley guy.

He was standing in my school. Wearing a police uniform this time.

"What are you doing here?" I threw him a filthy look.

"I do apologise, we were never properly introduced. I'm the new chief of police here in Ettney."

Hang on. If he was the new chief, then: "You're Noah's dad?"

"So you've met him already? Wonderful. Such a bright boy. I'm very proud of him."

"Sure." I folded my arms, and he picked up the hint.

"Don't worry, I'm not going to start rambling about destiny again. That was" — he looked around for a second — "a private matter. I'm here on official business today. Would you mind joining me in the staffroom? I have some questions I need to ask."

What were the odds I'd meet the new kid *and* his dad within ten minutes? I squinted at the cop. "You don't have a name badge or anything. How do I know you're for real?"

"It's been a quick transition, so of course it's been difficult getting everything arranged. I assure you the school would not let me in had I not proven my credentials."

That was true enough. Although our initial encounter at the hospital kept me firmly on edge, I followed him into the empty staffroom. It was weird being in here, like I was entering enemy territory. We sat across from each other at a desk in the corner.

He explained that he was here to ask me some questions about the accident; they were trying to put together a fuller picture of what happened. I couldn't answer most of his questions, as I hadn't been paying attention to much before the accident and the concussion had smacked any other details right out of my brain. The interview went on for some time, but before he finally wrapped things up, he paused. "There's another reason I'm here, Ari."

I raised an eyebrow.

"The truth of the matter is you should be dead."

"Thanks," I said dryly.

"Everyone who was near you died, either of burns or shrapnel. You were hit head-on by a metal barricade and smashed through a window, and all you ended up with were stitches on the back of your head."

"I also got a pretty mean migraine."

"Regardless, your survival was a miracle. Surely, you understand that?"

"I understand I got lucky."

"Luck had nothing to do with it."

"I thought you weren't going to start rambling about destiny again."

He ignored me and continued, "You didn't survive by chance. You survived because you were meant to. Everything happens for a reason. Your survival ... It has a greater purpose."

"A greater purpose?" My voice rose. "You think any of this had a *purpose*? What about the people who died? What about Adam, and Shaylee, and Mrs Annalund, and George, and the guy whose job you took? If I'm alive for some greater purpose, it means they died for that purpose or they just didn't matter, and you've got to be one sick, messed-up freak to think either of those things are true!"

I launched to my feet, slamming the chair against the wall, and stormed out of the staffroom. I didn't care if he was a cop. That last part was "private business," meaning the official interview was over. Noah seemed nice, but his dad was a creep.

The rest of the day was uneventful, a blurry haze of facts and figures, algebra and art. The tone of each class slowly lightened as everyone returned to routine, and by our last lesson, we were all pretty rowdy. I think our geography teacher was more than relieved when we all filed out at the end of the day.

I had almost forgotten about my impulsive plans with the new guy when Caitlyn nudged me and pointed towards Noah, who stood next to an old yellow truck. He waved and smiled.

"Have *fuuun*," Caitlyn sang, shoving me in his direction. She was never one for subtlety, and she'd always possessed a special knack for making things awkward for me when it came to boys. A rush of adrenaline hit me, but I tried to play it cool.

"Hey," I said.

"Hey."

We had walked into awkward second-conversation territory. The first one is easy, the third is better, but the second is somehow always a bit strange. I'm never quite sure how to act. The first conversation, if it's really good, ends with a familiarity that I'm never sure how to carry over into the second. Should I start casual, or like it's our first conversation all over again? How comfortable should I be, and how comfortable is he? Did our first conversation not go as well as I thought, and now he's regretting the invitation for a second? I was silent for an uncomfortably long time. My ears burned. They had to be bright red, lit up like a flare.

"So, this is awkward," he said as a wry smile spread across his face.

"Sorry, I'm not very good at this."

"Good at what, exactly?" he asked.

"You know ..."

"Talking?" He grinned.

"Shut up!" I laughed and shoved him gently into his car door.

Awkward moment over. My shoulders dropped. I could relax now.

"I met your dad," I offered.

"Oh." His eyes said it all. "And?"

"Nothing. I just met him." I didn't want to embarrass Noah. Mum had ensured I knew exactly what it was like to be embarrassed by a parent.

"Yeah, well, whatever he said, sorry. He can be a bit ..."

"Intense?"

He smiled. "That's one word for it. Anyway, are you ready to go? Do you need to call your mum or something so she knows you'll be late?"

"How very responsible of you," I replied. "But exactly how late am I going to be?" I tried tilting my head in a flirty way, but it was so strange and staged it looked like I had a neck spasm.

"Not heaps, but it's a bit of a drive to where we're going."

"Should I be checking your truck for a shotgun and a shovel?" I joked, only a tiny part of me seriously wondering.

"Sorry, I'm probably not giving you enough information. Dad says I do it all the time—only give half the answer. It's a thing. But, seriously, you can trust me. Besides, if I were a serial killer," his voice lowered in a mocking threat, "I wouldn't need a shotgun."

"Fine, but my friends know I'm with you," I played along, laughing, "so if you leave me in a ditch somewhere, they know who to come after. Josh and Caitlyn will totally kill you!"

"I'll keep that in mind." He grinned.

I returned it, attempting to be cute. Ugh. I had no idea if it was working. I climbed in the passenger-side door as he got in the driver's. The door creaked as I slammed it shut, and the cabin was warm and musty.

"Sorry about the wheels; the only other one we have is the cop car. Obviously, Dad doesn't let me drive that one."

"It's fine." The truck was old but felt solid.

He looked over his shoulder to reverse, arm resting on the back of my seat. His hand accidentally brushed my neck as he retracted it. "So, this Josh guy. You dating or ..."

"No! No. Nothing like that." I cleared my throat. Hopefully my denial didn't seem too strong.

"Hooked up?"

"No! I'm not like that."

"Sorry, that's not what I meant," he apologised. "So, friends then."

"Yeah, just friends. Well, best friends."

"Sure."

Silence. Neither of us had a new topic for discussion.

Before I even noticed, we were coming up on the site of the accident. If you want to get across Ettney, you have to go through Founders Road, the centre line of our town—and the place where I was blown through the front of the café. But my house is near school—and I was asleep when we came back from the hospital—which made this the very first time I'd passed this way. My stomach clenched.

The charred remains of a telephone pole still lay on the ground, and a huge black scar cut across the pavement. I closed my eyes, but it still came back. Glass shattering. Flame and dust and debris and death, the child still screaming in my ears, Adam's eyes lifeless under the barricade. And a new memory from moments before I hit the window.

Shaylee, screaming, her hair on fire, skin blistering as she was eaten by the flames.

Gagging, I opened my eyes.

"Are you okay?" Noah asked.

My pulse raced, and my skin was burning. I didn't want to talk about it. Slowing my breathing down, I tried to answer. "Yeah, sorry. Just a bit carsick. Can I roll the window down?"

"Sure," he replied. The concern in his voice was comforting, and the fresh air coming into the cabin helped. I pushed the thoughts out of my head.

Taking a deep breath, I smiled. Everything was going to be okay.

FIVE

The Western Highway is a key road that connects all the towns in our region. It winds slowly across the landscape, following the ridges and hills and giving amazing views of the mountains and plains around our town. The sun was still fairly high, but later on it would blaze a brilliant, deep orange as it cast fiery red streaks across the sky. I'd seen it a million times before, but it had never stopped being beautiful to me.

When I was a child, Dad and I used to watch the sunset at Carlyle's Lookout, a spot not many people knew about despite the absolutely breathtaking view right to the horizon. It was our own private sanctuary, and as the cool air started drifting in from the south, we would sit on the warm car bonnet together. Dad would wrap me in his arms, and we would watch as stars blinked into being across lush green farmland, the lights of towns and isolated homes switching on as twilight came. With the electric stars below and real ones in the purple sky above, I used to pretend Dad and I were floating in space, worlds away from trouble, and that we could stay there forever. Even the constant fights at home seemed to fade into the distance, and for a moment, it would feel like everything was okay.

I tried to recapture that feeling as Noah's truck edged onto the highway, but it was just beyond reach, dried up the same as the now yellow grass and skeletal trees. Five years of drought had scourged the land, and even the once huge Murrugal River now trickled across dead hills. As we drove, red dirt swirled at the sides of cracked asphalt. The highway itself was in reasonable condition, but the edges were badly maintained and full of gaps.

The car jolted, and Noah swore.

I smiled. "Out here we drive towards the centre of the road if there's nothing the opposite way. You can really smash your suspension up on the edges if you're not careful."

"Oh. Sorry. I'm a townie at heart, I guess." Noah moved the car to the middle of the road. "Good thing we're here already."

He slowed to take an exit. The Boulders. Of course.

Swinging around into our field of view were the imposing lumps of rock known as the Boulders. Huge semi-spheres made of red sandstone, they were a popular tourist attraction for people passing through. There were close to thirty of these giant bulbs gathered together, each at least ten storeys high, and between them were dozens of walking trails. As a girl, I always imagined a bunch of giants had been playing marbles and left their game half-finished. The thought made me a bit nervous any time my family went walking there, as if those giants would return one day and finish what they'd started.

This was all part of Ettney National Park, and there were signs reminding us to register our walk with the Parks Department, and stick to the trails, and take an emergency locator beacon. No one ever bothered to do that with the Boulders. It was a straight forward walk, not like in the mountains. Every few years, people went missing up there, leaving all their things behind. A few weeks before my accident, three teens from Cawley High had disappeared up there on a camping trip. Creepy stuff. They'd most likely fallen off a cliff or drowned in the river, but it was enough to freak people out. Nobody local went to the mountains. Not if you could help it.

"I know what you're thinking," Noah interrupted my thoughts.

"And what is that?"

"You're thinking you've been here a hundred times before, and I must be a real moron to bring you here considering every local I've talked to comes here all the time. Right?"

I didn't answer. He was right, but I didn't want to make him feel bad. Being here with him sure beat the last time I was here—a school excursion on a scorching day with twenty other sweaty, tired students listening to Mr. Gregson drone endlessly on about local history.

"Trust me," Noah said. "This, I guarantee you have never seen before."

We followed the winding road down into the parking area. Signs warned against everything from lighting fires to hunting with a bow and arrow, and we pulled into a dusty space marked out by a faded line of paint.

The empty lot meant no one else was around, and the sun was dipping lower on the horizon. It had been a long drive, but we had about an hour and a half of daylight left. Plenty of time to walk one of the smaller tracks.

Noah stopped, looking slowly between three different entrance signs, yellow letters etched into green logs with the names and lengths of each track.

"Do you even know where you're going?" I laughed, walking over to stand next to him. The day was cooling down, and I was close enough to feel the heat radiating off his body.

"Just give me a minute. I've got to remember which trail it is. Trust me." He looked straight into my eyes, and his intensity and the smell of his skin formed an intoxicating mix. My stomach jumped, and my breath left for just a moment. "This way." Noah had made up his mind and started down the centre of the three paths. He glanced back over his shoulder. "We might have to hurry. We need to get there before sunset."

I frowned. "Get where?" His obscure answers were frustrating.

He smiled and kept walking, so I tried to go with the flow.

After about half an hour, we reached the first of the Boulders. The towering amber form overshadowed the trail, and as we passed between the giant figures, they seemed to swallow up the trail. I felt like an ant scrambling through pebbles in the schoolyard, insignificant and tiny. The sky, tracing narrow spaces between the boulders, was beginning to fade into a warm orange. Clouds were streaked bright yellow, and I stared at the tiger pattern formed by the intersection of rock and the sky beyond. The sunset was going to be incredible. It was a shame I was going to miss it down here in this maze. The Boulders blazed red towards their tops as the sun hit them, but the light reflected and filtered down, bouncing from rock to rock until finally it came to rest as a cool purple blanket covering us down on the darkening path.

A few trees and shrubs dotted the edges of the worn track, which was littered with footprints and rubbish. A bird screeched close to my head, startled, and flew out of a bush. It flapped up between the stones and out into the quiet sky.

Noah stopped, and I almost ran into him from behind. "Here. It's definitely here."

"If you're talking about old cans and a freaked-out magpie, then yes."

"What did I say about trust, hey?" He disappeared into some underbrush on our left. There was rustling, scraping, and then the soft clink of rubble against stone. After a minute, Noah's face reappeared. I couldn't see his neck or body, and the gleeful look on his floating head made me snort with laughter.

"Come on!" His hand took mine, and he pulled me gently into the leafy understory. Several steps into the scrub, we came to the side of one of the boulders.

There was a dark hole about half my height. It looked like I could just squeeze through. Fresh stones and rocks were scattered around the entrance, like it had recently been dug out.

I frowned and dropped his hand. "Are you sure this is safe?"

"Nope." He smiled, and his enthusiasm was contagious. He stretched his hand out toward me.

With a deep breath, I grabbed his outstretched palm and followed him into the dank tunnel. Only a few steps in, the crumbling walls widened into a dark space. I couldn't yet see the perimeter, but my footsteps made long echoes. This place was big.

"Where are we?" My voice bounced around the expanse.

"We're inside one of the Boulders. I don't know if they're all like this, but this one is mostly hollow."

Details emerged as my eyes adjusted to the dark. Large rocks littered the floor of the cavern, which was about the size of a basketball court and as wide as it was high. Crystal stalactites clung to the ceiling, left over from when this whole place was underwater. Local historians thought the Boulders were formed by some sort of ancient flood plain, and the evidence here of swirling water backed up their ideas. Dust twisted in eddies around our feet.

I'd been holding my breath and exhaled slowly. This place felt sacred, like we were the first ones to have ever set foot in it.

"How did you even find this?"

Noah didn't answer my question but smiled at the wonder in my eyes. "Cool, huh? But that's not the best bit." He checked his watch. "Any minute now. We made it just in time."

Just then, the whole cavern came ablaze, orange light flooding down the walls to fill the dome. The change was dazzling.

A tiny hole in the top of the boulder was open to the sky, rimmed by stalactites that formed a natural lens. As the sun set, it hit the crest of the boulder at just the right angle to reflect light through the stalactites and down into the chamber, setting the whole place on fire with the setting sun.

A pool of water toward the far end of the cave reflected that light, causing shimmering ripples to dance back up along the walls to the roof. A smile burst out of me. After everything that had happened recently, it was so good to have some beauty back in my life. I didn't speak. It would have ruined the moment.

The blaze faded after a few minutes, swallowed up once again by the dark as the sun dipped below the horizon. Lights appeared on the cavern roof. Thousands upon thousands of sparkling diamonds lit up the whole dome.

They were glow worms, waking up to shine their own galaxy in the stalactites above.

It was magic.

I drew closer to Noah and nestled against his shoulder as he put an arm around me. His heart beat a strong rhythm through his chest, and mine tried to join it. He was a bit taller than me, and his breath brushed past my forehead. His eyes caught every single light in the cavern as he smiled at me. I returned it. There was nothing more to do except be in the moment. And try to remember to breathe.

SIX

We lay down on a flat rock to get a better view of the glow worms. It was cold, and I moved closer to Noah to stay warm, and because I wanted to be near him. Maybe I was just emotional from everything that had happened lately, and he was a useful escape, but this was the first I'd felt all right in a long time. He put his arm out, and I rested my head on his chest. "Why'd you bring me here?"

"You're different, Ari. Special."

I'd been hearing that a lot lately. I still wasn't sure if it was good. "I don't get it."

"You don't have to." We said nothing more, and one by one the glow worms blinked back out, bathing Noah and I in a purple gloom a lot darker than before. Noah glanced at his watch, the electric blue face illuminating his face for a moment. Concern etched his forehead. "Light's almost gone. Better get you home."

He switched on his phone's torch and lit up the tunnel as we picked our way over debris and back to the entrance. It was dim, only allowing us to see a few steps in front of us, but

Noah knew where he was going and managed to lead us back out onto the open track. There was barely enough light now to make out the difference between the rocks and the sky, and the only clue we weren't still inside were the stars.

We stood on the path for a minute, getting our bearings. No use heading blindly off in the wrong direction. "How did you even find that place?" I asked.

"It's a long story," he replied. "Guess I got lucky."

I frowned. He wasn't telling me the whole story.

Before I could complain, he continued, "It seemed like such a special place that I wasn't going to tell anyone about it, but then I saw you, and …" He looked into my eyes.

My heart felt like it was going to leap out of my chest and fly off like the bird we startled earlier. Noah leaned in, brushing my hair back from my cheek. I closed my eyes.

A blast threw me to the ground.

My arms scraped across the gravel, and my skin burned. Flames cast red streaks in the air above my head.

Noah pulled me up, his eyes wild. "Run." he ordered. "Now!"

A second flame burst behind us, blistering my back. There was something wrong about these flames. They weren't normal.

Someone yelled behind me, and three more blasts went off, one after the other. They were getting closer.

Someone was *shooting* at us.

Smoke swirled in plumes, and I lost Noah. The flames burst again, one on my left, another on my right. I had to run, and it didn't matter in what direction. If I stayed still, I was dead.

Holding one arm up to shield my eyes from the smoke, I chose left. Another bolt of fire exploded above my head, and I swore.

The flames lit up the scrub around me, and in a few seconds, the whole bush was on fire. After years of drought, it was desperate to burn. Ash choked the air, and an ember singed my hand. I swore again.

The fire spread across the path in front of me, and I skidded to a halt. I had nowhere to go but back. The shooter was herding me, forcing me back. I turned to find a way out.

Three figures stood in a swirling vortex, a tornado of fire burning around them, twisting up into the sky. They were half concealed by smoke and debris, but I could see they were cloaked in hoods, each with a black and featureless mask over their face. They stood unaffected by the flames. It was like a portal to hell. Together, they stepped towards me.

I froze. I was completely trapped.

A hand gripped mine, and I jumped. Noah stood behind me. Somehow, flames no longer blocked our escape.

"Face them," he ordered, tugging me backwards. "Don't let them out of your sight. Don't even blink." Our hunters still advanced—and they broke into a jog. "Scratch that!" Noah shouted. "Run!"

Flames again filled the air. Sprinting as fast as we could, we rounded a tight corner in the trail and hit a six-way intersection. The path forked off in all directions. Noah took the one on the right, and I followed. A short way down, he dove behind a huge rock beside the path and pulled me after him.

The figures stopped at the crossroads, unsure which way we'd gone.

"Close your eyes," Noah whispered.

"What?"

"Just close your eyes and don't open them until I tell you, no matter what you hear. Trust me." He reached out and squeezed my hand.

I closed my eyes. The backs of my eyelids glowed orange, lit up by flames. There was a low rumble, and the ground started to buck. A mind-crunching crack split the air, and an avalanche followed, spraying dust and rock over my face. Debris cut my cheek, but I kept my eyes closed, fists clenched. Sweat dripped down my forehead.

Then the air cooled. The world behind my eyelids returned to black.

"Open your eyes." Noah's voice seemed to come from far away, even though he still held my hand. The crack had dulled my hearing, hopefully only for a few minutes.

I opened my eyes, and sweat poured into them. The fire had gone, and so had the figures. In their place was a smouldering quarry of stone that had broken off the tallest of the Boulders and blocked the path. And strangest of all …

Noah's eyes were bleeding.

"We need to leave," he said. "Now. That only slowed them down."

"W-What happened to you?" My voice shook.

"Doesn't matter right now. Let's go."

"We need to call someone, we need the cops, and you look like you need an ambulance!" I fumbled for my phone that was still safe in my back pocket.

"Ari, there's no reception out here. Besides, we can't call anyone. Not right now." He put his hand on my shoulder. "Trust me. I'll explain everything when we get out of here. We need to leave."

"No!" I shrieked. This was the second time I'd almost been killed in as many weeks, and something inside me had snapped. I shoved his hand from my shoulder and stormed a few paces away. All of the tension and fear and stress from the accident and the last few terrifying minutes came screaming out. "I'm not going anywhere until you tell me what the hell is going on!" I slumped against the rock, sobbing.

He stood still for a moment, and took a deep breath. "Ari, you've probably worked out I haven't been entirely honest with you. But I think now it's—"

A ball of flame exploded next to his leg, burning it badly. He cried out and fell to his knees, no longer able to support his weight. Smoke rose from the wound, and as it cleared, I saw it looked like someone had carved out a chunk of Noah's leg with a chainsaw. It smelled like burned meat. Gagging, I looked away—to see a figure behind Noah, moving towards us both.

I screamed.

"Ari! Run!" Noah called. I wanted to help him, but I froze. I couldn't run. I couldn't move. Fear made sure I couldn't save him.

Another fireball burned Noah's arm, appearing from nowhere and disappearing just as fast. He choked on the pain.

Again, I tried to run to him, help him, carry him to safety, and again, my feet stayed still. But I couldn't look away. Smoke poured from his mouth.

His eyes glazed over, and the whole world stopped. My feet finally sprung free, and I was at his side as he slumped toward the ground, right into my arms. But I wasn't strong enough, and we fell backward, his body trapping me.

"Noah! Noah!"

He didn't move, and he wasn't breathing.

The figure came for me, just a dark mask under a hood. It moved like an animal, lithe and deadly.

I cried. *Not like this. Please, not like this.* I wouldn't get to say goodbye.

There was a white flash.

SEVEN

I woke screaming. It was cold. Three wooden slats formed the bench I lay on, supported by chains screwed into the wall. I frantically looked around. I was in a dank, dim room. A single yellow bulb lit obscene graffiti scratched into the concrete walls. The whole place smelled like sweat and urine.

I checked myself over, and nothing hurt too badly, aside from the burns on my face and back. There were wound dressings on my arms, and one on my face, but I had no memory of treatment. An awful headache pounded behind my eyes. My shirt was wet—covered in vomit. The smell made me want to puke again. Standing, I walked to the end of the room, but was unsteady on my feet, like the world was off balance. It was gross. I held myself up against the cold concrete wall.

On one side of the room was a wall of thick glass—reinforced panels separating my half of the space from the rest. It was locked with a triple-bolted door. I was trapped.

"Hey!" I yelled, wincing at the noise. This was one hell of a headache. Pressing my face up against the glass, I tried to see into the corridor beyond. It was lined with big, serious posters featuring warnings about the dangers of drink driving and other crimes typed in equally big and serious fonts. A tiny square cutout in the door was the only air supply into this room, and it allowed in the faint crackle of a two-way radio.

I was in the police station. *Thank goodness.* At least this place was safe, although it looked like I was in the drunk tank. I'd heard all about the 'tank' from a girl at school whose dad was in there all the time. It was the holding cell they put drunk people in until they sobered up.

But why the hell was *I* here?

"Hey!" I called again.

A guy in uniform appeared in the hallway. He was in his twenties, short, but cute. My face burned as he looked at me, studying the multi-coloured chunks dripping down the front of my top. He unlocked the door and threw me a clean shirt.

I caught it and held it up, away from me. *Don't do drugs!* was written across the front. Probably left over from some promotional drive.

Without a word, the policeman turned around so I could change. I did, and without turning back around, he asked me to follow him to an interview room.

Mum was waiting for me there.

She stood and hugged me, and the previous night returned in all its horror. My knees buckled, and I sank toward the ground. Mum caught me and held me upright as I sobbed.

After a few minutes, when I began to settle, the officer cleared his throat and said, "We want a nurse to check you out. Just to make sure everything's okay. The ambulance cleared you last night, but she'd like to ask you some questions just to make sure."

"Can Mum come with me?" I was still in shock, and for the first time in my life, Mum was the only thing keeping me tethered.

"The nurse will come in here, and your mum can stay. I'll give you some privacy."

"What happened?" Mum asked as soon as the door closed behind him. "When they brought you in last night, they said you were screaming about fire and monsters and things. They did a blood alcohol test. Just how much did you drink?"

"Drink?" I repeated dumbly. "Nothing! I was out with Noah and—" I tried to find the words to explain. I couldn't tell her what had happened to Noah; saying it would make it real. If I said nothing, there was still a chance it was a dream.

"Ari, you don't have to lie to me. Your blood-alcohol reading was really high; they were surprised you were still conscious. They couldn't control you. You kept thrashing around, grabbing equipment. They couldn't even tie you down. With that much booze in your system, it was dangerous to use a sedative, so they brought you here and left you in the tank to simmer down. The nurse has been keeping an eye on you, just to be safe."

"I wasn't drinking," I insisted. She was one to lecture me about that. With her track record, it was surprising she hadn't ended up in the tank herself.

"The boy you were with—"

"Noah." It hurt to even say his name.

"He was drinking too, and his truck ran off the road. Somehow you managed to crawl free, but the underside of the car was so hot, it started a grassfire and … "

53

My eyes burned. She didn't have to finish her sentence. I had seen him die.

But this story was wrong. All of this was wrong.

"There was no drinking, and we weren't even driving. There were these people, somehow they started a fire, and Noah got hit with it, and—"

Mum slapped me across the face.

I froze.

"Don't you *dare* lie to me, Ari, don't you dare! A boy is dead, and you were with him. For all the cops know, it was *your* fault. There's going to be an investigation. So stop *lying*!" This was the mother I knew.

My eyes watered. My cheek was throbbing. I wanted to speak but had no idea what to say. I was trapped.

The door opened. The nurse paused in the doorway a moment, frowning as she took in the scene. Her eyes settled on me, and her smile snapped back into place, all business again.

She ran a few quick checkups to make sure I was fine. Apparently, I had already been admitted to our tiny town medical centre and checked out, although I had no recollection of any of this. The nurse had seen me last night when I was out of control, and I felt a little betrayed when I realised she was the one who had recommended I be locked in the tank.

She asked me if it was okay if Mum left for a bit. I nodded. Mum looked suspicious but went into the hall. When the door closed, the nurse said, "Sweetie, it's all right to admit you were drinking. The police did a test at the station, and I did my own at the med-centre to make sure you would be all right. Your reading was high. Very high. You were so wild, I couldn't keep you in the med-centre. We don't have the facilities to deal with how out of control you were.

You're not in trouble, but it's going to help the investigation if you own up and tell the truth."

I wanted to scream that none of it had happened. That Noah had died in front of me at the hands of a bunch of hooded demons. I went to say it, but the words caught in my throat. It sounded crazy. Maybe it wasn't real. Maybe I had been drinking ... although I couldn't remember that. It did sound like a teenage thing to do, and the tests wouldn't lie ...

Confused, I shrugged and looked away.

"Anyway, you're all clear, aside from some residual alcohol in your system," she went on, kind but serious. The cheer in her voice was definitely forced. "You got very lucky last night. If you have anything you're concerned about, please give me a call at the clinic. And sweetie"—she took my hand—"I'm so very sorry about your friend."

I swallowed the lump forming in my throat. "Thanks."

With that, she was gone.

The police decided not to hold me—after all, I hadn't been charged, and there was no evidence I had done anything wrong, except the drinking. Apparently the chief, even though Noah was his son, had put in a special word in my defense. They would be around again in a few days to ask me some follow-up questions, and they gave me the number of a grief counsellor to talk to when I was ready.

Mum drove me home in silence. Actually, we spent the rest of the day in silence. I couldn't talk, and Mum didn't want to anyway. I think she felt guilty for slapping me, not that it was the first time.

When I got home, I was still covered in dust and sweat, and the smell of bile lingered. Plus, I wanted to be alone. So I waited for the shower steam to warm up the bathroom; it was always freezing in there, even in summer. The dressings were okay to come off; my burns were only minor. I removed them as I waited.

Once the chill was out of the air, I undressed and stepped into the shower. The water was warm, and the burned skin on my arm and back stung bad. My tolerance for pain had grown recently, so I grit my teeth and stayed under the shower spray.

Instead of washing, I gave myself a once-over to make sure I was alright. This was the first time I'd seen myself properly since waking up in the cell. An irregular red blotch covered half my stomach, and I reached down and tried to rub it off, using my fingernails when my palms didn't work. On impulse, I put my now red finger in my mouth, trying to determine whether the mark was dirt or maybe tomato sauce.

It was salty and metallic. Blood. Dried, caked on blood.

It couldn't be mine. I wasn't hurt badly enough to bleed that much, and there were no injuries on my front at all. The blood had to be Noah's. It must have soaked through the shirt I was wearing when Noah fell on me.

If I'd had anything left in my stomach, it would have come back up.

I fell back against the cold tiled wall, sliding slowly down until I was on the floor, holding my legs tightly against my body as the red stain leached from me onto the crisp tiles. It swirled around and around until it disappeared down the black holes in the drain.

When it had disappeared, I yelled, and ranted, and cried. Eventually, Mum came in, worried. I was still naked under the shower head, but at this point, my whole school could have walked in and I wouldn't have cared. I just scrubbed at my stomach, trying to wash off his blood.

When my own blood started to come through from my scratching, Mum grabbed my hands to stop me from doing more damage. She turned off the water and wrapped a towel around me. My head leaned into her arm, and I cried. For minutes, an hour, maybe longer. It felt like days.

Finally, my eyes dried, along with the rest of me. I felt a bit better, although whether I felt more alive or less was another question entirely. Maybe I was numb. I was definitely cold.

Mum helped me get dressed and walked me to my room. She sat with me until I fell asleep.

EIGHT

Days went by. Two weeks, I think. It was hard to tell. I ate, slept, ate, slept, and ate again. Grief makes people fat.

I still hadn't reconciled the supposed car crash with what had actually happened, and my head was hurting, too. I had nearly died twice in as many weeks. Maybe something was wrong with my brain. On TV, people got knocked out all the time and never had long-term problems, except on soap operas. But this was real life. Once, my middle-aged neighbour Harry had fallen off a ladder trying to clean his gutters and landed on his head. The blow caused a haemorrhage that nearly killed him. I lay on my bed, contemplating the possible blood clot forming in my skull and was so engrossed in my thoughts I didn't hear Skye come in at all.

"You promised." Her voice made me jump.

Noah's funeral was happening later that day, and Mum had taken the afternoon off to look after Skye for it, but that meant she had taken the morning shift so I was booked in to watch Skye until after lunch. A few days prior, Caitlyn had come over for a while to help out, but I was distant, like we were separate for the very first time. She couldn't have understood about Noah if she'd wanted to, but she didn't even ask me about him or what had happened. I guess she was either trying to protect my fragile state or just didn't know how to talk about it. I couldn't blame her either way. But I didn't want to listen to her chatter, either. She rambled on about Chelsea and Taylor, our year's newest couple and the talk of the quad at lunch. About how she had developed a serious crush on Eddie, her study partner for history. About Kelly, who snapped the other day when they'd been using the burners in science and threw one across the room. Everyone said the flame had reminded her of how her sister died.

Caitlyn also talked about how her conspiracy-obsessed mum thought the accident was a secret plot by the Greenies to take down the oil companies and wouldn't stop calling the local radio station to voice her opinion on the morning show. And about the cafe starting to rebuild now the police tape was gone. About how unfair her dad was, taking away her phone even though she hadn't been using it after midnight like he said and how now she couldn't even call Eddie to ask him out. It was all so normal, and yet foreign. Trivial. It didn't fit into my new reality, where hooded monsters killed my friends.

I didn't tell her about the shadow man in the park, either. There was one moment, halfway between her cafe story and the phone saga, one moment where I nearly told her. I opened my mouth, breathed in, but the words got lodged somewhere in my chest. I was so close. The only thing that stopped me was where on earth to begin.

And so she talked on and on, and I smiled and I laughed and I railed against the evils of fathers who confiscate electronics. I was an outsider, watching my conversation, wondering if I could be genuine with anyone ever again. This was my new reality.

"Ari, you promised."

Right. I had promised to take Skye to the park. I wasn't quite ready to go back to the park near our place, the one where I'd seen the darkness. We were going instead to the Ettney Green, our sad, brown version of a town park about fifteen minutes away by bike. And I was meeting someone else there.

I dragged myself off the couch and threw on some decent shoes before rummaging around the shed for our bikes. We jumped on, and Skye called a race, shooting ahead of me and laughing at how slow I was to get started.

It was good to be out in the open, and I breathed deeply as we sped down one of the few hills in our town. For the first time, it all seemed so far away, like it had been someone else with Noah that night, despite his impending funeral. Right now, my brain was rejecting the memory, not wanting to acknowledge it had happened. Fine by me. Rounding the corner, I caught up with Skye, who gave me a competitive death stare and threw her tiny legs into even faster cartwheels, slamming the pedals around so fast her feet became a blur. I didn't have the heart to tell her I was barely breaking a sweat. She could win this one.

It was overcast but warm, the perfect day to be outside. I smiled. I couldn't wait to see Josh again. It had been a while since we had seen each other. I'd been avoiding him since the police station, because I knew he would be concerned and ask me how I was, and I didn't want to think about it. Still, he'd been texting me for days, and I felt bad about ignoring him. We were going to meet next to the little park at the centre of the Green. That way, I could keep an eye on Skye but still have a decent conversation.

I had no idea what I was going to say to Josh. I couldn't tell him the truth about what had happened. I wanted to keep that to myself for now, at least until I knew what was really going on. Who would help me, anyway? The cops thought they had things all figured out, and I felt like I was going crazy. I wanted to be sure I was definitely not mad before I started spouting off about monsters. It was like that old proverb:

Better remain silent and be thought a fool than open your mouth and remove all doubt.

Staying quiet about this would be hard, though, because Josh knew me well. Sometimes better than I knew myself. Plus, he was persistent. Annoyingly so, when he knew I was upset. He was protective like that. Last year, he pestered me for nearly a week until I told him about the fight Caitlyn and I were having over some stupid thing or another. Having someone care that much was both irritating and strangely comforting.

We reached the Green, which was badly named, as a long summer had scorched the grass to a dead and prickly brown. The trees were somehow still lush, though, and dotted the park with cool shade. There was normally dappled light filtering through the leaves onto the playground, but the clouds made everything a gloomy grey. Skye dropped her bike, the bell tinkling from the impact as she leapt onto the swings.

I watched her for a moment, hard at work on her usual project—trying to swing high enough to flip completely around the top. That had caused some impressive injuries over the years, but she never gave up. Always a dreamer.

"Hey, you." Arms wrapped around over my shoulders and held me tight for a moment, swinging me back and forth, before toppling me to the ground in a friendly scuffle. Smiling, Josh held his hand out to pull me back to my feet.

"I'm going to win that one of these days," I joked as I punched him in the shoulder. He feigned injury.

"Yeah, you're really—" He stopped. Looked. Tilted his head slightly to one side and just looked. "I'm glad you're okay."

"Me too."

"I'm sorry about Noah."

"Me too," I repeated.

"I guess you've heard the rumours."

"What rumours?"

"That you guys were drinking and he rolled the truck"

I sighed. "Yeah, I heard."

"It's all over school."

"Good to know," I shot at him before rethinking my tone. "Sorry."

"Is that really what happened?"

"Josh, I—"

"Because it just doesn't sound like you. Did he force you to drink? Was he trying to do something to you?"

"No. Leave it. I don't want to talk about it." There was a menacing cloud in my voice I did nothing to hide.

"Check me out!" Skye called from her swing. "I'm nearly there!" The swing clunked, warning she was swinging higher than it was designed to withstand. I smiled and watched her, hair flicking back and forth as she grinned wildly. She was determined to make it this time.

"Did he do something to you?" Josh continued pressing. I shook my head. "What did he do to you? I knew you shouldn't have gone with him. I knew it. He got himself killed, and he nearly killed you too, all 'cause he wanted to get in your pants."

I slapped him. Hard.

"Would you just drop it? Nothing happened!"

He'd been badmouthing Noah right to my face, ruining his memory, and I had to make him stop. I just wanted him to stop.

"You never know when to shut up, you know that?" I cried. "For once in your life, just mind your own business and try to think about someone other than yourself!" The last words were out of my mouth before I could catch them. I could see they stung worse than the slap. Josh was one of the most loving, selfless people I knew. The look in his eyes was devastating. I wanted desperately to rewind. "Josh, I'm s—"

I was cut short by a scream.

Skye had fallen off her swing, knees hitting the wooden box that held the woodchips in. She rolled onto her back, holding her knee, which was bleeding. Josh raced over and scooped her up in his arms. He carried her straight to a water fountain to wash her knee as she whimpered.

It wasn't a deep cut, just a graze, but it hurt her a lot and she couldn't ride her bike home. Josh picked her up and held her in one arm, pushing her bike with the other, while I walked mine beside them.

"Sorry for before," I began.

"No, you were right. I'm always pushing you. I should have dropped it. And I shouldn't have said that stuff about Noah. If you say it's fine, I believe you."

"Thanks. I shouldn't have said what I did either. I didn't mean any of it. You're the most caring guy I know. I mean, look at you."

Skye sniffled a little, a few tears still edging their way out. Josh patted her back and stopped to face me. "I just want to know you're okay. That's all I ever want."

I could tell there was something more he wanted to say, but he turned and kept walking. We were silent for the rest of the walk home. Skye was exhausted from all the drama, and when we reached the house, Josh washed her knee properly, bandaged it up, grabbed an ice pack, and tucked her in a blanket on the couch to watch cartoons.

It was amazing, watching him with her. He was like a big brother or a parent. I had never really seen him like that, not since the day he piggybacked me in the playground after I hurt myself. But this was different, or at least I saw him differently. He joined me in the kitchen, cheek still red from where I'd slapped him. He winced as I reached up to touch it.

"I'm so sorry!" I apologised once again.

"It's okay, your hand is cold. It helps." Grabbing my hand, he held it to his cheek. He'd missed my meaning, thinking I was apologising for making him wince rather than my violent outburst earlier.

"The one time my ice-cold hands aren't a bad thing, huh?" I laughed.

He smiled and said nothing, instead watching me intently. His hand gently scooped around the back of my neck, warm and strong. I wasn't sure whether it was the last few weeks of trauma and emotion, or whether my feelings for Noah were seeping into my friendship with Josh. Maybe it was his constant warmth and safety, or the way he carried Skye, but a dam burst inside me.

I kissed him.

It was amazing, and strange, experiencing someone you know and love in a whole new way, like you're meeting them for the first time even though you've known them for so long. It felt like déjà vu, fresh but familiar, like coming home and finding the furniture's been rearranged. I don't know how long we were there before Skye squealed.

We both jumped apart.

How long had she been standing at the kitchen door watching? She started to laugh, chanting that song about trees and babies. I went bright red and so did Josh, although maybe my slap still had something to do with that.

I yelled at her to go back to her cartoons, and then I quietly freaked out. I couldn't even look at Josh, but from the corner of my eye, I could tell he was grinning from ear to ear.

What was I doing? What would this do to our friendship? And what exactly did Josh want from this? I was so confused, and this was all wrong. Guilt closed around my lungs like a vice. Noah's funeral was in a few hours. He was barely cold yet, and I was cheating on him. Not that we were together in the first place, but I felt I owed him time, at least.

A lump formed in my throat, and I stared intently at the white tiles framing our stove. Josh shifted uncomfortably from side to side. He knew he'd made a mistake, but I had started it. Either way, we couldn't come back from here.

I should have said something, but after a long and strained silence, Josh meekly suggested he should go. I nodded, and he crept out the front door like a puppy with his tail between his legs.

Throwing myself down on my bed, I tried to figure out what to do. This was a disaster, but it was a disaster I had kind of enjoyed. I grabbed my blanket between both fists and squeezed it as tight as I could, wishing I could rewind and start the whole year over.

NINE

My phone buzzed on the table next to my bed and I rolled over to check my messages. It was Caitlyn. Josh had obviously told her what happened and she wanted to know all the details. I sighed, and threw my phone back onto the bedside table. It knocked over a glass of water, and I swore. The water ran down across the table and dripped over the side, making little dark spots on the carpet where it landed.

Hold on... I sat up in shock. The police had said I crawled free from the wreckage, and Noah died trapped in his seatbelt. How would his blood be on my stomach? The angle, the amount—even if the truck was on its side, the blood drips were all wrong. Noah had died on top of me, just like I remembered.

They were lying. The cops were lying.

Mum was still at work, and I tried to call to tell her. She didn't pick up. I hung up and sat on the end of my bed for a moment.

This was big. What I had seen was real. That shadow was real. It was the same thing I saw in the park, I was sure of it. For some reason, it was stalking me.

I picked up the phone to dial the station and tell the cops about the new evidence I had for my version of events, but my finger froze over the call button. I had no evidence, not really—it had washed down the shower drain. Plus, either the police were lying, or something else had happened entirely, something even more sinister. Either way, someone had set it up. Moved me, Noah, and the truck, set the whole thing on fire to cover up his death. If the blood tests were right, if my blood really did show the presence of alcohol, they either forced me to drink it or poured it down my throat when I was unconscious.

My skin crawled. What was I involved in?

I stared at the drops on the carpet, trying to figure out what on earth I was supposed to do. My thumb hovered over the call button, but I was frozen. There was no good next step, none that seemed safe. Minutes passed, and I still had no solution.

My phone buzzed in my hand, and I jumped. It was a Caitlyn, asking if I needed a lift to the funeral. I looked at the time and swore. It was in just over an hour and I was nowhere near ready.

I scooped my hair up into a ponytail, but that seemed too happy. I wanted to show respect, so I brushed it out instead, and it fell across my eyes. That was okay. It took me three tries to get changed. I didn't own much black. The first outfit was a pair of jeans and a black t-shirt, but that was way too casual. The second was a cocktail dress I found in Mum's closet, but that was cut too low for a funeral; I could practically see my belly button. Classic Mum. I finally found a plain black dress in the back of the wardrobe Mum had bought me "just in case I needed it." I almost never wore dresses, so I looked myself up and down in the mirror. I could see my knees, which was weird. I would also have to shave my legs to avoid being mistaken for an escaped gorilla in a dress.

The funeral was quiet and poorly attended. Almost no one at school had known Noah; he had only been there a day, and a lot of people in town were sick and tired of funerals by this stage. The whole police force showed, though. As Noah's dad was the new chief, they were either keen to support him or suck up to the boss—or both. The casket was closed, for obvious reasons, but his photo sat atop the dark teak coffin. He looked younger there and happier somehow. Less burdened. I had never known him that way, but it was nice to think of him as a child, running around and getting into trouble.

I didn't cry. I had pretty much run out of tears by this point. I looked over at Noah's dad. His last name was Hackman—I'd learned that from the funeral notice. He wasn't smiling, not today. He was broken.

A girl sat next to him, bright green eyes smouldering against dark skin. Her dress was black but shorter than mine. She looked my age, perhaps a year or two older. Definitely too young to be Mr. Hackman's wife. Maybe a family friend or adopted daughter. At the end of the funeral, they talked in hushed whispers. I tried to make out what they were saying, but they saw me watching and stopped the conversation.

This was the first time I had seen Mr. Hackman since Noah's death. Considering my involvement, I figured I owed him an apology. As I approached, he turned to me. "Ari. Glad to see you're okay."

"Thanks. I wish Noah was okay too."

"So do I, dear."

There was an awkward silence.

"I'm Rachel." The girl stepped forward, extending her hand and saving me from conversational suicide. "I'm a family friend," she offered without my asking. "You were there that night, weren't you?" I nodded. "It must have been awful."

I didn't really want to talk about it, so I nodded again and looked away. Out of the corner of my eye, I saw her give Mr. Hackman a knowing glance. There was a crack in the conversation here, and I was going to pry it open. "It's funny, I don't remember the accident at all."

"No?"

"I remember flames, sure. But they weren't coming from the car."

Hackman jumped in quickly. "That's right, it started in the grass underneath and spread to the cabin later."

"That's not what I meant. The fire I remember wasn't anywhere near a car. We hadn't even made it back from the Boulders yet."

Hackman's eyes widened, as did Rachel's. "What exactly do you remember?" she prodded.

He put his hand on her shoulder, his voice dropping to an almost inaudible whisper. "I don't think it's right to make her relive the accident, and I don't really want to hear the details either. It's been hard enough."

She looked at him for a moment. Nodding almost imperceptibly, she looked back at me. "I'm sorry. He's right. I shouldn't have asked."

"It's okay. I did have a question for you though." I looked dead at Hackman. "Can I see the crash site?"

"I don't think that would be a good idea," he said immediately.

"It would, though. It would help me get closure. I've been seeing a counsellor to help with the trauma, and she thinks it's a good idea." That last part was a lie. I'd refused to talk to anyone.

He paused. "I'm sorry, no. It's still a crime scene."

"Isn't the investigation over?" Rachel asked.

He looked like a teacher about to snap at a difficult student. "The investigation is over, but the crime scene remains intact."

"That's strange," I said.

"That's how it is!" His voice cut through the air like a ruler smacked on a desk. It had a similar effect.

Everyone stopped talking and stared at us. Hackman turned red, and several seconds passed before noise in the room resumed.

"If you'll excuse me, Ari, I need to speak to Rachel in private."

I nodded and walked away. I had to leave anyway; as much as I wanted to eavesdrop on their conversation. Caitlyn's mum had come to take me home. She was a sweet lady, and I couldn't keep her waiting.

As I walked out the door, their body language said it all. A hushed but heated argument, and Rachel was giving as good as she got.

TEN

There were three knocks. Loud, sharp raps against the small window in our door. I opened it a crack. "Rachel?"

"You wanted to see the crime scene?" Her voice was hushed and urgent.

I nodded.

"It's nearly dark. Bring a torch, and try to be subtle."

"Mum, I'm heading out for a walk!" I called.

She responded from somewhere inside the house. All good. I felt bad for lying, but the truth would prompt questions I wasn't ready to answer.

Rachel's car was parked outside, a tiny, beat-up runabout that barely fit the two of us. The suspension was shot, and I felt every pothole and pebble on the road as she drove.

"Why are you doing this?" I asked.

"You deserve to know the truth," she replied.

"What is the truth, exactly?"

"You'll see." There was silence, except for the rumbling of the car. Rachel checked the rear-view mirror.

"What, are we being followed or something?" I joked.

"No, I made sure of that."

I stared at her. "You're not kidding, are you?"

"I thought they might be watching your house."

I swallowed. "What exactly am I involved in?"

"You remember the night Noah died, right?"

"Yeah. The accident."

She slowed to take a corner. "Except there wasn't an accident. You remember that much. You weren't supposed to, but you do. That creates a problem for them."

"For who? The cops?"

"Not just the cops."

I swore. "How many people are in on this?"

"More than you want to know, trust me." She indicated left, and we pulled out onto the highway.

My hands were shaking, and I sat on them to get it under control. "What really happened that night?"

"Just wait."

The sun had fully set now. A set of headlights pulled out onto the road behind us. Rachel watched them, worried.

"Is that them?" I asked.

"I don't know." She slowed down, and the headlights approached. They were going fast; if they got much closer, they would run up the back of us. I gripped the dashboard with both hands. A horn blared, and the other driver yelled as he overtook us, suggesting we take our driving and shove certain unmentionable things into other, even more unmentionable things. Rachel relaxed.

It felt safe to speak again. "Why couldn't you tell me everything at home? Why bring me out here?"

"There was no way to know if we were alone. Give me a minute, I need to concentrate." She scanned the road, looking for the right place to stop. Slowly, she pulled off the

73

edge of the highway onto rubble that cracked underneath the wheels.

We drove down a dirt road. More accurately, it was grass growing in the center of two tyre tracks, ruts cut by occasional use. We were nowhere near the Boulders. Not even close. Trees flew by us in the headlights, and their bony fingers touched overhead, creating a canopy.

Police tape loomed ahead, and Rachel stopped in front of it. I got out. The air still smelled of ash and burned plastic. The headlights of Rachel's car lit the clearing, sending giant shadows into the undergrowth. Noah's truck was flipped, smashed into the side of a burned-out tree. The vehicle was a charred white skeleton, plastic and steel melted off the body like skin. Black stumps surrounded the crash site like it was an altar.

"Anything feel familiar?" Rachel whispered.

I shook my head. I had never been here before. A breeze picked up, scattering ash into the air.

Ari.

"Yes?" I turned to Rachel.

She frowned. "I didn't say anything."

I shivered. "So what's going on? I need to know the truth, and I don't want to stay here long."

"Come with me." Rachel stepped under the police tape, and I followed her. She walked around the back of the truck, into the darkness. Her torch clicked on. "This'll be cleaned up tomorrow, now that the investigation's officially closed, and now you've started asking questions. I wanted you to see for yourself." She leaned down and dug around in the charcoal. I knelt next to her. The wind blew ash into my eyes, and they stung. Rachel pushed her hand into the pile and

74

pulled out something black and charred. A face, burned by the fire. I screamed and fell backwards.

"Ari, it's okay. It's just a mask. They burned everything here to contain the evidence, but this piece survived."

I took a deep breath and composed myself. "I remember them. They wore those masks. They wanted Noah."

"They wanted you."

My skin crawled, and I looked around in the darkness.

Rachel's voice changed. "You can feel it, can't you?"

I nodded. I could see nothing in the night. There were stars, but their light was sucked up by the canopy above. Even the torchlight only extended to the first row of trees.

Rachel moved closer to my ear. "I hoped this wouldn't happen, but we're not alone. It's watching."

Ari.

"Time to go." Rachel stood and grabbed my hand. "Stay calm, and walk slowly. Keep your movements small."

"What is it?"

"No time for that. Try not to talk about it, or even think about it." We edged towards the car, ducking back under the police tape. Rachel dropped my hand and slowly got into the drivers' seat.

Ari.

I jumped in the passenger side as the car roared to life. Rachel spun the car around and sped away. She turned the headlights off. "The darker the better. Use the torch. Shine it ahead of the car."

I held the torch to the windscreen. It barely lit the path ahead, but it was better than complete darkness. I turned but couldn't see anything following us.

I felt it, though. The hair on the back of my neck stuck straight out.

Rachel swerved as an animal ran across the road, and we almost drove off the side of the path. She corrected at the last second, and the wheels spun out in the dirt, sending dust everywhere. She was scared, even more scared than I was.

We burst out onto the highway. Rachel switched the headlights on and floored it. "You've got a lot of questions, I know. But I can't answer them. Not now. We need to get you home, and I need to get back. I can't tell you more, not now. It might put you in more danger. If it thinks you know—"

"But—"

"Just drop it!" she yelled. The rest of the trip was silent. When we pulled up outside my house, the front light was on. "Don't tell anyone about this," Rachel warned.

"Who would I even tell? If the cops are in on this, I can't trust anyone."

"It's not just that. Anyone who knows is in danger. Anyone you tell you put in harm's way." Her eyes were dark, and I believed her.

"Am I safe?"

"I think so. Just leave the light on tonight, okay? I need to do some things, but I'll be back for you, I promise."

"Sure." I tried to sound confident, but my voice cracked.

"Ari, you'll be fine."

I closed the car door and walked inside. Everything was so familiar, but I still felt weird. I lay awake on my bed for hours, scrolling through dumb videos on my phone, but I wasn't even watching them. I typed the word 'Unseen' into my browser, but stopped before I hit *Search*. I had found nothing last time, and they might be watching my online activity. Whoever 'they' were.

I shook my head. This was ridiculous. I was totally paranoid. Maybe I should call Josh, so he could talk me back down to earth. My finger hovered over the call button, hesitating. Because if Rachel was telling the truth, I could put Josh in danger just by talking to him. She seemed genuinely scared for me, and she knew more than I did about all this.

Finally, I locked my phone, and put it down on my bedside table to charge. I had to try and sleep. There was nothing more I could do right now. I turned my bedside lamp on, got changed, and got into bed. I didn't think I'd be able to sleep, but eventually, I did.

My eyes snapped open. Pinpricks ran the full length of my spine and around my scalp. Something had woken me, but I didn't know what.

It was dark. Mum must have turned my lamp off when she got home. Normally, the streetlights reflected little puddles of light through my blinds onto the ceiling, but tonight it was so black I couldn't tell if my eyes were open or shut. I blinked. It made no difference.

A breeze chilled my cheeks. I must have left the window open. I was about to get up to close it when I suddenly felt certain I shut it before going to bed. The breeze crept across my forehead and down my ears. That wasn't normal.

I fumbled for my lamp, and it fell off my bedside table. The crack meant it wouldn't be working any time soon. I grabbed my phone off charge, and the screen lit up.

It wasn't a breeze.

Above me, barely outlined by the pale blue pixel light, was a shadow. That was the only way to describe it.

It had followed me home from the crash site. It had found me.

I tried to move but couldn't. My legs were frozen too.

The thing clung to the ceiling above my bed like a spider, only way bigger. It had no face and barely had a body. Ten legs gripped the ceiling, and a single dark lidless eye reflected the light from my phone. It was covered in black, wrinkled skin, and two of its legs stretched out, covered in hard shells like cockroach wings. I had seen it before somewhere, in a nightmare or another life, in the desert …

My phone locked itself, and the room went dark. I fumbled for the button and hit it, fingers shaking. The screen came back on, illuminating the ceiling again.

Only, the spider creature had changed.

It was human now. But covered in scales. And it was headless, its neck stopping too early. A scaly black bone stuck out where the brain stem should've been, and the ends of its limbs spread into tendrils, blurring into snake-like ropes of smoke. The face was gone, but I could still feel it watching me. My phone went dark again.

I tried to press the button once more, but my hand was shaking too much. My phone dropped to the ground instead, hitting the lamp with a crack. I couldn't muster the courage to move any further. I was blind in the dark.

The creature leaped on top of me. It pinned me to the bed. I gasped, and tried to scream, but no sound came out.

A finger traced the outline of my face, down my neck, down my chest, and stopped just below my ribs. It was cold. Too cold. The ice seeped through my clothes, through every layer of skin and into muscles and organs.

The tendril stabbed me, a needle past my lungs, right to the center of my stomach. The cold spread, following my veins, pumping into my heart and out into my hands and feet. It burned, and I couldn't catch my breath to scream. My veins pulsed, the tendril pulsed. My body was on fire.

I must have blacked out from the pain, because the cold blue light of dawn was suddenly creeping through my window. Whatever the shadow creature was, it was gone.

ELEVEN

When it was light enough, I got up, even checking under my bed in case the thing was hiding there. I looked at my stomach, where the cold had been, but there was nothing there, and I wasn't sore. It felt silly, now, in daylight. It was a dream, for sure. A horrible dream, but a dream nonetheless. The whole thing was weird, I had been hit on the head way too many times recently, and after all the strangeness of the last few weeks my brain was probably glitching.

I wanted to call Rachel nonetheless, just to tell her about the dream. It had felt so real, I needed to talk it out with someone. My phone was broken under my bed, which was weird. It seemed it had hit the lamp, which was busted like in my dream. Maybe in the thrashing around from my nightmare I had knocked it onto the floor. That part of the night was real. Of course, even if my phone had worked, it wouldn't have mattered. I didn't even have Rachel's contact number. I had no way to reach her.

As I stood, I heard Skye leave with Mum, who had obviously let me sleep in. Mum would drop Skye at school and then head to work. She had a double shift today, so she wouldn't be home till the following morning. Skye would walk home after school, and it would just be me and her tonight.

I didn't like the thought of being alone, even with Stewie snuffling around in the yard. The nightmare still had me creeped, and even without it, there were some really disturbing things happening. I felt like I should call the police, even though I didn't know what I would tell them. Plus, all evidence pointed to the fact that at least some of them couldn't be trusted. Without knowing if I could trust them, there was no way I was going to take that risk. Noah had already died because of whatever this was. I called Josh without thinking.

"Ari?"

"How did you know it was me?"

"Psychic powers. And also caller ID."

I laughed. "Sorry, bit paranoid at the moment."

"Not going to school today?" He sounded concerned.

"No. Not up for it. Want to skip it and come over?"

"Always. Be there soon."

I staggered to the bathroom, exhausted. My pyjamas were dry with old sweat, and they practically cracked as I took them off to shower. I stood in front of the mirror for a moment, to check that I was definitely okay.

There was a black dot on my stomach that wasn't there before. I tried to rub it off, but it was stuck. It looked like ink. I hopped in the shower, shivering as the water warmed up, and scrubbed at the dot as hard as I could. It didn't make a difference—just turned my skin bright red and raw. In fact, scrubbing it seemed to spread it further. And no matter how hot I made the water, my stomach still felt freezing cold.

What was happening?

"Hello?"

I swore. Josh was here already. I jumped out of the shower and wrapped myself in my white fluffy towel. "Just a minute!" I called.

"The door's open; I'll just come in."

I squeaked in protest and ran to my room, throwing on an old pair of jeans and the first t-shirt I could find.

"Ari?" The door to my room opened. I had dressed just in time.

"How about you knock next time?" I snapped, breathing hard.

"I did. I was knocking at the front door for like ten minutes. I was getting worried."

"Well, just. Yeah." I had nothing.

"Nice shirt."

I looked down. I had thrown on a joke T-shirt Josh had given me last year. He'd made them for me and Caitlyn. It was custom printed with a photo of his face, and the words "Josh's groupie" on it.

I grinned. "Pretty much your dream girl right here."

He smiled and said nothing. My cheeks went hot. What a dumb thing to say after yesterday.

"So, what do you wanna do?" he asked.

"Nothing."

"Sounds fun." He paused. "Are you okay? You seem … different."

I wanted to tell him what had happened to me, what I had experienced the night before. I wanted to tell him about my nightmare and Noah and the cover-up and the accident scene that made no sense, but with him here it all suddenly felt so far away, like it had happened to someone else. Telling him now would make it real. I wasn't ready for that.

I shrugged. "Yeah, just tired."

We spent the day watching old cartoon reruns from our childhood that made me nostalgic for the good old days. So much had changed recently that my childhood felt like someone else's life. Sitting there with Josh reminded me of one time, before Dad left, when Mum and I were sitting on the couch together. She was feeding baby Skye, and this silly cartoon came on. I don't even remember what it was now, but Mum thought it was hysterical. She laughed like crazy, and I laughed with her. We felt so connected then, like she really understood me. Baby Skye even managed a giggle. Dad had come home and joined us, and soon we were all in stitches, not so much from the cartoon anymore but from laughing at each other, with each other. Together. It was nice to remember that moment, before the world got so complicated.

The front door opened. Skye was home from school. The day had gone quickly.

The afternoon grew cloudy and cold, and the warm breeze morphed into a chill that whistled through our back screen door. It had changed fast. Really fast. Years ago, Dad had put in a small black fireplace so we could save money on heating during the winter. We had stacks of trees in our backyard; it was a deep yard with five giant grey ghost gums. We used to pick up fallen branches for the fireplace, but these days Mum would get wood delivered and cut up into logs.

I ducked outside to collect some from the pile out back, watching for falling branches from the gums as their leaves thrashed wildly through the air, frenzied by the frantic weather. The birds were quiet now, hiding in that mysterious place they disappear to before it rains. The sun was setting, and the clouds further darkened the shadows under the trees, deep purple mixing with green and brown and turning them all the same shade of murky grey. The air crackled. A storm was coming.

I was in the middle of grabbing my last handful of kindling when the wind disappeared. There was silence, just for a moment. I thought I heard a sound and slowly turned to face it.

Nothing.

But something. The wind picked back up, and I ran to the house without looking behind me, in case something was there. Sprinting up the porch stairs, I dashed inside and slammed the door behind me, panting. Josh saw the wild look on my face and ran to look outside through a crack in the curtains. After a moment, I dared to join him.

There was nothing in the backyard but trees and a very startled owl nestled on a crossbeam under the porch roof.

"Sorry," I said, embarrassed. "I spooked myself."

Josh held me close, his hand on the back of my neck, and I felt safe again. Skye seemed oblivious as she continued playing with some chipped wooden toys Josh had found during a clean-out of his grandparents' place. The toys looked really old, and paint was coming off in places, but to Skye, they were brand new. She had never seen wooden toys before. If you wait long enough, everything old is new again.

We defrosted some sketchy-looking lasagne from the freezer and had a quiet meal. After, Josh got the fire going, and it soon began to warm the house. We sat in silence, although the night was anything but quiet. The wind crashed through the canopy outside, rain smashed against the window, the fire crackled and hissed where the firewood hadn't quite dried, and Skye clunked the toys together as she played in front of the fireplace.

There was nothing good on TV, so Josh and I just sat next to each other on the couch. I nestled into his arm, watching the flames and Skye. They were strangely similar, Skye and the fire. Both so alive, so untamed and unpredictable. She jumped up and twirled around, her skin glowing red with light from the flames, hair spinning in dark circles around her. She was the fire itself, a glowing ember, a dancing flame.

I can't remember falling asleep, but when I woke, the fire was low. Josh was slumped across me, and Skye was curled up on the rug in front of the fire like a cat. I gently rolled Josh off me, and he grunted in protest. Skye was light, and it was easy to carry her to her room. She was already in her pyjamas, so I laid her straight in bed. She stirred. "Is Mum home?"

"No, not yet," I replied. Was she ever?

"I want to stay up until Mum's home."

"She's doing an overnight. She's not going to be home until morning."

Skye started to cry quietly. Not a tantrum, not even a sob. Just slow, soft breathing and a tear trickling down her red cheek.

"It's okay, I'm here." I held her close.

"I know. I missed you when you were in hospital."

"I missed you too."

"One day, you're going to leave, aren't you?" she asked.

"What makes you say that?"

"Mum told me one day you're going to go off to the city and you're going to leave me."

"Well, I might … But I won't be gone forever."

"That's what Dad said."

I swallowed the lump forming in my throat. I'd always thought Dad leaving had affected me more than it had my sister. But I guess it doesn't matter how young you are, it still blows your world apart. There was nothing I could say now. Any words, and I would have lost the plot completely.

"I love you, Ari." Her eyes were still red, but a smile pushed its way through.

"You too, little one." I kissed her on the forehead and turned out the light. The glowing nightlight at the end of her room cast star-shaped patterns on her walls.

Back in my own room, I got changed and flopped onto my bed, feeling more alone than I ever had before.

TWELVE

It felt like only moments later that I woke to the sound of Skye calling my name from her room. As I sighed and dragged myself out of bed, I checked the clock. It was just after three.

"Ari!"

She must have had a bad dream. As I trudged down the hall, something felt off. I put it down to the questionable lasagne and opened her door. Skye was sitting up in bed, sweat pouring down her face.

"Bad dream?" I asked.

She nodded.

"It's just me and you here, and Josh out on the couch. You had a nightmare. It's all okay." I walked over and sat on her bed, stroking her hair for a while. That always calmed her down. It calmed me too. Even now, when I was still creeped out from the night before.

The stars from her nightlight twinkled on the walls around us, and we both began to breathe a little easier. Skye drifted back to sleep.

"Thank goodness for nightlights," I murmured under my breath and gently stood to leave.

Just as I reached the doorway, there was a sharp gasp. I turned, and Skye was again sitting bolt upright in bed. Her eyes were wide, and she whimpered. "There's something here."

Her blanket ripped off the bed, and her body was thrown into the air. She hung like a doll, suspended from her stomach by a long black shadow, as black tendrils seeped from inside her mattress like fog. Her head turned to me, and her eyes bled smoke. I froze, heart thumping. I wanted to run, but I couldn't leave her.

She spoke, but it wasn't her voice.

"*PUELLA ELECTIS EMPROBAS AETERNO.*"

There was something else inside her.

The stars from the nightlight shrunk. Darkness leaked out of every wall, soaking up light and sound and feeling. I wanted to run, but I couldn't leave Skye, not like this.

Her little body slammed back down on her bed, the tendrils gone. For now. She was breathing but still seemed to be unconscious, so I grabbed her and ran out the door.

Into an inferno.

The hallway was on fire. But I didn't stop. My feet blistered as I reached the kitchen, and I turned to see a ball of flame forming in the air behind me. The orb exploded, blowing me off my feet and into our island bench. My rib cracked against it, but I kept hold of Skye and pulled myself up. Around us, darkness leaked through the walls. It was bleeding through the paint, stretching towards me, trying to grab hold of my arms, my hair, any part of me that brushed close enough. It was hungry.

I stumbled out to the front room as smoke filled the house. Something stopped me, and instead of opening the front door, I glanced through the tiny window next to it. Outside were nine forms dressed in the same robes as the demon figures from the night Noah died. If I ran out the front door, I knew I would be killed instantly, smoke blasting out of my mouth like it did Noah's. I had to take the back door.

As I hoisted Skye higher over my shoulder, the two edges of my broken rib ground together. I winced but stumbled towards the back door as my lungs filled with smoke. A dark coil reached down towards me from above. The walls were on fire and the ceiling was black, but it wasn't from smoke. It was covered with the darkness. Slimy, crawling darkness, like the one from the dream. The dream I now knew was real.

Black snakes reached for me, dripping from the ceiling like spiders from a nest. I froze as they came perilously close. The chill ran across my scalp and rippled through my hair as one made contact. I had the horrible feeling it *liked* me.

Warmth. In my hand. A wonderful warmth, alive and strong.

Josh.

His hand in mine unglued my frozen body. My feet moved as he led the way to the back door. The tendril lost its grip, but others stretched for me, reaching to pull me back. One snaked towards my head, and I ducked. A huge section of ceiling collapsed onto the couch behind us, sending sparks and ashes into the air. Tripping over the doorjamb, I stumbled outside, smacking my shoulder into the porch railing. The stairs were hard to navigate with Skye's added weight, but I made it down and across the yard, careful not to be seen from the front of the house.

I felt safer under the trees at the back of our yard, although I knew we wouldn't be for long. The only way out was over the fence into the yard behind ours—the Johnsons'. They were away on holidays, and thankfully, they took their huge, angry dog Basher with them. Josh took Skye, and I climbed up and checked over the fence. The Johnsons normally had a trampoline pushed up against the fence on their side, and today was no exception. I jumped over the top, landing safely on the trampoline surface, and Josh hoisted Skye to me. I lay her down on the canvas for a moment to catch my breath. Josh leaped over too and nearly overshot altogether. I stood, the canvas rolling under my feet like a boat in a storm. The Johnson's yard was on the higher side of the street, so from here I could see over the fence, and our roof, and get a good view of the road.

Our house was soaked in flame. There would be nothing left. A section of roof tiles collapsed, sending up a plume of smoke punctuated by spark and fire. The extra burst of light allowed me to see the whole picture.

There were more than twenty cloaked figures standing on our street, although they clung to the shadows so it would be hard to see them if you didn't know to look.

As lights came on in houses up and down our street, the figures made their move. Some disappeared into the shadows, and others made their way down either side of our house toward the backyard, their flares still lighting up the house. They were trying to ensure I burned to death.

The fire bled an inky darkness that snaked along the ground of our yard. I felt it searching. It was looking for me.

"What the hell is that?" Josh whispered.

"I don't know." My broken rib made it hard to talk. "It came for me last night. And I've seen it once before, at the park."

"It's after you."

"No kidding."

"What about the guys in drag?"

"I don't know. They were there when Noah died. They killed him."

Josh swore just as one of the tall, cloaked figures made his way to the backyard, darkness curling around his feet like the tail of a cat. He pulled back his hood to get a better look at the destruction, revealing a familiar face. The face I saw when I woke in the hospital after the accident.

Nathan. The medical intern who treated me. He turned toward us, and his eyes disappeared into dark shadows.

"She's over here!" He sprinted towards the fence, the others following close behind. A ball of flame lit up our yard as I grabbed Skye, spun around, and tore through the Johnsons' side gate, out towards their street. The path here was made of pebbles, and I slipped and stumbled, barely catching Skye as she bounced around in my arms.

Seeing me struggle, Josh grabbed Skye and threw her over his shoulder as we made it to the front yard. The Johnsons' fence out front was high, with wrought-iron spikes; we had to use the gate. Josh swore again as he reached the huge barred entrance. There was a lock on the gate, probably to keep the house safe while the Johnsons were away. I cursed their paranoia. We were trapped. I closed my eyes and waited, lungs heaving.

"Ari, what the hell are you doing? Move!" Josh yelled. He put Skye on the ground while he wrestled with the lock. A ball of flame flickered in the air above my head, lighting the scene like a strobe, freezing each moment in time as it sparked on and off. I turned around.

Nathan was around the corner of the house now and almost on top of us. Josh grabbed a fallen tree branch, ready to fight.

The light grew, still flickering off and on. Skye was sprawled flat, knocked out by whatever had grabbed her in her room. In the strobe light, I saw Nathan knock Josh to the ground, his hands around his neck. The light sparked again—Nathan pressed on Josh's throat. I had to do something.

There was a spark. A blast. Metal grinding metal. Josh drove his thumb into Nathan's left eye, spurting jellied mess over his face. Nathan screamed and rolled on the ground, blood dripping off his cheek. I felt sick.

"Come with me. Quick."

I spun around. Hackman stood in the open gate behind me. The lock was now a glowing, molten blob. Josh stood to face us, his hands soaked red. He looked from me, to Hackman, and back again. The cop car was parked out front, headlights blazing through the dark, engine running. We both knew this was not the time to ask questions.

Josh scooped up Skye, and we both dove inside the car. Hackman slammed his door shut and hit the pedal as more cloaked figures ran into the Johnsons' yard. The wheels screeched as Hackman floored it. A light exploded on the road ahead, and Hackman swerved to miss it, clipping a parked green van. Lucky I'd put my seatbelt on. The car stalled from the collision, and Hackman tried to restart it, but the engine only coughed.

I twisted to look out the rear window. The sky was streaked with smoke, and the flames from my house were above the trees now. A dark shadow spread across the ground in front of the Johnsons' house. Josh was wheezing from Nathan's choke-hold. The patrol car's engine coughed again.

"Come on!" I screamed.

Nathan's face appeared at the window. Bloodied and snarling, he stared us down with his right eye, the other shut tight but bleeding badly. Hackman turned the key again, but the engine only hacked like a smoker. The back door ripped open, and Nathan's arms clawed into Skye's legs. Screaming, I held her tight, but I wasn't strong enough. By the time Josh saw, she was gone.

Nathan had her.

I tried to leap from the car, but the engine cleared its throat and lurched forward, locking my seatbelt. I couldn't get it undone.

"Stop, Hackman!" I screamed. "Stop!"

He didn't, and the tyres screamed on the tarmac.

There was a white flash.

THIRTEEN

It was dark. Four arms pinned me down, and over the ringing in my ears, I could just barely hear a man's voice barking orders to keep me still.

"Let me go!" I bucked against the restraints on my hands and feet. I couldn't see anything.

"Ari, you're safe. You need to calm down." A hand pressed gently on my shoulder. I tried to bite it.

"Take this blindfold off!" If I could just *see* my surroundings and captors, I would have a chance to escape. "At least let me see you!"

"You aren't wearing a blindfold, Ari." The voice sounded the tiniest bit sympathetic. "You're blind."

I froze. The heat drained out of my body. I lost the will to fight.

"Only temporarily, we hope," the voice added.

"Who are you?"

"I'm sorry, I thought you'd recognise my voice, but I forgot about the hearing loss. Your ears will be fine soon. It's me, Noah's father. I apologise for the restraints, but you went off the deep end. You wouldn't stop screaming, and you were going to hurt yourself or someone else. Not for the first time, either, mind you. At least this time we don't have to put you in a cell." He paused. "Do you think if we loosen the restraints you can refrain from thrashing about quite so wildly? There's a lot of expensive equipment around you that we'd rather like to keep."

I paused for a moment, then nodded. The bonds around my wrists and feet were removed. My ribs hurt, but not as badly as they should have. Whatever they'd done, it had helped my injuries.

"Skye?" I asked.

"Alive, we think."

"Why didn't you stop? Why didn't you let me save her?" I spoke in a whisper. I had no energy to yell.

"We were outnumbered as it was. If I'd stopped, we all would have died. I had to keep us safe. I had to keep *you* safe. As it was, you had some rather terrible bruising on your brain. Tends to happen when you get knocked unconscious as many times as you have. Fortunately, one of my colleagues is quite talented in medicine of an experimental nature. The bruising is taken care of. It would be a shame to rescue you, only for you to end up a vegetable."

"They've got her." The shadow people had taken my little sister, and somehow it was because of me.

"They do," Hackman said gently. "But we can get her back."

"Josh?"

"Recovering in another room."

"I want to see him."

"You will, when you're both ready. In the meantime, you need to rest. We're working on a way to get your sister back, and you'll need to be ready when the time comes." Hackman placed a hand on my shoulder again. This time I let it stay. "I'm sure you have a lot of questions." I could hear the smile in his voice. It only made me angry. "But the most important thing to know right now is that you're safe, and we're on your side."

"Does my mum know where I am?"

"Honestly, we aren't sure where she is," he said. "She wasn't at work and hasn't returned to your house. We have people out looking for her, but we think she's been taken too. I'm sorry."

I shook my head but was too numb to cry.

"Do you want some time alone?"

I nodded. Hackman's hand left my shoulder, and several pairs of feet shuffled out of the room, followed by a short click as the door shut.

It's strange how darkness removes the perception of time. With no way to know if minutes had passed or hours, I couldn't tell how long it was before coloured blobs congealed in front of my eyes. My vision was returning.

Slowly, I made out the room around me. The ceiling and walls were formed from rock, but whether the room was natural or etched out by hand was difficult to tell. At least the damp smell made sense now. I was in a cave of some kind. My bed was made of green vinyl, with aluminium struts forming a support base. A few medical-looking machines sat around me, lights blinking. I was tired of waking up in strange, cold rooms like this.

A fluorescent lamp hung from the ceiling, and the whole place looked military. The most imposing feature was the solid steel door held shut by an enormous metal bar that appeared to lock from the outside. A small glass window sat in the door at head height, but the glass looked pretty thick and it was covered in bars. I was trapped.

The ringing in my ears finally subsided enough for me to make out beeps from the machines around me and hear conversations taking place outside in the corridor. A dripping sound slipped under the door from somewhere in the hallway. This wasn't the police station, and it wasn't a hospital. Maybe it was a mental ward. That would explain an awful lot. Maybe I had cracked. Maybe, since Noah's accident, I'd been losing my mind, remembering things that weren't there and hallucinating awful creatures. It was almost comforting to think maybe the whole thing wasn't real.

There was a small plastic dome on the ceiling in a corner of the room. A red light blinked inside its dark shell. They were watching me.

I tried to sit up and managed to slip off the edge of the bed. That's when I became conscious of my clothing. Gone were my smoke and dust-stained pyjamas, replaced in my sleep by a grey hospital gown that revealed far more of my back half than I was comfortable with. Facing the camera, I re-tied the back, trying to get it as tight as possible so I felt more covered. I wished they'd at least left me my underwear. This vulnerable feeling was not comforting, and neither was the cool draught blowing under the door. I checked myself for damage. Nothing seemed amiss, aside from my vision, which was still obstructed by spotty blobs every time I moved.

That was three times now that I'd been knocked unconscious. Hackman said they had experimental medicine here. Hopefully they could prevent any brain damage from my impressive number of head injuries.

Still, I realized that each time I'd awoken in a strange place, Hackman had not been far behind. Almost as if he was watching over me.

There was a loud thunk. The metal bar over the door slid to the left, and a familiar face entered the room. Rachel.

"I'm really sorry," she began at once. "I was hoping to get back to you before ... well, before everything happened. Again, I'm sorry. Things were going crazy here, and I couldn't make it out to you." The door shut, and the metal bar clanked back into place.

"You're a part of this."

"We're all a part of this," she said, sitting next to me on the bed.

"What do you mean?"

"Sorry." She smiled. "Cryptic is kind of the way we talk around here. How's your eyesight? I've been hit by one of those ultra-bright flares before too. Hurts like hell."

I shrugged. "It'll be fine, but I'd feel better if I knew what was going on."

She smiled. "Fair enough. You up for a walk?"

Helping me off the bed, she motioned at the camera. The little red light didn't respond, but someone got the message, and the door unlocked.

I followed Rachel out into the hall. It was shorter than I expected, only a few doorways that looked identical to mine on each side. Maybe Josh was behind one of them. A musty smell blew down the corridor.

"It feels like a cave," I said.

"It is. We're about five storeys down right now, in an underground cavern network we call the complex."

"I didn't know there were caves near Ettney."

"Not many do. We're deep inside the national park, about an hour from town. We've kept the complex well hidden since we found it over a century ago. Of course, we've done some upgrades since then."

This has been here a hundred years? I shook my head in disbelief.

White lights hung from the cavernous ceiling, and cabling was bolted to the walls, probably running power or the security camera feeds. Rachel led me to the end of the corridor and unbolted a second metal door. These people had the place locked up pretty tight.

As if reading my mind, Rachel continued, "Sorry about all the security. We've been on high alert since you were attacked. It's to keep bad guys out, not to keep you in. Especially if you were their target."

Somehow, that managed to make me feel better and worse at the same time. I wanted to ask questions but didn't know where to begin. The door opened onto a metal stairwell that led down into a larger, dome-shaped cavern. This area was several storeys high, rimmed by a web of steel gangways and stairwells, doors leading off in all directions. Rows and rows of chairs sat in the middle of the cavern, enough to seat a few hundred, and all pointed towards a central podium. There was no one else around, although the faint drone of activity echoed around the dome from somewhere deeper in the complex. This place was huge and well organised.

As we descended the staircase, I studied the massive image etched into the floor below: two offset triangles forming a six-pointed star, the points arranged in pairs rather than evenly spaced apart. Inside the triangles was another, smaller one, with a circle at the very center.

"This is the Apex," Rachel explained. "It's our main meeting place."

"Seriously, who are you people?"

She smiled. "We call ourselves the Kindred."

"That's ... arch."

"I know, it's kind of dramatic. The powers that be have a taste for theatrics; you should see initiations."

We descended eighteen steps to the floor—I counted them in my head, something I had done since I was little. Crossing the floor of the dome, I looked up. From here, I could just make out the ceiling. A few floodlights were stuck up there, and they provided the only source of light in the Apex.

"So, are you guys a cult or what?"

Rachel laughed. "No, nothing like that. We're more like an army."

I shivered, although it wasn't cold. "I didn't know there was a war."

"There's a war all right, and it's bigger than you could possibly imagine." She read my expression. "No, we're not terrorists, and we're not crazy either. You've seen enough by now to know you shouldn't take your world at face value. There's a lot going on beneath the surface."

She was right. I had seen so much weird stuff I was ready to believe anything. I nodded. "It's the duck effect."

"What?" she laughed.

"On the surface, a duck looks really calm when it's swimming, but underneath, its legs are going full speed. I thought the world was normal, but there's some pretty insane stuff happening behind the scenes."

"That's one way to put it. You've started to see the truth."

"Those black things—the guys in robes?"

"All part of this. Of course, they're not on our side."

"They're your enemy."

"Your enemy now, too."

I fell silent, taking this all in. None of this felt real, but it had to be.

Down here, it was like the colours of the world were still the same, but someone had turned the brightness down. Everything was darker. Two masked and hooded figures stalked across the Apex floor, disappearing through two huge doors on the wall behind the podium.

Rachel read my expression. "Don't worry. Those are good guys. They're our trainers, heading out for a practice session. Want to take a look?"

I nodded. Rachel was the first person to give me coherent answers to any of my questions, and I wanted to keep the ball rolling on the transparency front. What I had seen so far was strange, certainly. But that was nothing compared to what was coming.

FOURTEEN

The training ground was a huge cavern about the size of a football field. From where I stood at the second-level entrance, it looked like a giant open-plan office, with hundreds of walls joined to form cubicles slightly taller than their occupants: hooded figures who stood in front of various objects.

Upon our entry, many of them stopped and stared up at us, and even though most of the cubicles were empty, it still felt a lot like I'd just interrupted a busy day at Hell's head office. The cavern was lit by torches scattered along the periphery, casting giant shadows that swam around the walls, and the figures wore dark hooded outfits like I'd seen before.

I shrunk close to Rachel, whispering, "Those masks — that's what the guys at my house were wearing!"

She shook her head. "Similar outfit, different side. Like I said, these are the good guys. Both sides of this war seem the same if you don't know what you're looking for. It takes some getting used to."

One of the masked figures waved at Rachel, and she smiled back. "Hey, Max! Got a newbie here. Show her what you've got!"

Max nodded and probably smiled, but the mask covered his face. He definitely didn't seem scary, not like the hooded figures at my house.

Rachel closed her eyes. "He can only take one observer so far, and that's already impressive."

If I was meant to understand what she was saying, I missed it.

"Watch the tree!" Max called to me, pointing to a big dead fig tree that lay near the side of the training ground, close to where Rachel and I were standing.

A few seconds later, there was a colossal crack, and the whole thing burst into flames. Heat and smoke billowed up towards me. I swore. The tree split apart, and not just from the fire. It splintered and broke, dark lines running its full length. It was torn limb from limb, ripped apart, and disappeared completely in a burst of sawdust.

"Is he done?" Rachel asked.

"I have no idea."

She opened her eyes. "Wow, he vaped it. Show-off." Max gave her a thumbs up. I got the distinct impression he was flirting. Rachel turned to me. "Cool, huh?"

"I still don't even know what I saw."

"In a word: resonance."

Resonance. Again, that word. I frowned, and Rachel continued. "You know how when you're in the car you can feel the engine vibrating? Not heaps, and you hardly ever notice it, but it's always there whenever the car is on? Or when you crank your music really loud and you can feel the bass buzzing through the floor?"

I nodded.

"The lower the sound, the bigger the buzz. Everything in the universe vibrates at its own particular frequency." She placed her hand on the guard rail and looked out across the cubicles. "At the tiniest, most microscopic level, this whole cave and everything in it is vibrating. The tables. The walls. The stairs. You. Me. We're all buzzing at our own frequency. It's what holds the atoms in our bodies together. It's what stops us from flying apart."

"That's comforting."

"You know when it's really quiet, like dead quiet, and you hear that weird ringing in your head? People think it's just their ears playing tricks on them. But in those moments, when you hear that ringing, you're actually hearing the sound of the universe vibrating around you, like someone's plucked a giant guitar string."

"Whoever's playing needs lessons."

Rachel smirked. "Imagine you could change the frequency of an object. Imagine you could alter the resonance. You'd change what held that object together. You could alter the nature of the object itself. You could make it hotter, or colder, or pull it apart. Change the resonance, and you change everything."

It started to make a strange kind of sense. "Max destroyed the tree by changing its resonance?"

"Right. He basically unmade it at a subatomic level. Pulled its essence apart."

This was a lot to take in, and I fell silent.

One of the other figures let out a pointed cough, and Rachel took the hint. "We should go. Very few of these guys can train with any observation. We're messing up their tunings just standing here. That's why the cubicle walls are so high—prevents any accidental interference from others on the ground."

I still only understood about half of everything she said but nodded anyway.

She put her hand on my shoulder. "Max isn't the only one who can do that, you know."

"You too?" I asked.

"Me. Everyone here." She paused. "You."

"You think *I* can do that? Blow up trees and stuff?"

"Why do you think you're a target of our enemies? We've been keeping an eye on you for a while."

"You've been watching me?"

"Of course. Since the first accident, anyway. We knew there was something different about you. Your survival so close to the blast was highly unlikely. And if we'd noticed you, we knew our enemies would too. We arranged protection after that, although we should have organised a higher-level bodyguard. I'm really sorry you had to see him die. No one could have guessed how much of a target you would become."

Noah. He'd been sent by the Kindred?

"He was a recent transfer to our district," Rachel explained. "We overestimated his abilities. Unfortunately, the others got the better of him. They would have taken you too if I hadn't been close by on backup. We intervened, and Noah's dad managed to cover things up. It hurt him, though. I can't even imagine having to cover up the death of my own child."

She kept talking for a while, but I didn't hear it. I was dealing with some badly conflicting feelings. Noah had been lying to me the whole time I'd known him, pretending to be something he wasn't. But he'd also died trying to protect me.

I was mad, and grateful, and shocked, and broken-hearted. I couldn't figure out what to feel.

Noah had died because of me. No one should have to deal with that responsibility. It felt selfish to think, but it was true. My heart raced. "I want to see Josh."

"We haven't even begun your training," Rachel said.

"I want to see him." I was losing it. I had to see someone normal, something from my real life, to ground me before I went insane.

"That's not the right—"

"*I want to see Josh!*" I ran for the door. Rachel was faster and dove in front of me, grabbing my wrists. I tried to wrestle them free, but she was surprisingly strong for her size. I kept screaming, shouting, and scratching, until her voice broke through my anger.

"I'll take you to him. Ari, I'll take you to him. Just settle down!"

My cheeks were wet, and I was breathing way too fast. I doubled over, my vision blurring.

Rachel's hand was on my shoulder. "Ari, look at me. You're panicking. Just slow your breathing down, and look at me."

I forced myself to make eye contact, and it helped. Rachel breathed slowly, encouraging me to do the same. Eventually, my heaving breaths became slower and more controlled.

"That's good. Slow it right down." Her voice was intentionally calming.

I eventually composed myself enough to apologise.

She shrugged "It's okay. That's a pretty common response when people first learn the truth. We grow up so strongly believing our own idea of the world that when we find out we've been wrong the whole time, it unhinges us just a little bit. I was the same, although a little less hysterical." She smirked, and I felt better.

"I still want to see Josh."

"You will. But for the time being, you need to clean up and rest. I'll talk to the powers that be and arrange it." She led me out of the training ground and back across the Apex towards my room. But instead of going all the way back, we made a detour down a long corridor.

Rachel turned into a room marked *showers*. I gasped as we rounded the corner. The shower room was most definitely in use. I've never been good in public changing rooms, and this one was mixed gender.

I tried to avert my eyes as best I could and stare at the floor, the ceiling, anywhere but the other occupants of the room, both male and female.

Around the perimeter of the cold, circular cavern were ten shower heads, out in the open, no walls or curtains between them. White tiles were poorly installed along the floor and up to about waist height on the wall, at least one attempt to make things normal. In the center of the cavern was a circular bench where towels and clothing sat ready for their owners. Thankfully, nobody seemed to notice us come in, and everyone kept their eyes squarely on the wall in front of them. It was as if they didn't even notice the others in here.

"We've picked you up some clothing," Rachel said, oblivious to my reaction. "It should fit. You look about my size. You can change here."

I glared at Rachel. "Are you kidding me?"

"What? You do look my size."

"No, not that. I mean there are *people* in here. There are … *men*!"

"So don't look."

"What? What if they look at *me*?"

She sighed. "We have no secrets here. The Kindred believe in total transparency. Complete honesty. Modesty is for those who have something to hide. Don't worry, you get used to it."

I didn't *want* to get used to it. All I could do was desperately stare at the ceiling, but the flush I could feel spreading from my ears to my cheeks must have been obvious, because Rachel took pity on me. She asked the other occupants to go once they were finished. They smiled at me as they picked up their stuff and walked out the door, not even bothering to cover themselves with their towels. I tried very hard to keep my vision squarely at eye level. If I'd been with Josh or Caitlyn, I would have burst out laughing as soon as they left, but since Rachel already thought I was being ridiculous, I managed to control myself.

She left too then, giving me some privacy. I got undressed as quickly as possible and showered facing the wall, paranoid that someone would walk in and see me. God forbid they decided to bring Josh in here as well. I would never be able to look at him again. These people were the good guys, but they had some really strange habits.

As I showered, I inspected the black dot on my stomach. It had grown. It was cold to touch, even under the hot water. I tried to scrub it off again, but it didn't work. Hopefully it wasn't some kind of disease.

I dried myself and put on the clothes Rachel had given me: a white button-up shirt with no sleeves that hugged me tightly, along with a knee-length black skirt. I felt a little like a businesswoman. Even the underwear they provided fit perfectly. That was weird. Hopefully Rachel had picked them out, not Hackman.

On the way out, I glanced in a mirror on the wall. The bruises from the accident had all but gone now, and although I could still feel the stitches in the back of my head, they remained invisible. There was no longer any evidence of that fateful day, at least not on the outside.

My damp hair hung in waves over my shoulders. It looked a little messy, but I liked it. Inhaling deeply, breathing in the shower fog and musty cold, I tried to prepare myself as best I could for whatever was coming.

There was darkness on the horizon. For all the awful things that had already happened, I couldn't shake the feeling that the worst was yet to come.

I swallowed hard. *Pull it together, Ari.* I had gone to the edge of sanity and looked over, but at least I was still here. And as long as I was still here, there was a chance I would see my family again. I was trying not to think about them, not right now. Spending any time on that road would lead me right off a very nasty cliff.

Rachel was waiting for me in the hall, and she led me back to my room. She didn't say it, but I was definitely under guard. I still had to earn their trust.

In my room, I fell onto the bed and was asleep before I knew I was tired. I dreamed of Noah, and Skye, and flame, and shadow, and death.

FIFTEEN

"He's ready for you." Rachel beckoned me from the door.

I followed her out of my room and down the hall. Josh's room was two corridors over, but the hall looked identical to mine. The only difference was the lime stains down the wall, caused by constant dripping from who knows where. I stepped in a puddle of water outside his door, and it was cool under my bare feet.

Rachel bashed on the door, and it creaked open. "The girlfriend's here," she joked and stepped back to lean against the wall opposite the door.

I opened the door fully and walked inside. Josh lay on his bed, his face covered in bruises. A large gash was stitched up across his forehead, and his arms were all scratched. In the corner near the door, a hooded and masked figure kept watch.

"Ari?" Josh croaked.

I ran to him. "It's me, I'm here. Everything's okay. What happened to you?"

"You know how my mum's always harping on about wearing a seatbelt? Turns out she's right. But don't tell her that." He laughed, and then winced, grabbing his ribs.

"You shouldn't be making jokes right now."

"The alternative would be screaming. Jokes keep me distracted."

"Jokes it is, then." I reached out and stroked his hair. "Look at you."

"Yeah. When the car exploded, I was thrown onto the road. I went via the windscreen. In retrospect, that was a bad choice."

I smiled. "You really should be more careful."

"They haven't told me much. Are we in the hospital? Do my parents know I'm here? They're overseas. Were they able to get a hold of them?"

I shook my head. "No to both. Josh—"

"They won't even know I'm missing," he interrupted. "What about your mum?"

Tears fought their way into the corners of my eyes. "Taken."

"What do you mean *taken*?"

After a deep breath, I explained everything. Where we were, who was watching over us, what had happened. But I didn't tell him I was the one being targeted. I knew he would react badly to that.

When I finished, he was quiet, thoughtful for a moment and frowned.

"You know this is nuts, right?"

"You saw the flames. You saw the shadow."

"So I'm nuts too. There's a whole heap of nuts flying around at the moment."

I started to giggle.

"Yeah, I just heard that back," he laughed.

My giggle broke into a full-blown snort, which made Josh laugh even more. He was still wincing, but he didn't care. My stomach began hurting, too, and every time we tried to get ourselves under control, we started back up again. What made it even funnier was the motionless masked figure in the corner. He looked so serious, like a stern teacher, and it set us off every time we looked at him.

Eventually, I asked him to leave for a moment, so we could compose ourselves. He complied, but I could have sworn he was smiling underneath his mask.

It was good to laugh. Still, we settled ourselves down, and Josh got back to business.

"So, what's the plan? We getting your family back or what?"

"I'm honestly not sure. There's a plan, but they haven't told me what it is."

"How much do we really know about these guys?" Josh whispered with a glance towards the hallway, where the guard stood next to Rachel.

"I know they've saved my life at least twice now. I know they want to get my family back, and I know Noah was one of them. That's more than enough for me."

"Let's push them for more." Josh sat up slowly and swung his legs around so he was facing the door. "Hey, you!"

"Rachel," I prompted.

"Yeah, Rachel!"

She came inside.

"What's the plan?" Josh pressed her. "We need to get Ari's family back. You've been in here a bit, you seem to know the answers. So, what are we doing?"

"I don't really think it's wise for me to discuss things with you."

"Even things that have to do with me?"

"Any Kindred plans at all."

"Good Lord! 'Kindred plans'? It's not a bloody picnic we're talking about, it's a six-year-old girl and her mum. Ari's mum."

"You don't have the clearance to—"

"Screw clearance!" he yelled. "Ari doesn't have the clearance to find out what you're doing to get her own family back? They're probably holed up in some cell somewhere, trapped by this 'enemy,' who, by the way, we have no name for. We don't even know what this so-called war is about. You're being so damn obscure about everything, and you want us to be on your side? You're thicker than a rhino's rectum if you think we're just going to sit here and help you without knowing more. Ari deserves answers, and based on these scars"—he pointed to his face—"I think I deserve answers too." He stopped to catch his breath. The guard had moved closer to the door, watching.

Rachel pursed her lips. "You do deserve answers. But I'm not the one to give them to you. That's better off coming from someone higher up the food chain than me. I can't give you clearance, but he can."

"Who?"

"Hackman." She swiftly turned and left the room, closing the door behind her.

I smirked at Josh. "Thicker than a rhino's rectum?"

"Shut up," he laughed. "It worked, didn't it?"

I smiled. "Hopefully. Thanks."

"Anything for you."

I wasn't sure how to respond, so we sat in silence until the door opened and Hackman entered. I almost didn't recognise him in the robe he was wearing. It was black, with an insignia sewn into the top left corner, where a pocket might go. The symbol was the same one painted on the floor of the Apex: two offset triangles, a smaller one inside, and a circle in the center. It was obviously some kind of logo. I pictured some hip graphic designer with thick-rimmed glasses working tirelessly to create the logo for a supernaturally powered clandestine organisation. It made me snigger.

"Everything all right?" Hackman asked, frowning at me.

"I like your logo," I giggled.

"Thanks." He'd either missed or deliberately ignored that I was mocking him. "The first triangle represents the real world. The second, turned triangle is the true reality that most can't see. The inner triangle and circle stand for our unique sight, something that will make more sense to you as time goes on." He paused and sat on the edge of the bed. "I hear you're ready for some answers."

"It's about time," Josh snapped.

"I'm sorry, I've been busy in strategy meetings."

"You important or something?" Josh asked, still abrasive.

"You could say that. But I would prefer to have the bulk of this conversation with Ari, as she is, after all, the one with the most at stake here." Josh took the reprimand and sank back into his pillows. Hackman turned to me. "In fact, I'll answer any question you like, my dear girl. But not here."

"Josh can't walk yet."

"I know. He's not cleared for this conversation anyway."

"Hey!" Josh butted in. "You're not taking her anywhere without me. Who knows what you'll do."

"If something was going to happen to Ari, it would have happened already. She's perfectly safe here. We're on the same team, Josh. I want her safe just as much as you do."

Josh opened his mouth to protest again, but I stopped him. "It's all right. I feel safe here."

"Excellent," Hackman said. "Now, if you'll excuse us, my boy, I need to explain some things to your girlfriend."

Josh didn't correct him, and I frowned. There was probably an uncomfortable conversation on the horizon.

Hackman left immediately, and I followed him. We didn't speak, not until we reached the Apex. He sat on one of the chairs in front of the podium. I turned another around and sat opposite him. Behind him, I noticed two enormous doors I hadn't seen before. Carved patterns danced across their surfaces. The first time I walked through the Apex, I'd thought they were artwork carved into the wall, but now I saw the enormous bronze hinges.

Hackman saw me looking at them. "Beautiful, aren't they? The South Wing doors are older than this entire complex."

"What's inside?"

"Something very special. One day, you might be lucky enough to enter. It has been decades since the doors were last unlocked. That was a truly momentous day for the Kindred. I do hope that day returns soon."

I turned my attention back to Hackman. "You're part of the Kindred, I know that, but I don't even know what the Kindred is. Where did you come from?"

"The first stories of the Kindred date back beyond ancient times." His voice echoed off the cold stone walls, sounding grandiose. "There are records of Egyptian soothsayers who could transform the world around them, Roman philosophers with deep insights far beyond their time, alchemists in the Dark Ages conspiring to change the nature of metals, and Eastern mystics who could raise objects with their minds." He saw the look on my face. "Believe me, or don't, but until this week, you wouldn't have thought a man could burn objects with his will. Surely your worldview isn't so limited that this extra knowledge is too much of a stretch?"

He made a good point.

"The ancestors were a scattered people, individuals emerging in pockets of history, clusters of those who could tune like us. They didn't understand what their ability was, or even the potential of what they were doing. But whenever they appeared, great upheavals in history were sure to follow. Society moved forward in huge leaps any time our people emerged from the genetic soup. Babylon, Assyria, Rome, India, China, Britain—the United States, they were founded in no small part thanks to people like us."

He leaned forward in his chair, becoming more animated. "Five hundred years ago, there was an acceleration. More and more people were born with the ability to tune. They found each other, formed groups, appointed leaders. They began to realise the true potential of what it was they knew. Two camps formed, each following radically different philosophies, one of peace and the other chaos, one of order and the other bloodshed. These groups became the Unseen and the Kindred, and we've been at war ever since."

Whoa. This was bigger than I thought. Far bigger. This place, these people, this war, all of it was ancient. My school friends, my neighbours, the world was surrounded by a war they had no idea was being fought. How many had gone missing, taken like my family or murdered like Noah? How many had been caught up in this secret war? How many had been killed in the crossfire? They deserved to know. The world deserved to know.

"You think the world should know." It was like he read my mind. "It's a common response, but you're mistaken. If the world knew what was happening, if they knew what was going on, they would turn against both sides. They would hunt us all down, burn us at the stake like they did in the witch trials. They wouldn't care who was on what side, who was right or wrong. Their first instinct would be to seek out and destroy every last one of us. We're different, and that makes us a threat."

I couldn't deny his logic. The world always fears what it can't understand.

"Both sides would be forced to fight back to keep ourselves alive. Many would die, far more than now. The day might come when the world knows the truth, but neither side is ready for that to happen. Not yet."

As much as I didn't like it, he made sense. Besides, this wasn't my war, not really. I wasn't interested in some cosmic battle being fought for centuries. I couldn't even really imagine it. The scale of this was insane, and I just wanted my family home.

"If you want your family back, join us." Again, he seemed to read my mind. "We can assist you, but we need your help to save them. We're dangerously understaffed at the moment. There have been escalating attacks recently, and we're struggling to keep ourselves defended. You're special, Ari. I get the feeling you don't even yet know how special you are. But you can save us." He took my hands in his, eyes looking earnestly into mine. "You can save all of us."

A door slammed open, shattering the silence. There was a scream, and then another. "Get him to med wing, now!"

Three men burst through the door, blackened and bleeding. One of them was holding a child, a boy no more than five or six. He was limp, one side of his face burned. He looked so much like Adam, lying broken in the café. I swallowed the lump in my throat.

Two of the men stormed through the Apex and out the opposite door, taking the boy with them. The other approached us, breathing heavily.

Hackman stood. "What happened?"

"They found the school. They found the kids."

Hackman dropped back into his chair as if he'd been sucker-punched. "How many?"

"Twelve. Riley here's the only one we could ..."

"They're attacking your children?" I swallowed.

"They took your sister," Hackman snapped. "Do you really think they have boundaries? The schools are where we teach our children to defend themselves, to use their abilities." He buried his face in his hands. "They look like small private schools, nothing more. We've kept them secret. Until now."

"Sir?" the other man prompted.

There was no response.

"Sir, what do we do?"

Still nothing.

"Sir, we need to move quickly."

"You're right." Hackman's voice was barely audible. "Evacuate the other school. Do it now. Send a message to the other networks. They'll need to get their children back inside. Raise our defense level. If the Unseen have identified the schools, I'd bet they know a lot more than that."

The man nodded and hurried off to complete his orders. There was silence for a long time.

"I'm in," I finally said.

Hackman raised his head. "What?"

"I'm in. If this is what these guys do, if this is what they're capable of, they need to be stopped."

"Are you certain?"

"They killed Noah, they're killing children, and they've taken my family. They have to pay. I'm in. I have no idea what this even means right now, but I'm joining the Kindred."

SIXTEEN

Rachel poked me awake. It was morning. At least, I assumed it was morning. The lack of natural light made it difficult to follow the passage of time, and I hadn't had my watch or phone since the attack. But for the sake of sanity, I was prepared to call it a new day. It's funny the lies we tell ourselves about reality so we can continue maintaining at least some sort of normal.

I hadn't talked to Josh since my conversation with Hackman. He'd been sleeping when I returned, and I hadn't had the heart to wake him. He would've just pushed me for answers, anyway, and I didn't really want to tell him what I'd learned. It felt sacred somehow. I knew something special, and it wasn't meant for everyone. Besides, he probably would have tried to talk me out of joining the Kindred, and he probably would have succeeded.

Today, I was to attend a ceremony where I would be formally adopted into the Kindred. *Adopted* was the exact word Rachel used. It was comforting, in a way, although a bit too permanent sounding for my tastes. It didn't really matter — in the end this felt like the only way to get my family back. Hackman had rushed my approval through, maybe in case I changed my mind.

I was still wearing the clothes Rachel had given me, so got straight up and followed her down the corridor towards the Apex. As we neared the end, I could hear voices seeping through the gap between the door and the ground. There were too many to make out any one speaker, but I got the impression there was a massive crowd on the other side.

"Are you sure about this?" Rachel asked. "Once you commit, there's no going back."

My heart danced on my stomach. "I'm sure."

She cracked open the steel door. It screeched in protest, and the voices in the Apex fell silent. I stopped on the threshold.

People flooded every walkway, every staircase, and the entire perimeter of the cavern. Hundreds of them, all watching me. I squinted into the darkness that cloaked them, trying to make out who they were. Some were dressed in the worn jeans and flannel of farmers, others in business suits, and some wore police and ambulance uniforms. There was a distinctive red dress that appeared to belong to the local reporter, Jane MacArthur. She'd interviewed me about the accident while I was in hospital, but I'd never seen the article. I couldn't be sure it was Jane, though, because I couldn't see her face. I couldn't see anyone's face. Everyone, save for a few near the central podium, was wearing a grey mask that covered their entire head, right down to their neck, like a sack or bag. Eyes gleamed at me through shoddily cut holes in the masks, but I couldn't see anyone well enough to make out distinguishing features.

I turned to Rachel and jumped as a masked figure looked back. She had put on her own as we entered the room.

She prodded my back to get me moving, and I trod to the centre of the Apex. The only clear faces in the room were the three figures now in front of me. They didn't wear everyday clothes that I could see; instead, each of their grey masks was pulled back and attached to a robe that fell all the way down to fold around their feet. They were standing in a triangular formation, with Hackman at the back left corner. Next to him was a bald figure that was neither overtly male nor female. The tall woman at the front wore a coat that was longer than the others'. She was clearly the boss.

Startling blue eyes met mine, so light they were almost white. She looked about forty, with white-blond hair clipped extremely short. A blotchy scar on her neck extended down into her coat. I couldn't see how big it was, but it looked like she'd been seriously burned at some point, her skin melted into twisting ridges and valleys.

After a moment of dead silence, she spoke. "Maria Carpenter. Ari. Welcome."

Her voice was warm, which offset her appearance. She smiled, softening her features a little and putting me at ease. I felt my shoulders drop slightly. I hadn't realised how tight they were.

"Look around you."

I turned slowly in a circle, looking up at several levels of masked figures surrounding me like ravens perched on a power line.

"From today, these are your brothers, your sisters. You are special, Ari, and so are they. We are a family. We are everywhere. We are here to protect you." She spoke now to the room. "Kindred, welcome your sister."

The room let up a short, sharp shout, but I couldn't make out the word. It hung in the air for a moment before evaporating into the walls.

"We know you, Ari," the woman went on. "Possibly better than you do. You are different. You have a singular and special ability. This has been a force running through much of your life. An undercurrent towing you out into the deep before you were ever aware of it. You have felt isolated. Alone. You see the world more clearly than others, and that clarity separates you, places you outside the everyday so many others enjoy. You see things no one else can see. You notice things no one else will notice. That makes you special."

My heart raced. She was describing how I'd felt my entire life, although I'd never put words to it before.

"I know you because I *was* you," she continued. "I stood where you stood. I asked the questions that are burning in your mind. I too was on the outside, and I too have the ability that is beginning to awaken inside you. Everyone here is just like you. We felt alone because of that ability, even when we did not know it existed inside of us." She nodded at the others. "They came here, as did I. Now I belong and have the privilege of being mother to these Kindred. We are going to change the world."

The room barked in enthusiastic agreement. The whole ceremony had a ritualistic tone, as if this had been run many, many times before. It was a liturgy.

On cue, Hackman spoke. "We have been a family since the beginning of history. We trace our ancestry from before the written word. We have always been, and we will always be. For countless generations, we have used and developed our skills to keep the world on track. In war, in peace, through the rise and fall of civilisation, the great leaps forward that mankind has taken, we have overseen that change. We are the guardians of the plan. In time, you will become a guardian yourself."

The figure on the right spoke now. "We exist for the betterment of humanity. We move the world along without its knowledge, clandestine philanthropists for a greater and unified world. There are those who have tried to destroy us. Many times, over many centuries, we have found ourselves at war. At times, we have been at the brink of extinction, but we rise, and we rebuild. Despite opposition, despite the hatred and bigotry of our enemies, we remain, and we will always remain. Let it be so."

The room chorused an echoing "Let it be so."

The woman spoke again, this time only to me. "Do you accept adoption into the Kindred?"

I coughed. It felt like a big moment, so I paused before answering, "Yes, I do."

"Then bring forth the shade!"

Hackman stepped forward holding a mask the same as the others were wearing. He winked and went to place it on my head, but I stepped back.

The room chuckled, and the woman smiled. "Do not fear the Shade, Ari. It is both for protection and posterity. For all the trappings and rites of our organisation, we are just everyday people. We are teachers, doctors, businessmen, students, factory workers, and unemployed people. Most of us have ordinary lives doing ordinary things. The Shades date back hundreds of years, to a time of a great oppression. We have always been besieged, of course, but there was a season we did not know who to trust. The Shades at our gatherings protected the identity of Kindred, allowing us to meet without fear of being identified by traitors and enemies.

"That threat is past, long past, but you know what they say about old habits. We all have our rituals. Humanity craves routine and procedure. It is what makes us belong. While the masks may be unusual to a new initiate, in time, you will embrace the anonymity and safety it represents."

I relaxed a bit. She was right—I had my own little rituals, even down to which shoe I put on first every morning. I nodded at Hackman, and he placed the Shade on my head. It was rough and smelled of hay. The eye holes restricted my vision a bit, but I could see well enough. The crowd cheered, and the woman smiled gently.

"Upon your acceptance, then, I welcome you into the Kindred. We pledge your protection, as you now pledge to protect us."

Rachel nudged me. Apparently, I was supposed to say something.

"Uh, I pledge to protect you," I offered weakly.

"We pledge to serve you, as you now pledge to serve us."

Realizing the routine here, I pledged to serve.

The woman smiled again. "And we commit now, together, in the sight of the Apex and the gathering of the Kindred, to act in the betterment of mankind and towards the destruction of our enemies. Let it be so."

The crowd echoed, and this time I joined in. "Let it be so."

I couldn't help but smile. There were still a lot of unanswered questions, but these people had my back. I felt safe, a lot safer than I had in a long time, even before the accident. Someone was watching out for me now. I didn't have to fight the world on my own.

The crowd began to file out of the Apex, and when I turned back to ask the woman more questions, she had disappeared, along with Hackman and the third figure. Soon, I was alone with Rachel. It was a relief to have the crowd gone. I was unnerved by the attention, used to disappearing in crowds rather than being the focus. Rachel removed her Shade mask, and I followed suit.

"They've assigned me to train you," she said. "They want us to start immediately."

She walked to a staircase on the edge of the Apex, on the opposite side from where I came in. Two flights up, we stopped outside a door marked *Training Room*. Rachel opened it, and we stepped inside.

It was a long, thin room with a table at the other end. Objects were scattered along it: cups, pens, lightweight stuff, as well as some heavier things on the floor like barbells and tyres. There was even a large mannequin with a target scrawled on its front. Scorch marks and dents scarred the grey foam panels that lined the walls, and in places, the foam was burned right through to a shiny metal backing.

"All recruits start here, then move to the training ground." Rachel closed the door behind us and led me to one corner of the room. "We can sit around and talk about resonance all day, but you'll pick it up faster if you're learning as we go. This room is shielded, so it doesn't matter if you make mistakes."

"You really think I can do this stuff?"

"You'd be a pretty bad Kindred member if you couldn't. Weren't you listening before? Anyway, everyone on the planet can to one degree or another, but some are more naturally skilled than most. The room is soundproofed, which should make it easier to focus on the resonance around you."

The room had no echo. The foam deadened the acoustics so every word disappeared as soon as it was spoken, sucked up by the walls. The low hum present in other rooms of the complex wasn't here. It was strange being surrounded by this much silence, like the world outside the door had just stopped existing. Rachel was still talking, but my mind had been wandering. I tried to catch up.

"So, in essence," she was saying, "tuning is the first step. You've got to become aware of the resonance before you can change it. Want to give it a go?"

I nodded, pretending to have heard everything she just said.

"You can shut your eyes if it helps you focus, but only during the initial stages of tuning. Without sight, it's nearly impossible to change resonance, and that's going to be important later."

I closed my eyes. The still, deadened—and now dark—room became a void, like when I dunked my head underwater in the bath.

Rachel talked me through it. "Focus on your inside. Tuning starts with you and then travels out."

I focused on my stomach. It was hungry. Not good. I changed to thinking about my lungs instead. It was like one of those breathing exercises they made us do in health class.

"Now, hear the world around you," Rachel said. "Not sounds, not my voice or your heartbeat or anything else. You're listening for the vibrations themselves."

I tried to hear past the sound of Rachel's voice. Deeper than the sound of my breath. Past the shuffle of Rachel's feet as she moved, the scrape of my clothing as I breathed in and out, my heart beating in my ears. Then, for a moment, everything stopped. There was nothing. No sound, no voice, no breath, no heartbeat. The world ceased to be, and I ceased to be in it.

I was caught up in the stillness of the room, and more than that, the stillness of the universe. All noise eventually is silenced. In eternity, the world stops spinning, the sun lies dormant, the flame always flickers and dies. Caught in that moment, I faced the void, the darkness outside myself and in. It was terrifying, and exhilarating. It was death, and resurrection. I stopped, and yet I was beginning again, absorbed into galaxies and stars and planets to be reformed by them into new life. I drifted inside that moment forever. I had completely ceased to be.

Then, from nowhere, a new sound. A hum. Quiet, barely audible. It came from nowhere and everywhere. It grew stronger, a low, pulsing tone.

A higher frequency joined the first. Then a third. A fourth. I was surrounded by sound, although it wasn't in my ears. I was hearing from another part of myself; some deeper, inner sense had awoken. It came from the back of my mind and deep in my stomach.

The tones grew louder. Some were pleasant, some were piercing, and all were overwhelming. They grew until my legs shook. It hurt, and it wouldn't stop. I screamed but couldn't hear it over the noise. A tidal wave broke in my mind.

I fell.

SEVENTEEN

The floor was cold. Rachel stood over me, one hand on each of my shoulders. The corners of my mouth were wet.

"Bit of a fall there," she said. I nodded and sat up, trying not to overestimate my ability to stand just yet. "What did you hear?"

I did my best to explain what had happened. The nothingness, the silence, the multitude of tones that had dissolved my mind.

Rachel frowned. "No one has ever ... Normally during the first tuning session, we don't hear anything. Most people are lucky to even hear a pencil or a cup. Sounds like you heard *everything*. All at once. No wonder you were shaking. Nobody is built to hear that much resonance in one go. I've never heard of it. Not except for ..." She appeared to catch herself.

"Except for what?"

"Can you stand?" Ignoring my question, she pulled me to my feet and unlocked the door. "I think that's probably enough for today."

"I want to keep training."

Her brow furrowed so hard her eyes nearly closed. "You sure?"

"The sooner I learn this the sooner I can find my family. I want to keep going."

After a brief hesitation, Rachel conceded, and once I pulled myself together, we were ready to start again. She cleared the room of all the objects except a white porcelain coffee cup, to reduce the amount of resonance in the space. Apparently, that would make it easier for me to focus.

I repeated the process of slowing, focusing, breathing, listening, and again, the cacophony returned, this time with much less intensity. Rachel took a more active role this time, determined to guide me through it and avoid the results of the last attempt.

When the resonance began to form, she said, "Now that you're tuning in, I want you to hear the cup. I've never trained someone who has reached your level so fast, so I'm not entirely sure how to explain this properly. You're jumping in halfway through the process. The best way I can describe it is to think about the cup. Hear the cup. Just think cuppy kinds of thoughts."

I smiled. One part of my mind stayed empty, and the other part focused on the cup. It was like I had two brains, each performing a different function.

The background noise faded. The sonic tidal wave receded, and all the other tones disappeared. One clear note rose above the others.

"What do you hear?" Rachel asked after a moment.

"One sound. It's sort of high, but pleasant. Rounded."

"Does it sound cuppy?"

"As strange as that seems, yes. It's definitely the cup."

Rachel's hand lightly touched my shoulder. "I want you to open your eyes very slowly, but keep the resonance tuned. I'm going to close my eyes, and you're going to look at the cup and nothing else."

I slowly opened my eyes, keeping the clear, high tone ringing strong. I stared at the cup for a moment. The tone began to lift. It rose, higher and louder, like feedback from a microphone placed next to a speaker. The tone went ultrasonic, and a spiderweb of cracks spread over the white porcelain of the cup. There was a flash, and the cup blew apart in a shower of dust and shards.

I swore and turned to face Rachel, whose eyes were now open—and wider than before. "How did you do that?" she demanded.

"You told me to."

"I told you to tune, not blow the damn thing apart. You shouldn't even be able to …"

Rachel escorted me back along the corridors to my room faster than I could protest. She locked and bolted the door from the outside, her eyes still so wide it looked like she was wearing glasses. I called after her, but it was no use. She glanced at me through the window for a second before disappearing down the hall, probably to find whoever was in charge of this place and let them know what was going on.

What *was* going on? I had just destroyed a coffee mug with my brain. Just what kind of ability was this? Was I an agent of destruction sent to blow up fine china? I slumped down on my bed.

The door glared at me, the deadbolt a reminder that I was trapped. Was I dangerous? Could this ability—resonance—

shatter the door like I'd shattered the mug? Could I use this to *kill*?

I shuddered. Why did my mind go there? No matter how I tried to think about something else, the thought kept coming back. If I got good, if I really tried, maybe I could create blasts like the one that had killed Noah. The others seemed to have that power. I could use mine to get my family back.

But if it came to it, I couldn't kill someone. Even if it was right down to the wire—them or me—I couldn't do it. At least that's what I tried to tell myself.

I touched the cold spot on my stomach. It chilled my fingers. Nobody likes to think they're capable of evil. We like to pretend the darkness isn't there, the capacity for hate, violence, murder. We all quietly convince ourselves that we could never do such a thing, all the while watching those who do and wondering how they went so wrong. But inside all of us is a little part that could. We hardly ever notice our shadows, but that doesn't mean they aren't there. Sitting safe in my room, it was easy to gloss over the darkness and tell myself I would rather be killed than kill.

But I secretly knew that might change if the circumstances did.

When I got bored, I yelled at the door for a while, demanding they let me out. Nothing happened. I tried to use my new ability, but for some reason all I could hear was static. That wouldn't work for now.

Hours passed, and I heard nothing. I was hungry and needed the bathroom badly. Hoping for the first time that someone actually was watching me through the camera, I crossed my legs and jumped up and down, which is universal language for "I need to pee."

After a short wait, the door unbolted, and Hackman stood at the entrance. "Are you all right?"

"I need the bathroom."

"You don't need my permission."

"The door was bolted!"

"Yes, I noticed. Why, exactly?"

I explained what had happened in the training room and how Rachel had locked the door. Hackman frowned. "I'm unsure why she bolted the door. She didn't mention anything to me when I saw her earlier."

"Should she have?"

"Yes. She probably went straight to the Mother."

"The what?"

"The woman at your initiation. Everyone in the Kindred has a title denoting their status within the ranks. You are a Junior Sister at the moment, as you've just joined. Rachel is a Sister. My son … Noah, he was a Brother. I'm an Elder Brother, in charge of my own portion of the Kindred. Mother keeps watch over us all."

"Big Momma, huh?"

He frowned. I obviously couldn't joke about the Mother. "She is a truly remarkable woman. I do hope you get to meet her outside of her official duties. As one of the Arch Elders, she is kept quite busy."

"Arch Elders?"

"Each complex has at least one Arch Elder, part of the Kindred Council, who direct and coordinate our affairs across the globe. They are known only as Mothers, or Fathers of course."

I shrugged. "Right. Can I go to the bathroom now?"

"Yes, you're free to move about whenever you want. I'm going to have a word with Rachel about your treatment. She shouldn't have locked you in here, regardless of what happened in training, and she certainly should have informed me."

Shrugging, I wandered past him and out of my room. Strange that, up until today, I'd thought of it as my cell. Something had changed today that caused my mind to relabel the places around me. This space was now *my* space, the training room was *my* training room, this facility was *my* facility. Now that I belonged, I felt ownership.

The bathroom was shared, like the shower block. At least there were cubicles here. Thankfully, there was one thing the Kindred didn't mind keeping secret.

Two male voices entered the room. Chatting loudly, they entered the cubicles on either side of me. I would wait until they were gone before doing what I needed to do.

The voice on my left spoke. "That girl from this morning, the newbie. There's something about her."

"It's her eyes, man. They're cool. Weird, though."

I frowned. Was that an insult or a compliment? I decided to take it as the latter.

"No, it's just … her resonance. It's something else."

"I get you. She's got a sort of field. Like gravity."

Was that a fat joke?

"Yeah, it's like you're drawn to her somehow."

"Go for it, man."

"No, I don't mean it like that! Plus, what is she, twelve or something?"

I scowled.

"Hear what happened in her first training session?"

"Yeah. No wonder the Elders are excited. If she's as good as they think she is, they could bring the timeline forward by decades."

Something caught in my throat, and I coughed.

The guys fell silent, now aware there was someone else in the room. I waited until they left before I came out of my stall.

Timeline? What timeline?

The word was ominous. I was obviously more important to these people than I knew.

EIGHTEEN

Josh smiled as I entered his room. "Hey, you."

The guard walked out of the room to stand just beyond the door. He closed it behind him. Apparently we could be trusted a little now, although the security camera still watched from the corner of the roof. Rachel had said all the security around Josh was to keep him safe, because if my family had been taken, he could be a target too.

Josh propped himself up on the bed, and threw the newspaper he'd been reading on the ground. The headline read 'THREE MISSING AFTER HOUSE FIRE'. I reached for it.

"You don't want to read that," he said.

Picking up the newspaper, I glanced over the article. "They think we're dead?"

Josh nodded slowly. "The three of you, yeah. Your Mum, Skye, you. Nobody knew I was there, and nobody knows I'm missing either 'cause my parents are overseas."

"Caitlyn, my dad, everyone thinks we died in the fire." Sitting on the bed, I put the newspaper down next to me, and stared at the wall.

"Caitlyn's been texting me," Josh said. "The Kindred took my phone, for security or something, but they let me text her back to keep your cover. They made me tell her I went out of town for a job trial, and that I can't come back. They won't let me tell her you're alive. Caitlyn hates me right now. She thinks you're dead and that I don't care and that I can't even be bothered calling her. She's trying to organize a funeral for the three of you. Your dad's a mess apparently, so she's taking the lead."

"A funeral? Oh no — you can't let her do that. You just can't."

"I'll do my best. When we get out of here maybe I can tell her the truth and she'll forgive me. Maybe."

Sighing, I looked into his eyes. "When we get out of here? I hadn't even thought about that. Once I get Mum and Skye back, I kind of thought everything would go back to normal."

Josh took my left hand in his. "Ari, I don't think that's going to happen. It's never going to be the way it was."

Flipping open the newspaper with my free hand, I gasped at the photo they used for the story. My house, what was left of it, lay in ruins, still smoking in the daylight. There was nothing left. I squeezed Josh's hand.

"I'm really sorry," Josh said. "No word on Stewie, either."

My eyes were wet at the edges, and I shut them tight. "Screw this," I whispered. "Screw all of this. I wish I could go back before all this happened, erase everything, and start again."

"Me too, although there's one moment I'd kind of like to keep."

The kiss. I had to tell him about Noah, about how confused I was.

"Josh, I —"

The door burst open and Hackman entered. "Ari, I've been searching for you. You're due in training. Now."

"I've got to go, sorry," I said, standing.

Josh nodded, and smiled. "Go, practice those crazy mind powers of yours. How else are we gonna kick some Unseen butt?"

The training session was supervised by Hackman. Rachel did the ground work, but he acted as overseer. We spent hours in the training room as I focused on different kinds of objects, learning their resonance and tuning in faster and faster.

Tuning grew easier, so the environments became more complex. I no longer felt overwhelmed by the amount of noise and could tune in more specifically to what I was being asked to hear. Different objects produced difference resonance, and I grew comfortable identifying each by their sound. I heard the world around me in a whole new way. The table was a low sound, rounded and constant. Feathers were higher and laced with static. Paper was hard to hear at all. Metal pulsed quietly. Even the room had its own resonance, but it was so constant I didn't notice it often. Nothing more exploded, which was both reassuring and a little disappointing.

"So," I asked between tunings, "why do you close your eyes when I tune?"

"I think it might be easiest if we show you," Hackman replied.

"Try to focus in on something." Rachel closed her eyes along with Hackman, as they had done each time before.

I was learning how to focus on resonance without closing my own eyes, and it was easier to keep them open now to direct my tuning faster.

There was a clay pot sitting on the table. I knew the sound of earth and rock, and expected the deep whine of clay. The rest of the world tuned out, and my focus narrowed as tunnel vision took over. Static burst through my head, and my tuning dissolved into a ringing buzz that hurt like crazy. I staggered, losing focus completely.

A moment later, the room returned to normal, along with my hearing. "What was that?" I panted.

"We opened our eyes," Hackman said.

"That was you?"

"Sort of," Rachel jumped in. She was generally better at answering my questions than Hackman. "You've already learned that keeping your eyes open makes it easier to focus on the resonance of an object. And you accidentally discovered that with extra focus, you can actually change the object you're tuning."

"When I exploded the mug."

"Right. The act of observation changes the event," Hackman said.

I frowned.

Rachel tried to help. "You know how people act differently when they know they're on camera? Like when you watch those reality shows, you know they aren't really being themselves."

"Because they're being watched."

"Right. They might fight more or less than usual because they know someone else is looking. The fact that someone is watching changes what would normally have happened."

It started to make sense. A few months ago, Andy's Supermart had installed a security camera because of shoplifters. I was always self-conscious when I saw myself on screen, and even though I wasn't doing anything wrong, I could never act naturally knowing someone was watching me. Even my walk felt weird on camera.

Rachel sat on a small wooden stool. "Whether you realise it or not, when you look at an object, you change what that object is doing. Regular people don't notice, but it actually shifts the resonance of the object. We all perceive resonance slightly differently, so when I look at something that you're trying to tune in to, the resonance gets crossed. It's like trying to cram two radio stations into the same frequency."

"So when you guys opened your eyes," I said slowly, "there were three of us observing at once. Three stations trying to use the same airwaves."

"Exactly. And it happens whether we are trying to tune or not."

"So I can only tune in to resonance when no one is looking?"

"Correct," Hackman jumped in. "Even if someone is observing through a secondary device, like a camera."

That explained the static I got when I'd tried to tune back in my room. Someone was watching through the camera.

Hackman sat on a rusted metal chair, crossing his legs and leaning back. "However, the most powerful of us have learned to use our ability even when others are observing, to cut through the static and override the observations of others. The majority will never be able to tune that well. Most of us can only operate when nobody is watching."

Noah's actions during the attack started to make more sense. He'd made me close my eyes, and that's when he'd brought down part of the Boulders on top of the cloaked figures. They must have been powerful, because they were firing at us even while we stared at them. If they were that strong, hopefully they really were dead now. Hopefully they hadn't somehow survived out there, waiting to kill me whenever I left this place.

Wishing that scared me. During a fight with Mum or Dad, I might have said something like, "I wish you were dead," but I'd never really meant it. It was just a stupid teenage outburst. But this desire was so much deeper. In the most honest place in my heart, I wanted those people to die. I wanted whoever killed Noah to be lying on the floor in front of me, breath gone, blood draining out while I ripped them apart with my new power.

Hoping neither Rachel nor Hackman could tell what I was thinking, I took a few deep breaths, swallowed my anger, and looked up.

They were staring at me.

Rachel's mouth gaped wide open, and Hackman looked intently at a spot just above my waist. I looked at my pants, convinced my fly was open—and a little disturbed Hackman was staring at it.

But that's not what he was staring at.

A dull orange light glowed level with my stomach, a small ball just in front of me. It was ethereal but warm, radiating from a central point with small, fiery tendrils spiraling out from the middle. Frightened, I jumped back, and the glow disappeared.

Hackman spoke before I could. "Ari, this is important. What were you just thinking about?"

"How did you do that?" Rachel asked. Without waiting for my answer, they began to speak, ignoring me completely. "She can flare."

"Naturally. Without any coaching."

"Why now, though?"

"The resonance training. It's amplified her natural tuning."

"We were looking at her. She broke through the interference."

"Without even trying."

"That level of ability ... It's almost unheard of."

"Almost."

"Imagine the possibilities."

"Hey!" I broke in, mad they were talking about me without explaining what was going on.

Hackman turned to face me. "Ari, that orange glow was the beginning of what we call a flare. You know how you've been learning to tune in to objects?" I nodded. "Well, a flare begins by tuning in to the air itself. It's much harder to do, because air is so intangible and expansive. But when you accelerate the resonance of the air around you, it warms up. If you heat it enough, the oxygen in the air will catch fire. With enough training, you can create these pockets further and further away from your body."

Noah's death now made sense—the reason smoke had poured out of his chest. Someone had accelerated the air in his breath until it caught fire inside his lungs.

Noah had been burned from the inside out.

My stomach lurched. The pain would have been horrific.

"It's not an easy ability," Hackman continued, ignoring the sick look on my face. I was sure my skin was now pale. "But you created a small flare naturally. That's incredible."

"What were you thinking about?" Rachel demanded.

"I—nothing really." I didn't want them to know what I was feeling, to see that dark place inside me. Not just yet. Maybe not ever.

Rachel frowned. I wasn't the greatest liar, but she glossed over my answer anyway and moved on. "Regardless, you've gotta be careful with flaring. It's exhausting trying to focus on that much resonance. It can wear you out pretty fast. Try to use it as a last resort."

I imagined using this against the men who took Skye, setting the air inside their lungs on fire, burning every last scrap of flesh inside them until they died of their wounds or the agony, whichever came first. It felt good.

A small glow, barely visible, formed in front of me. I was flaring again. Quickly, I thought about something else before the others noticed. Focusing on my hatred seemed to cause the flare, and the glow disappeared once I was distracted. Hackman was talking, but I wasn't listening. I tried to pay more attention, and it helped me stay under control.

"It's extremely difficult to flare with interference," he was saying. "The fluid nature of the air and the already high level of focus required means that any level of interference will destroy a flare before it's fully ignited, unless of course you're extraordinarily gifted. It would be difficult for you to form a full flare, even with your natural abilities, without exceptional levels of training. Most never make it to that stage.

"That's why stealth is one of our greatest assets," he continued. "Distraction, disruption, secrecy—these are our first lines of defence but also our greatest offence. The less noticed you are, the easier it is to use your ability. Plus, the more you can keep your line of sight on your enemy, the harder it is for them to use their power."

In other words, if I'd been more alert and observant that night, Noah might still be alive.

I tried not to dwell on the thought in case I started to flare again. "Why don't you guys use guns?" I asked. I hadn't seen any at all so far.

"They're almost useless in battle with our enemies. A well-trained fighter can melt the bullets inside them in a few seconds, or worse—make the gunpowder explode and destroy the person holding it. In our kind of war, carrying a gun would be like carrying a grenade with the pin out. Projectile weapons in general are pointless against our abilities. Even blades are risky." He thought for a moment. "The best way to learn stealth is to try it, so I'll schedule a live training session for this afternoon."

"A live what?" I repeated.

"A battle. In the arena."

Rachel smirked. "You up for it?"

I swallowed hard. "Bring it on."

NINETEEN

The afternoon came sooner than I was prepared for.

On the way to the arena, Rachel explained what was going to happen. The arena was where recruits proved their abilities under controlled, live-combat situations. There would be real people trying to take me out—mostly high-level trainers who'd developed enough control of their abilities to create flares that stung without actually injuring. "Kind of like paintball," Rachel suggested, grinning. It wasn't reassuring.

My job was simply to survive without being hit. It was a timed exercise, and the longer I could last, the better my performance would be. If I could last five minutes without being hit on my head or torso, it would be considered a pass. That would qualify me to join a Kindred unit as a trainee, bringing me one step closer to retrieving Skye and Mum.

Rachel would be with me for the first two minutes, coaching me through whilst the combatants went easy. After that, a siren would sound, Rachel would leave, and the others would throw everything they had at me. At five minutes, the battle would be over. My goal was to be standing unhurt at the end of it.

Rachel and I crossed the Apex, and Rachel gave a short rap on the shiny steel door leading to the west wing. A face appeared in the small window. "Live fire," Rachel said.

The face nodded, and a bolt in the door slid back. It swung slowly open, and my eyes watered from the stench of antiseptic, so thick I could taste it. This part of the complex was different from the east wing, where my room was. The roof of the east wing was rock, the corridors over there raw and leaky. It felt old and dingy. Over here, on the other hand, the corridors were made of shiny steel, and bright white fluorescent lights bounced off every surface, making it hard to distinguish between walls, ceiling, and floor. It was so formal, the air itself stood at attention.

Six doors lined this corridor at perfect intervals, three on each side. The first on the left was ajar, and when I peeked inside, I saw it contained a large wooden table surrounded by chairs. It looked like a meeting room. The second was set up like a lecture hall, but the other doors were closed.

We headed straight on, and the next corridor was identical to the first, except all the doors were shut. The third and fourth corridors were clones as well. The fifth had one very important distinction—each door here had a small embossed sign that read: *Confinement*. They kept prisoners here. None of these doors had windows.

After several disorienting turns, Rachel and I reached the final door. There were three guards on each side of it. Security was tight here. The door whirred as it opened, and we stepped into an airlock. The first door closed behind us, and then the door in front of us opened.

Air. Beautiful, fresh, clear air rushed over me. I breathed deep, sucking in every last drop, feeling it trickle down my throat. For the first time in days, I was outside.

"Welcome to the arena." Rachel stepped over the threshold, beckoning me to follow.

The place was a dump. Literally. Fallen trees and logs were interspersed among burned-out cars and piles of rotting garbage. The clear air I'd experienced so briefly was gone, replaced by the thick odour of trash.

The arena was enormous, almost as big as the airfield outside of Cawley. It was so big I had trouble believing no one from the outside had found it yet. Although, if they had stumbled upon it, it wouldn't have looked suspicious. It just looked gross.

Around the edge of the dump was a rim of huge rocks, placed to mark the boundaries of the arena. I knew we were deep in the national park, and trees towered beyond the rock line. Twilight had sapped the world of colour, and it was hard to see much farther than the rocks.

Three trainers arrived behind us. They wore modified versions of the masks worn in the adoption ceremony. These were slimmer fitting but curved out at the sides, partially obstructing their peripheral vision. They looked a bit like horse blinders. Rachel said this was normal attire for group attacks, as it reduced the chance of accidental interference from others on the same side. I didn't need one today, because I was on my own. Their limited field of view would be my one advantage.

I took my first steps into the arena—and sunk up to my ankles. The whole place was mud. Frustrated, I sighed. This was not going to be the greatest fun.

We trudged into the centre, around rocks and trees and the skeletons of cars. A large pile to my left was made of food scraps.

The trainers took up positions around the outside of the arena. I couldn't see two of them as my view was obstructed by logs and garbage. We reached a burned-out school bus in the centre of the arena, a yellow one that looked really old. The side of the bus was blackened, but I could make out letters spelling *hool* drizzling down the charred panels like chocolate sauce.

Rachel motioned for me to step inside. The bus creaked as I climbed the stairs. The molten plastic and fusty chair foam smelled so bad I could practically see the fumes. I knocked one of the chairs, and a plume of dust blew into my eyes, scratching them. Holding them shut for a moment, I could at least *hear* Rachel explain the plan.

"The first two minutes won't be too bad, so let's work on strategy. Outnumbered like this, your best bet is evasion and stealth. Your flaring isn't really up to scratch, so don't try anything like that this time around. Juniors like you survive best by hiding, not fighting."

I blinked, and my eyes cleared. Rachel prodded my back, and I obediently moved towards the end of the bus.

"The enemy normally operates in small, mobile parties. They're designed to surprise and overwhelm you. So if you find yourself in a scenario like that, get to cover quickly. They aren't great at long, drawn-out stand-offs. You want to see them without being seen—the interference you create will wear them down a lot faster. Of course, the interference will also tell them you're within eyeshot, and they can narrow down where you are. So it's a trade-off."

The seats had melted into their frames, and busted seat springs poked through my jeans as I tried to sit. Standing was definitely the better option. At least we had a decent view of the arena through the broken windows.

"They're going to know we're in here." I rubbed my stabbed behind.

"Of course. They've run this training countless times, but it's still the best place to defend." A glow drew my attention. One of the trainers was warming up, starting flares in a circle above her head. When my eyes fixed on her, they disappeared. "See? By observing, you've interrupted their pattern. But remember: some of us can flare despite interference."

"All this fire out here in the middle of the bush … That's pretty dangerous, isn't it? Especially in this weather?"

"There's a river just beyond the rock fence that acts as a fire break," Rachel explained. "Plus, we've always got a crew on standby to deal with outbreaks. The last thing we want is someone to head up here investigating a bushfire. We've got it covered." She grabbed my hand and squeezed it lightly. "Ready to go?"

I nodded, and Rachel waved to someone off in the darkness. A siren blew, and the trainers entered the arena.

"Okay, time's ticking. This is where things get fun." Rachel pointed out a number of big boulders and logs that lay around the edge of our clearing. "We can't actually move objects, we can't lift stuff in the air and throw it like in the movies, but we *can* modify them."

She pointed out a log nearby, and I tuned in. It was a familiar sound now; many of the objects I trained on were made of wood.

"Remember what happened on our first training day, when you murdered that poor innocent mug?" Rachel asked.

I nodded, smiling even though my hands refused to stop shaking.

"Try it again, but this time don't let the resonance hit so high. Tune out before the whole thing breaks apart."

I tried to concentrate on that feeling, on shifting the resonance. The sound changed, as with the mug. It rose higher and higher, like a jet engine warming up.

There was a crack, and the log blew apart in a cloud of fog and sawdust.

"Sorry," I said.

"That's okay. Try it again with another. But now that you know the shatter point, stop just before you get there."

I chose a gnarled old tree stump that was at least an arm's-length across. The trainers had been heading at me for a while, and the stress made it harder to focus. I tried twice to tune before finally locking in. This stump sounded like the last one, and the resonance rose just the same. I stopped short of the highest note, and flames arced out of the stump. In a second, the whole thing was on fire. I grinned. Cool. If I lit up enough of the surrounding area, I could reduce the approaches the trainers could take. I set another log on fire, to Rachel's approval.

"You're a natural strategist. Nice work." A flare burst in the air above my head. I swore. Rachel placed her hand on my shoulder. "At least one trainer is here, faster than I thought. But they can't see you yet. That was meant to drive you out. Stay down and try to spot them. The interference should give us an advantage, too."

I raised my head to peek out a shattered window. The glass was hard to see through, as it was spiderwebbed with cracks, but a few small pieces were missing, creating a perfect peephole. I could see without being seen.

A figure glowed in the firelight. The mask and hood creeped me out, especially because they were lit by the flickering flames. He was either scanning the area or looking straight at me.

"Got him." I ducked back down and crouched with my back to the bus wall. "Now what?"

"Here's where things get interesting. You're probably thinking you can just set someone on fire, but you won't be able to directly manipulate a living body. Too many different tissues and cells. It's impossible to tune in to a person, even without interference. Plus, this is only simulated, so we'd prefer you didn't melt our trainers."

I laughed, but it quickly drained away. Perhaps that had happened before.

"You want to use the environment to your advantage. If you can shatter the rocks behind them, you can distract them or potentially knock them out with flying debris."

"I don't want to hurt them. They're not really my enemy."

"These guys are sent out of the arena bleeding all the time. They're almost disappointed when they leave without a new scar. They'll be fine."

There was a big boulder right behind the approaching trainer. I pointed it out to Rachel.

"Perfect. He won't see it, so the interference will be low." She placed her hand on my shoulder. "This one is harder. You can't set rocks on fire. You need to raise its resonance and lower it suddenly. The change will break the pieces apart without shredding them. With any luck, bits will go flying everywhere."

I'd tried this the other day in the training room with a small stone figurine. A boulder was a bigger challenge. I tuned in. Adrenaline, interference, and pressure made it harder to focus, and static shimmered in and out of my head. Still, I managed to raise the resonance and then drop it fast. The boulder blew apart, and shards of stone shot across the arena. The trainer ducked as a large chunk flew over his head.

He took a moment to recover, but when he did, he started running towards the bus. He tried to flare while he ran, but I kept him in view and the interference left him blocked.

"Try another one—catch him off guard," Rachel said.

I was tuning before she finished her sentence. The trainer was close now, so I picked a boulder just in front of him. The boulder shattered, again missing the trainer's head, but a stray shard smacked him hard in the legs and he tumbled forward, face planting just a few meters away. He raised his hand.

"That means he's tapping out. You've defended yourself successfully, and he's giving up."

He staggered to his feet, blood streaming down his face. He'd smacked his forehead on a sharp piece of rock when he fell.

Rachel noticed the look on my face. "It's okay. He'll be fine."

I took a deep breath. This was not what I'd signed up for back at the Apex. Still, there were two more trainers out there, and if I could win this thing, I would have a shot at getting my family back. That was all that mattered. The siren blew a second time, signalling the end of the first two minutes.

"That's my cue to leave," Rachel said. "You've made it almost halfway, but now they're really going to put the pressure on. Those two techniques should be enough to last you until full time. Just keep focused, and you'll be fine. And don't leave this bus!"

She ducked out a broken window, and I was alone.

TWENTY

I had to get an eye on the other trainers. They would be approaching from the other direction—there were no logs or tree stumps on that side, which left a big hole in my defences. I crept down to the other end of the bus, towards the driver's seat. It was darker down this side, away from the flames. My heart slammed in my ears, drowning out the crackling logs. The world became still.

There was a flicker of movement.

I shifted my balance to the front of my feet, ready to run if need be, and peeped over the side of the driver's window, squinting to make him out.

A glow appeared ahead of me. No, it was in the rear-view mirror. The glow was behind me. I turned around as the flare formed at my side, too late to stop it with interference. It blistered my arm, and I yelled, falling backwards and cracking my head on the steering wheel.

Rachel had lied. This was nothing like paintball.

Adrenaline dulled the pain as my body went into survival mode. The other trainer had come up behind me while I was watching the first. They were now approaching from both sides, and there was no way I had time to take out both.

Twin flares formed in front of me, through the hole where the windscreen once was. I untangled myself from the bus controls and leaped away as flames punched the air, chasing me back toward the other end. The bus was lost. I had to run and ignore Rachel's instructions to stay in here. This was what good soldiers did. Improvise.

The back of the bus was my only way out. Burning-hot seat springs and melted upholstery grabbed at my clothes as I clambered past them. I dove out the back window, thankful the glass had fallen out a long time ago. There was a sharp drop, and I smacked my shoulder on the ground. The mud broke my fall a little, but not enough to stop the pain.

I scrambled to the nearest set of bushes and glanced over my shoulder. The trainers were heading my way. How long was left until the siren?

Staying low, I edged towards a boulder. I had to lose them. That was the only way to pass their test. Run out the clock. My arm burned from the flare, and when it scraped against the edge of the rock, I had to bite down on my shirt to stop myself from screaming.

From where I stood, there was a straight run to the edge of the arena. The rim of stones that formed the boundary would give me some protection.

The air went eerily still, with no sound but the crackling of the fires I had set. A fly buzzed over a nearby garbage pile, landing on a mouldy piece of plastic so old it was melted into the food scraps underneath. My breathing was loud. Too loud. Surely they could hear me.

Rachel had told me to use stealth and misdirection. If I could distract the trainers, make them think I was somewhere else, I would get a clean break to the safety of the rock line. They hopefully wouldn't expect me to bend the rules, and they'd stay searching for me inside the arena.

An old car sat rusting on the other side of the bus, barely visible over piles of debris. They wouldn't expect a rookie to be able to tune over such a distance, so they would think I was on the opposite side of the arena. That is, if I managed to pull it off, at least.

The sting from my arm made it harder to tune. I had to slow my breathing and forget about the pain. This had to work. I had to pass this test. I had to be out there, searching for my family. Fighting for them. I used that energy, the pure rage I felt for the Unseen, to focus. My tuning locked, and I channeled all the resonance I could muster straight into what sounded like the fuel tank.

The ground jumped, and there was a colossal thump as the car blew apart. They would have heard it all the way inside the complex. My ears rang. The heat was intense, so hot the skin on my nose blistered. That was a bigger bang than I was expecting.

I tore my eyes from the burning wreckage and ran blindly in the smoke, heading for the rock boundary. If the trainers found me, I wouldn't even know—I couldn't hear or see much of anything.

The edge came faster than I thought, and I smacked head first into the rock. Brain spinning, I had to sit down before I passed out. It was technically cheating, but I edged around the rock, through the small gap between the stones, and out of the arena entirely.

The air was clearer out here, and my breathing eased. I closed my eyes, rubbing them to ease the sting of the smoke. It had been at least four minutes by now, surely. Not long to go. My hearing still hadn't returned. I likely wouldn't even know when the siren sounded.

Steadying myself with one hand against the cool rock, I took a deep breath, ready to go back inside. The sky was dark now, and the space beneath the trees was black as death. Their tops glowed red, lit by the light from my fire inside the arena as it burned high above the rock fence. Deep inside the bush, the ground glowed red too, like lava seeping through a fissure. It was the river, reflecting the firelight that flickered in the trees.

My eyes adjusted to the darkness, and details emerged as if from fog. Smoke crept along the leaf-strewn dirt and crawled around trees, lifting its fingers to snake along bark and branches. The ringing in my head started to clear, and someone yelled over the crackle of fire.

Beyond the river was a shed of some kind. It was hewn from stone, cold and uninviting. It wasn't large, and I could barely make it out in the gloom. But looking at it gave me a weird feeling, like it didn't belong. Not here, not now. It shouldn't be here, in our time, in our world. It felt wrong. *Evil.* It glowed in the firelight, but it had its own light too, coming from a candle inside.

It wasn't a shed. It felt more like a shrine. A chapel.

It had no door, just an opening where a door should be. The candle flickered out, and the door went black. Too black. It wasn't just a hole in the wall, it was a *threshold*. A door to somewhere else entirely.

I blinked, and a man stood in the threshold. No, not a man. His face was wrong, distorted and dripping, as if he was a wax statue burning down. Bone protruded from his cheeks and eyes and chin. He didn't seem alive. It was not the thing I'd seen on my bedroom ceiling, but it was just as evil. And he was staring straight at me.

I blinked again, and when I opened my eyes, the chapel was closer. It had moved toward me. It was now on my side of the river.

The figure still stood in the doorway, and now that he was nearer, I could see him more clearly. He moved his mouth as if to speak, but it made no sound. His tongue lolled over his teeth like he was unsure how to use it. Had he ever been human?

His mouth continued to move, as if incanting some terrible truths our world should never know. I was drawn, magnetized. I had to go closer. The spot on my stomach burned colder than it ever had before.

The chapel moved again, and I was standing at the threshold, right in front of the awful man. His eyes had no irises, just black holes for pupils. I wanted to scream, but I was frozen.

He grabbed my arm, and his fingers melted into my wrist. They burned as cold as my stomach. I jerked my arm away, but his grip remained firm. He moved his face closer, almost touching mine, his throat clicking as he tried to speak. Skin dripped down his cheeks, and I could feel his breath, see the veins in his eyes. There was something in them I recognised, something I knew.

The siren blew, and he was gone, along with the chapel. I stared at the trees and river for a moment, to see if it had moved back to its original position. There was nothing there at all.

Shaking, I snuck around the stone and back into the fire and smoke. Rachel was calling my name.

"Over here!" I replied.

She saw me and walked over, smiling. "Ari! You made it. You passed."

In the distance, the trainers were heading back into the complex. One of them gave me a thumbs up.

"You did well, too," Rachel said.

"Thanks." I was still a bit shaky, and I felt cold.

She saw my face. "Are you all right? The test can be pretty intense."

"Yeah, I'll be fine."

I should have told her, but I didn't.

I couldn't.

The chapel was monstrous, and the man was a nightmare clothed in molten skin, but for some reason, I felt it should stay secret. The chapel had reached out to me, and no one else could know about the evil thing inside.

TWENTY-ONE

"Begin!" Hackman's voice cracked like a bullet.

We started again. *Focus, tune, wait, signal, shatter. Focus, tune, wait, signal, shatter.* Six of us were gathered in the training ground, running drill after drill in our cubicles. This particular drill focused on timing and speed. We had to synchronise our tunings together and cause the small wooden stakes in the ground to shatter simultaneously. The better we could time our attacks, the more effective we would be out in the field. Hackman's signal got faster and faster, so we had less time to tune between successive actions. You didn't have time to think when the Unseen attacked.

The last four days had been exhausting. Since passing the test, I'd been put straight into group drills. They started early and ran until none of us could stand anymore. I hadn't got a chance to see Josh. I was so exhausted from training I could barely think straight, let alone make it to his room at the end of the day. It was getting harder and harder to get out of bed each morning. I thought after the test I would be sent straight out to find my family, but that wasn't the plan. Of course, I had complained loudly to Hackman.

"Based on our understanding of the Unseen modus operandi, they will not harm them without us giving good cause to do so. It would be unwise of them to damage their bargaining chips, so to speak. Your family will be safe for the time being," he explained. "But if we are to have the highest chance of success, we must first be adequately prepared."

I complained a lot, but he wouldn't give in. When I thought about it logically, he did make sense. After all, I would be no use to my family or Josh if I was lying dead on the ground. In fact, the more I thought about it, the more I agreed with Hackman. A failed rescue attempt could be even worse than waiting a bit longer, as it would likely cause the Unseen to keep my family locked up even more securely than before. Or hurt them in retaliation. Why they took them was still beyond me, and no one here had offered any convincing explanation. I had to assume they were leverage against me and the Kindred. If I really was some part of a grand plan, important in some way to either side, it made cold sense to hold me to ransom.

"Cease!" Hackman called, sighing.

Each of us had destroyed our ten stakes in less than thirty seconds. Not bad, but not good enough for Hackman, apparently, and he stormed off to find more bits and pieces for us to explode.

I glanced at Rachel, who was tying her shoelace. She was assigned as my training partner. All of us newbies had been partnered with a more experienced Kindred member to speed up our training.

There were three pairs, including Rachel and I, and we all took off our masks and sat down to catch our breath. There was James, a tall lanky guy with wispy blond hair and an awkward smile that looked vaguely familiar, and his training partner, Vicki, who was a short, sultry firecracker with a shot of blue running through her cropped black bob. James was the newbie, and Vicki was about five years his senior, but from the way they'd kept looking at each other, even from the first day, I'd gotten the feeling something was going on. This was confirmed when I walked past one of the empty dorms and caught them, well, making efficient use of bunk space. They'd been too engrossed in their attempts to rearrange the sleeping bag to notice me, and I didn't mention it to them, but every time I looked at them, I went bright red, which must have been a dead giveaway.

The other pair was Frank and Nareem. They were both older, in their mid-forties, and got along like a house on fire. I'd never seen Frank around Ettney, but I'd stopped dead in my tracks when I first saw Nareem in here. He was the town's pharmacist and had apparently been Kindred for close to five years.

Knowing the way Nareem was usually treated by most of the townspeople, I wondered why he hadn't used his abilities on them. I sure would have. We didn't have a lot of non-white people in Ettney, not like in the city, so when he first moved to town, some ratty kids had spray painted the front of his pharmacy with a whole stack of awful, racist messages, and then one day his house got done. Mitchell Markson at school told me his dad was mad at Nareem cause the "filthy migrants kept stealing our jobs." I pointed out we'd been trying to get a pharmacist in the town for close to ten years but none of the white city folk wanted to move out here, and that also, Mitchell's dad was unskilled and didn't exactly want to work, so it wasn't like Nareem was stealing a job his dad could have gotten anyway. Mitchell didn't talk to me much after that.

The way the town treated Nareem made me mad. He was such a nice guy and always went out of his way to make sure Skye and I were all right. Once, when we were younger, Mum had gotten caught up at work and I walked Skye home from preschool. She tripped right outside his shop, and he came out and bandaged up her knee with a bright pink Band-Aid, which she was so pleased with that she immediately forgot all about the pain. He even offered to close up his shop and give us a lift home, but Mum didn't let us get lifts with anyone so I said no as gratefully as I could. Nareem seemed a bit confused by that. I think in his culture everyone helps each other out a lot more.

Then I'd walked in to the training ground for our first session and found out he was part of the Kindred. He was there for my induction in the Apex too, but with all the masks, I hadn't seen him. In fact, I had never seen the faces of any of the live-ins from the west wing, aside from Rachel of course, but she was staying in the east wing to keep an eye on me. They always wore masks when they were outside their rooms, and we weren't allowed to wander through there unaccompanied. It was a security measure; keeping real identities as compartmentalised as possible would protect everyone.

Hackman stayed with us in the east wing as well, although he disappeared frequently to maintain his cover as the chief of police. I wasn't sure why so many of them needed covers and outside lives, except maybe to keep them from getting cabin fever. Also, Hackman had hinted there was a much larger plan at work, one that needed Kindred in positions of influence in society. You couldn't get those hiding in a cave underground.

"You need to get your tuning faster," Frank told James, who nodded and shifted uncomfortably. Frank was a newbie like us but had that annoying habit adults have of thinking they know everything. Sometimes he acted like he knew more than Hackman.

Frank moved on to Vicki, who glared at him as he tried to tell her where she was going wrong. She had years of experience over him, and I quietly willed her to crack and teach him a lesson.

I leaned over to Rachel. "If he comes over here," I whispered, "you have my permission to set him on fire."

"Face or butt?" she grinned.

"Butt first, then face."

"That's a problem," she said. "I might have trouble telling which is which."

I snorted, and when he looked over, we had to pretend we were laughing at some inside joke that had nothing to do with him. Fortunately, Hackman returned before Frank started on us, although he had time to roll his eyes in our direction and sigh, "Kids," which made me want to punch his bulbous nose right back into his squashed little head.

We ran the exercise twice more, each time getting better and faster. Frank struggled a bit, which was deeply satisfying for the rest of us, even Nareem, judging by the look on his face. When Frank got wrung out by Hackman for missing two targets, I could barely hide my grin, at least until I saw the look on Frank's face. He was so deeply embarrassed, it was like someone had pantsed him in front of the Dalai Lama. Maybe for Frank, knowing what to do and being the best at it—even if he wasn't—was something he really needed. Struggling to master something was not just humiliating for him, it was crushing.

It finally hit me how I knew James. He'd gone to the same primary school as me, a few years ahead, but had transferred to Cawley when his parents moved for work. I never knew him well—in primary school, a four-year age gap is an eternity. Still, I remembered he had spent most of his time at school playing one of those fantasy card games with the strange-looking characters on them. Everyone thought he was the biggest nerd around. Back in primary school, I would never have pegged him for getting with a girl like Vicki. I don't think he would have, either. As I watched him, he smiled. He was clearly loving his new identity as a secret superhero, like one of the characters in his card game.

We trained for days, and to say I was getting impatient would be an understatement the size of Frank's ego. It felt like ants were crawling up and down my legs. I could barely sit still and was on edge constantly. It was exhausting being so tense, like a guitar string wound too tight for too long.

I was ready to snap.

TWENTY-TWO

I paced around my room. It was late on a Thursday, maybe. It was hard to tell day or time so far underground. My watch and phone were melted somewhere underneath the remains of our house, so any time I wanted to find out the time, I had to ask someone. It didn't really matter down here, so I didn't bother much.

The silence and stillness were beating me around the head, and I couldn't take much more. I had to *do* something.

Rachel's room was opposite mine, so I gently creaked open her door to see if she was still awake. She was lying on her side in bed, facing the wall, and as she turned towards me, her eyes were raw and red. It looked like she was crying, but when I moved forward to ask about it, she waved me away. I felt like that too sometimes, that I just wanted to be left alone with my sadness, so I didn't push it. She would talk when she was ready.

After a few moments, though, I started to resent her for it. It was my family who were missing, not hers. It was me who had lost everything. It was me who had watched Noah die.

She might have walked that journey before, but it was my turn now. The least she could do was pull herself together.

I shook my head as if to flick the anger out of my brain. My insides had been growing darker every day, like a sponge absorbing a bottle of ink. I heard somewhere that when you sleep, fluid drains out of your brain through your ears or something. My thoughts had been so dark I was half expecting to wake up one morning and find my pillow had turned a murky black. It was hard to remember what it felt like to be okay.

"I'm sorry," Rachel mumbled.

"For what?" I had the horrible feeling she could read my thoughts. After everything I'd seen, it wouldn't surprise me.

She sat up and hugged her knees. "For everything that's happened to you."

"It's not your fault, Rachel."

"It's all our fault, in a way. I mean, if the Kindred weren't here, if it weren't for the Unseen and the war and everything, your life would still be normal."

"So would yours, right?" I attempted a reassuring tone. Sure, I was selfishly mad at Rachel, but I didn't want her shouldering this kind of responsibility. No amount of blame would bring back my old life.

"You had no choice to be here. I did."

I sensed an opening. "Then what made you join?"

"We used to live in the city. My parents and me, and my older brother, Ben."

She'd never mentioned a brother before. I tried to picture her with a big brother. Sometimes I wished I had one, someone to look out for me, someone to pester, someone to stick up for me when kids at school were jerks. It was hard to imagine Rachel needing much protection. I hadn't seen her cry before today.

"When I was ten, my mum died in a crash way out west," she said quietly. "Dad was driving, and he spun off the road into the side of a tree. He told us she died quick, but I overheard someone at her funeral say she was in heaps of pain, and that Dad held her hand for hours until she died. Someone drove past the next day and found them. He went to hospital, but he never really recovered, if you know what I mean. To lie there, listening to someone you love dying, knowing it's your fault … No one should ever have to do that."

My mind went to Noah. If nothing else, at least it had been quick.

"Anyway," she sniffled, "two years after that, Dad killed himself, I guess from the guilt. Ben found him, and he was never the same after that."

I couldn't believe how calm she was, how she could talk about this with such cold language. Maybe this was how she survived. She switched off the pain somehow, retreating inside herself. I was doing the same thing more and more lately.

"We got bounced around a few foster homes, but none of them really worked out. They tried splitting us up, but that made things worse. Eventually, I bailed and ran away from my last placement when I was fifteen. Ben had already turned eighteen and gone to live on the west coast. I didn't have enough money to go find him, and I didn't get the feeling he wanted to be found anyway. I spent a year on the street, living off other people's rubbish and scabbing money where I could. I would spend hours lying somewhere, in an alley or a park. Sometimes, I was coming down; other times, I was high as.

"Anyway, this one night in summer—I remember it 'cause it was warm and a storm was starting to roll in—I was lying under this huge oak tree watching the stars get swallowed up by the clouds. It felt so amazing, and I felt so alive that night, like I hadn't felt ever since Mum died. I wanted to be absorbed into the air, just disappear and stay in that feeling for eternity. Not in a dark way, or a death way, but in a kind of alive way, like I had become the air and the tree and the stars and the storm. I thought about it for long enough, and I started to hear a sound. It grew, and pretty soon it enveloped me. I got scared and snapped out of it. That was the first time I tuned.

"A few days later, I got up a bit of courage and tried again. I got pretty good at it after a few months. That was when I realised I could change things. I managed to blow apart a few rocks and stuff in the huge park in the middle of town. Then it clicked: I could use this to get whatever I wanted. I started vaping shop windows to grab food. It was basically silent and really quick to get in and out.

"Eventually, I tried a jewellery store, but I hadn't counted on the interference from so many security cameras. I didn't even know what interference was at that point. I got stuck inside the automatic security bars, and the cops got me. I'd never really thought about the risks until then, and I'd been too desperate to care. But then, sitting inside a cell at the station with two drunks and a carjacker, I saw what I was. It was a shock, like the first time you see yourself on video. I'd become this awful, selfish person. The cops told me the shops I was hitting were family businesses, struggling shopkeepers; even the jewellery store was owned by a little old man who could barely pay his bills. My life was hard, but that was no reason to make it hard for others.

"The Kindred had caught wind of a girl running around town vaping storefronts, and they put the pieces together pretty quick. The next morning, a high-flying lawyer turned up to negotiate my release, and the cops mysteriously turned a blind eye to all the stuff I'd been doing. The Kindred really are everywhere.

"They took me in, fed me, helped me get a cover job, gave me a place to belong. Above everything else, they gave me just about the most important thing anyone anywhere can have: a reason to keep going. Purpose."

She stopped, apparently having run out of words. It was true, though. Purpose is probably the single most important thing that keeps any of us going. I think purpose is what keeps us alive. It's what keeps our hearts beating and our lungs moving and our brains sending those little electrical signals that do whatever it is they're meant to be doing—I wasn't really listening that week in science when we studied the brain. I never really liked science that much, not biology, anyway. I didn't like the part that reduces our lives down to animal impulse, our feelings and emotions down to physics and genetics and biological programming. I always felt like we were so much more than that, so much more than computers made of skin and blood and chemistry. Maybe that "more" I was thinking of was purpose. What keeps us alive, gives us the will to live. We need it, and that's how we're different from the animals. If you run out of purpose, you run out of life, like Rachel's dad. Without purpose, you stop.

Rachel had found her purpose in the Kindred, and I'd always found mine in protecting Skye—and now in getting her back. That was why I was here, and to be honest, I wasn't sure what I would do when I had them back. The drive to find them, the need to recover Mum and Skye, was all I could think about lately. It had taken over, and now it was what kept me breathing. Once I had them back, maybe I would stop, just run out of steam and keel over on the spot, or maybe revenge would replace it. Maybe I'd be kept alive by my hatred of the Unseen and everything they'd done to me.

"I'm sorry," I murmured, but my attempt at sympathy felt like putting a Band-Aid on an amputee. How could I possibly begin to understand the weight of what Rachel had gone through? My family were missing, but they weren't dead. Not yet.

My dad had left, but he was still out there, still alive. I always thought I had it the hardest, that my life was the worst around, that my parents' split and Mum's work and my constant feeling of disconnection was the worst life could possibly get. But Rachel's life, that was a whole new kind of suffering. Mine seemed trivial by comparison. I could be thankful for what I did have, even though it wasn't perfect. I still had a mum, and a dad, and a sister, and until recently, I'd had a home. A slow creep slithered up the back of my neck and grabbed hold around my skull. If I didn't get my family back, if I couldn't rescue Skye and Mum, my life would start to look a lot like Rachel's.

This was the first time I truly felt connected to her. She had always been nice to me, but it had never felt as genuine as right now. She had been putting on a front, and I was just now breaking through her shell, just by being in the right place at the right time. Perhaps now I could get some real answers.

"Your purpose is the Kindred," I ventured, "I get that. But I'm still not clear on what the Kindred's purpose is. I know it's about making sure things work or something, like there's some grand master plan to make the world a better place, but—"

"I need some air," Rachel said, standing. "Want to walk?"

I nodded. She'd changed suddenly, but I wasn't sure why. We made our way out of the room, down to the end of the corridor, and out onto the landing. Our section was mostly quiet, but I could hear faint bubbles of activity from other wings, mostly from the west, where the live-ins were. It was past midnight by my guess, but they seemed to operate on their own strange schedule down here, body clocks confused by the constant darkness. After only a week, I was having trouble getting to sleep. I could only imagine how much stronger the effect would be after months or even years spent here.

There were two security patrols, one on either side of the Apex, and they were just changing guard for the overnight shift. Security had been ultra-tight since the school attack. There were three people in each patrol, and they walked in a point formation.

As we watched, one patrol stopped right at the highest level, five storeys up. They spread out; from there, they could see the entire Apex. The other continued through where we'd entered, to the east wing.

We quietly made our way to the lower north-wing entrance, through the doors that led to the training ground. They swung silently open. Rachel closed them gently behind us and led me out across the floor.

We veered to the left, cutting through the cubicles set up across the giant cave. They were covered in scorch marks and debris. We reached the side of the cavern, a huge rock wall dotted with boulders and dark fissures. Rachel walked back and forth for a while, searching in the rocks, and then disappeared into one of the fissures. Her head popped back out. "Coming?"

I made my way over and squeezed through the claustrophobic opening. I had to turn sideways and suck in my stomach to get past some of the thinner sections. How had she even found this spot? It wasn't exactly a tunnel— more like a long crack in the rock caused by an earthquake or maybe just the slow shifting of the earth. It was a far longer fissure than I expected, full of twists and turns, and I had to feel my way through as it was now completely dark. The ground was wet, and the atmosphere dull and musty. Often my fingers came up against a damp rock wall that seemed impassable, until Rachel's hand thrust through some previously undiscovered crevice and grabbed me. It was probably twenty minutes before I got a glimmer of fresh air and the tunnel opened up to about an arm's width across. I could smell trees, sweet green syrup in the air, and then there was moonlight edging its way past the rocks and jagged edges to play at my feet.

The tunnel opened even farther, and the soft patter of water rippled in from outside, a nearby creek stepping over pebbles and twigs as it wandered off to join the larger Murrugal River.

We stepped out of the mouth of the tunnel and through a brisk shower of water. It had clearly been raining. Droplets fell across the mouth of the passage and collected in a puddle before heading down the tunnel into the cave system. We were on a moon-drenched outcrop that was only a few steps across, high up above the tree line, a rocky outlook jutting from the side of the cliff face.

We were close to the top of the cliff, which meant we had actually been moving slowly up as we sidestepped through the tunnel. I breathed in. A thick, leafy mist steamed into my chest. The night was warm, and for a moment, I almost forgot Rachel standing next to me.

"Nice, huh? I found this place a while ago, by accident. I was in the training ground and noticed a trickle of water coming down through the crack. The walls in there are always wet, so I wouldn't have noticed it otherwise, and that's probably why no one else has. I came back at night with a torch and found my way through. It was confusing at first, but you get used to the turns pretty quick. I ended up out here. If we're on high security and I need some space, I sneak out here for some fresh air. There's something special about this place. I think it's just the fact that I'm not meant to be here."

The last of the summer storms crackled over the distant mountains, but otherwise the sky was clear. Far away, I could see the glow of streetlights in Ettney. There was a huge patchwork dotted with farmhouse lights, and then the trees started at the edge of the national park. I hadn't realised how deep into the forest we were until I saw just how much canopy stood between me and civilisation. Rolling mounds of brushy foliage and wiry branches bumped up against each other, blurring into a thick blanket. It looked like broccoli, and the comparison made me smile.

"You asked about the Kindred," Rachel said.

I nodded, turning to face her. She was striking in the moonlight, her dark skin shimmering beneath eyes that shone emerald when caught at just the right angle in the half light. It was like she didn't quite belong here, like she was slightly out of place in the world.

She took a deep breath, about to speak, but stopped, looking over the side of the cliff. The undergrowth below had gone silent, and I looked down through the canopy, trying to see what she was staring at.

Through branches, sticks, and leaves, there on the ground was nothing. Less than nothing. A void surrounded by swirling tendrils of night. A shadow was here.

TWENTY-THREE

I dropped to the ground. It was a clear night; if the shadow was looking our direction, it would see us for sure.

This one looked different from the thing in my bedroom or the figure at the park. It was more like the one that had held Skye in the air—an ethereal, swirling darkness, like a fire burning black.

Out of the corner of my eye, I saw Rachel gesture, and I turned my head, but hair got in the way, falling in my eyes and mouth. I desperately brushed it away to see she was signalling for me to stay low and crawl back to the tunnel. There was no space on the platform for us to turn around, so I inched backwards, staying as flat as I could. Raising my head for a moment, I peeked over the edge. I had no rational reason to do so, and it was a pretty dumb idea, but there's something in humans that really wants to see whatever's about to kill us. The shadow was still there, motionless.

Ducking my head again I reversed toward the tunnel, my shirt riding up as I slid backwards. The moist rock made my stomach slimy, but there was no time to care about that.

Rachel was already inside waiting for me, having ducked in as soon as we saw the shadow. Now I was on the ground, though, the base of the tunnel was too thin to slide through. It was wider at waist height, and the only way I could get inside was to stand. When I did, I would be exposed again, but there was no way around it. I had no idea if it could even reach us up here, but Rachel was scared and that said a lot.

We needed a distraction. If I could get the shadow to look the other way for a few seconds I might be all right.

I crawled forward, and Rachel figured out my plan. "Ari, no!" she hissed. I didn't care. If the shadow saw us here, the Unseen would know our location. I wouldn't be responsible for that.

There was a big, sturdy tree just beyond the shadow. Time to start a bushfire. If I got lucky, the whole place would be burning in a matter of minutes. The shadow would be forced away, and it would seem like a natural event. Focusing on the tree, I took a deep breath and tuned in to it. Flames shot out of the trunk, lighting up the forest.

The shadow didn't leave, like I'd planned. It moved towards the fire, gliding silently across the ground. A tendril reached out and wrapped itself around the tree. I felt sick—the tendril looked like an oesophagus. I'd seen one at a museum once, taken from a body for an exhibit on the digestive system. This looked like someone had reached inside the shadow and ripped its throat out, attaching the entrails to the outside like limbs. It pulsed, rhythmic striations flowing from the fire to the shadow. It was feeding.

The flame died, and the shadow swelled with pleasure. So much for a bushfire.

But the thing was still distracted, so I took a deep breath and positioned my arms on either side of my body, ready to push up and duck in through the mouth of the tunnel. I counted to three and jumped to my feet, leaping towards the entrance. Rachel beckoned frantically, and I looked back just in time to see the shadow turn towards me.

My shoe caught a rock, knocking it over the side of the cliff. It skipped off other rocks, slowly but surely bouncing towards the shadow on the ground. *Click. Click. Click.*

Thud.

A scream. A scream like nothing I had ever heard before. Inhuman, like a wolf being tortured. It knew I was here. It was coming.

Rachel pulled at my arm, and I jumped into the cave. The screech echoed off the tunnel walls, deep into the fissure. It came from everywhere.

The shadow was from the same place as the thing in the chapel. They didn't belong here. They were the opposite of here. They were wrong, an abhorrence, an abomination in the universe. The cold spot on my stomach burned. Whatever this evil was, I was connected to it. It had marked me, and the mark was calling to its maker.

The tunnel felt infinitely smaller. Where once it had only pressed on me, now it crushed. In the dark, I saw black, throaty tendrils reaching out towards me, grabbing my skin and pulling at my clothes. I swallowed hard. It was all in my head. Perhaps.

We were moving faster this time, and I scuffed my legs and hands. My knee stung, and I reached down to check it. It was bleeding. Could the shadow smell blood?

The tunnel opened out, and I sensed we were close to the end. I breathed deeply; even the musty cave air felt fresh after my panic in the darkness. Rachel was comfortable enough to talk now, but we didn't lose pace. The conversation was breathless. "I don't think it saw us."

"It turned towards me," I panted.

"It's not as perceptive as you'd think."

I hadn't asked about the shadows before. Keeping them to myself made them feel like just a bad dream, so I'd been too scared to ask. If someone answered, I would know they were definitely real, that the cold spot on my stomach was real. Something else had stopped me too, a strange impulse that seemed to come from deep inside. But now that Rachel and I had encountered one together, I couldn't pretend anymore, I couldn't keep up the fantasy that I was losing it. I had to ask. "What is it?"

"It's bad. Those things are the worst kind of bad you could imagine."

"Those? You mean there's more than one shadow?"

"Far more. The most anyone has ever seen at once is twelve. One of our units stumbled across a cluster of them by accident and radioed back to let us know. They went missing after that. The Shadows work with the enemy, maybe lead them. We've never seen enough of them to know for sure. I should probably tell you —" She paused. "You called it a Shadow. Where did you hear that name?"

"I didn't. It just came to me. It seemed right."

Rachel frowned. "We call them that, too. It's odd you picked the same name." She furrowed her brow, studying me intently.

"I've seen them before," I said, changing the subject. "Those Shadow things. One came to my house. It took hold of Skye."

Rachel stopped. "It took her?"

"It talked through her."

"They've never talked before," Rachel said, her voice tense.

"They weren't real words, at least not a language I know. It was different." I stepped over a large rock in the middle of the tunnel. "That was the second one I saw. Maybe the third, but I can't be certain."

Rachel grabbed my shoulders. "You've seen three?" Her tone scared me.

I took a deep breath, which was difficult in the musty air around us. "After we went to the crash site, the one the cops faked—I think it followed me home. It was above my bed."

Rachel swore. "What did it do?"

I wanted to tell her how it had grabbed me. How it changed me. I wanted so much to tell her of the sickness taking root in my stomach. I opened my mouth to speak, but stopped. The same force inside me that kept the chapel a secret wanted this a secret too. I could feel it tugging at the edges of my mind, pulling me from the truth. "Nothing," I lied. "It left. Probably scared it off. I'm tough like that."

My joke fell flat, and I was thankful for the dark blanket around us. Before she could press me further, I changed the subject. "What was it doing out there?"

"Who knows? Maybe it was coincidence. Maybe it was looking for us. Maybe it was hunting."

"Hunting?"

"Everything's got to eat."

I remembered the teens who had gone missing. The people who'd disappeared up here over the years. Nobody from town ever came to the mountains, and now I knew the urban legends were anything but myth. Those hikers had been hunted.

We reached the end of the tunnel and lowered our voices, not wanting anyone in the training ground to hear us. It was unlikely to be occupied, not in the early hours of the morning, but we didn't want to take the risk.

"We should tell someone about it," I whispered.

She shook her head. "If we do, we'll have to explain how we saw it and where we were. Heading out there is a pretty big breach of protocol. No one else can know. It was probably a coincidence, it being there the same time as us. Let's keep it to ourselves for now. Actually, maybe don't tell anyone you even know they exist."

I wasn't sure why she wanted me to lie, but I nodded. I felt connected to her now. We could trust each other. I didn't want to wreck that, especially considering that, right now, she was probably the only person I could truly say that about. Except Josh, and he didn't know half the stuff going on with me.

As scared as I was, I thought we should at least wait around to see if it had followed us. I didn't want to be the one to jeopardise the security of the entire Kindred. Rachel agreed, and we found a spot behind a log in the training ground that gave us enough cover and let us comfortably see the crack in the wall.

After an hour, nothing had come through. We were home free.

We moved far away from the training ground entrance before we stepped into the patrols' eyeline, in case they got suspicious about where we'd been. They looked pretty tired anyway, and their heads were starting to droop, so it was unlikely they were alert enough to wonder why we were in the training ground this late at night.

It was a quiet walk back to the east wing, and when we got to our hallway, Rachel said, "If you see one again, you need to tell me."

Nodding, I closed the door of my room. I'd been borrowing some of Rachel's pyjamas, and while they didn't fit properly, it was better than sleeping in my clothes.

I stripped the sheet from the bed and wrapped it around myself to change, facing away from the security camera and whoever might be watching. That's when I took a moment to inspect the black spot on my stomach.

It had grown. It had started the size of a fingernail, but now looked like I'd been hit by a baseball. The mark blurred, and I blinked, certain I was just overtired. The blur didn't clear, and I bent over to get a closer look.

There were tiny dots moving around the outside of the spot, and the mark pulsed like an ink blot on a wet sheet of paper. I placed a finger on my skin. It was slimy and wet, like mould.

I'd known it for a while now: I was marked. A target. Prey. But something had changed tonight.

The Shadow had called, and something in me had answered.

Now, we were connected.

TWENTY-FOUR

Josh sat in the corner of his room, bouncing a ball he'd managed to scam off one of the guards. "I'm going crazy. I'm honestly going to crack and just scream or something."

"Me too." I paced around the room. I was tense, and bored, and stressed, and exhausted.

"Plus, I'm sick of these *bloody cameras!*" he yelled at the security dome above him.

I stopped pacing. "They really are everywhere, aren't they? The only place I haven't seen them is in the Apex and the training ground. Couldn't have a private conversation in here even if I wanted to."

"There's none in the showers, either," he said.

"Yeah, but those are all creepy and open. You never know who might walk in."

Josh stood. "I've only used them late at night when it's quiet. The whole mixed gender thing is super weird. I've always hated public bathrooms at the pool, and this is so much worse. Also, *Hackman* was in there yesterday."

"Oh, gross!" I laughed. "I was going to use the showers last night, but I was too tired. Thank the Lord! I don't think I would have ever recovered from that mental scarring."

Josh stared into the distance, looking sick. "I don't think I ever will. It's a good thing you didn't come back anyway, 'cause I went in there after he left."

My face flushed at the possibility. "If we're both going late at night, it's lucky we haven't crossed paths yet. Maybe we need a signal just in case, like leave a shoe at the door or something so we don't accidentally run into each other."

"Sure," Josh nodded. "Shower shoe. Good plan." He was red, too. We both stood awkwardly for a moment.

"So about the other day," I said.

He raised one eyebrow.

"When you said there's something you don't want to erase. You meant our kiss, right?"

Josh nodded.

"Thing is, I'm not sure if I — I mean, with everything that's happening and all ..."

"It's okay," Josh said quietly. "You're dealing with so much right now. I keep trying to put myself in your position, feel what you're feeling, but I can't. I — I just want to feel you, you know?"

I snorted, and Josh went bright red. "That's not what I meant! I was... oh for ..." He looked at his feet, downcast, and my laugh subsided. His words were careful this time. "I was trying to say, I know you're having a worse time than me, and I get that it's complicated, and that's okay."

My laugh subsided, and I held his hand in mine. "You're sweet. And thank you."

He smiled.

"I've got to go," I said. "Training starts early again today."

"All good. And shower shoe?"

I nodded, grinning. "Shower shoe."

We had been training every day, tuning faster and faster, and I even felt I had flaring under control. I could now create a small flare anywhere within about ten steps of myself, which wasn't hugely useful, but I was able to shut it on and off at will. It only ever worked when I thought about Noah, but I could switch those emotions off inside now, which brought the flare back under control. I didn't feel so much like a loose cannon anymore. I was starting to feel like a weapon. A blunt one, but a weapon nonetheless.

We reached the end of our training mid-morning, and Hackman called us all together to make an announcement.

"Ten days ago," Hackman began, "Ari's family were taken hostage by the Unseen. So far, the Unseen have made no demands, but we have it on good authority that if something does not happen soon, they will most likely get bored with them and do something drastic."

I glared at him. "You told me they'd be safe. Either you were wrong, or you lied to me, but if anything happens to them I —"

"No plan survives a battle, Ari," he snapped. "Things change. Intelligence changes. The point is, we intend to take action by the end of the week."

"But you —"

"This will be a highly coordinated, highly planned attack focused on the clean extraction of Ari's family." He ignored me now, speaking to the group. "Many of our units are currently deeply embedded in key positions, and several others are engaged ... elsewhere. The remainder of our units are devoted to keeping this facility safe and will need to stay to continue that defence. This means we only have three units to deploy.

"Considering Ari's connection to the mission, this unit will be involved. It will be the first field experience for some of you, but it is a critical one, and the most experienced of us will take the lead. Our first task will be reconnaissance before the main action, which should take place tomorrow evening. Tonight, several of us will head out to the suspected safe house and review the lay of the land, as well as confirm the presence of Ari's family before we attack."

Finally, something was going to happen. Relief and nerves hit me at the same time.

"The reconnaissance team will be led by myself," Hackman continued, "and it will be made up of the following: James, Rachel, Vicki, and Ari."

Frank and Nareem looked crushed, but they had been struggling to work as a team over the past few sessions as Frank had grown progressively more arrogant. Maybe Hackman was trying to teach him a lesson.

"We will meet in the Apex this evening at five. That will give us enough time to prepare before sunset."

Late that afternoon, before it was time to go, I ventured back to see Josh.

When I walked in he was lazing on his bed, reading another newspaper he'd borrowed from one of the Kindred. He put it down as I entered. "Hey there sunshine."

I smiled. "Hey. You know you look about fifty years old reading that?"

"That's cool. I heard you like older men."

"Ew!" I punched him in the arm, and he laughed.

"How go the superpowers?"

"You know me, I've saved the world already."

"We can go home then?"

"Yeah, done and dusted." I grinned. "Seriously though, I'm heading out tonight. We might have found Skye and Mum."

Josh smiled, and then frowned. "That's great news about your family, but they're actually sending you out there?"

"I want to go."

"I don't like it. You're not a soldier."

"You don't have to like it. And you'd be surprised what I'm capable of."

There was an awkward silence.

I sat down next to him on the bed, and he sat upright. "I don't want to lose you," he said, slipping his hand over mine.

I laid my head on his shoulder. "You won't."

He gently kissed my neck, just below my ear, sending tingles down my back. I closed my eyes and leaned into him. He kissed me again, and I kissed him back, trying to forget about the danger I was walking into. I was still so confused from Noah, but I didn't care despite our last conversation. Josh was like a drug, a way to forget all the darkness inside me. I needed him.

He slid his hand around my waist, brushing my skin with his fingers. I realised too late, and he pulled his hand back in shock. "You're so cold!" He gently lifted my shirt up a bit to look at my stomach.

The black mess was still there, still pulsing, still growing.

"Ari," he breathed. "What happened to you?"

I shook my head. "I don't know."

"You need to get that looked at! You're injured."

"It's not an injury," I said.

He froze. "What is it?" he asked quietly.

Josh seeing the mark somehow broke the spell that had stopped me talking so many times before. Facing away from the camera in the corner, I told him—in whispers, so they wouldn't hear me—about that night in my room with the Shadow and the ice. The chapel stayed a secret, though. I had a feeling it wouldn't let me speak about it even if I wanted to.

Josh listened intently, his eyes as dark as his voice had been. When I finished, he sat in silence for a while. Finally, he said, "You have to tell them."

"What?"

"The Kindred," he explained. "If that's some sort of tracking signal or a predator's mark, you might be in more danger tonight than you think. What if the Shadow can smell it, or track it down like a GPS locator? It's too dangerous. You can't go out tonight."

I frowned. "You can't tell me what to do, Josh."

"I think I've got a right. I've been stuck in here for two weeks because of you, and you've come to see me what, three times?" As soon as he said it, I knew he wanted to take it back. My face burned, and my eyes narrowed into slits as I stood. He tried to recover. "I didn't mean that. I wasn't—"

I slammed the door on the end of his sentence.

TWENTY-FIVE

That evening, we gathered in the Apex. Vicki sat on the ground, leaning against James's knees. He looked nervous, and I didn't blame him; I was freaking out myself and trying desperately not to let it show. Hackman was his usual calm, unnerving self, and he maintained his weird smile as he began the briefing.

"We're heading into the heart of Unseen territory tonight. They are not as centralised as we are—instead, their facilities are scattered across the region. Their safe houses are generally smaller and easier to hide, which is why pinpointing the location of one is nothing short of a miracle.

"Tonight, we're heading to an old farmhouse which has been, for all appearances, abandoned for some time. Three days ago, one of our Sisters in deep cover was on her way to work and drove past the entrance to the property. Fresh tire tracks and a newly broken window suggested squatters, and when she tried to tune, the interference was enormous. That level of interference is only present in large crowds or

Unseen facilities due to their awareness training. She saw a woman and child through a window, and they matched the description of Ari's mother and sister. Our job is to get close to the property and ascertain defensive positions, as well as any entrances. We will also work out the best approach for tomorrow night. The two other units involved will stay back and enter only if conflict occurs. We don't expect any need for them, but they're our backup tonight."

Hackman gave us our entry plan, showing us a map and a few photos of the property. There was a long driveway and several large silos off to one side of the house, across a big dirt clearing. The only cover for our approach would be a set of trees along the driveway, and a few closer to the house. As the farm was derelict, one of the paddocks had waist-high grass, but the rest was barren—ploughed but left unplanted. That happened a lot in our region, especially since the drought. So many farmers had left, trading their work boots for jobs in the city driving trucks and working in supermarkets. The neglect would make it tough for us to get close without being seen. Our best shot would be coming across the paddock of the farm on the opposite side of the road to our target, a big field of corn that would give us cover to the fence line.

We donned grey-green khaki jumpsuits, not the traditional robes the guards wore. These were more practical and would keep us hidden. We didn't wear the blinker-style masks and hoods worn by the trainers and advanced combat units, either. We needed the widest field of vision possible; after all, this was meant to be a recon mission. In and out.

I followed the group through the east wing. This was the first time I would enter the outside world in more than two weeks. The arena didn't count. Not to me, anyway.

We walked through eight or nine different corridors; they were so similar I lost count after a while. They were all hewn from rock like the corridor outside my room, bare stone left to weep water, unlike the clinical steel of the west wing. But the last corridor was different. The walls, ceiling, even the floor were dull metal. Six guards stood at the entrance, three on each side. They were heavily armed. This was the first time I'd seen actual weapons in here.

"What's with the guns?" I asked Hackman.

"Look around you."

I did and counted eight different security cameras in this section of the corridor.

"This is a different kind of war and requires a very different kind of security. The cameras stop the Unseen using their abilities to break in. Unfortunately, they also stop our people from tuning in defence. In this situation, for once, guns are the most elegant solution."

It made sense, but they still made me nervous.

Hackman knocked on the large metal door, another airlock like the one that led to the arena. A masked face appeared at the small barred window and nodded. A clunk, and another, and the door swung open. Beyond was another corridor like this one, identical guards with identical guns, and another metal door at the end. This security was intense. There was no way the Unseen could get in here.

The guards were motionless as we passed. They were so still it felt like a mark of respect, like they were saluting with their bodies. The whole thing felt like a funeral. The final door opened into a dark tunnel in the rock, similar to the secret one in the training ground, but not as claustrophobic.

The light was dim, and we shuffled through the tunnel until it opened out into a mess of shrubs and lantana. Hackman ducked, and we followed, crawling through a low gap in the bushes. There was a steep path on the other side, and wooden sleepers in the dirt formed steps that led to a clearing. A few steps down, I looked back; the tunnel was impossible to see from here. No one would find the compound by accident.

The clearing was basic, a small open area like a campground. A huge tree sat in the middle, a beautiful old oak that twisted and curled, covering most of the clearing with shade. There were three large patches of ground that looked as if they had been disturbed, dug up and backfilled somehow, but the only real indication this wasn't a typical campsite was the ground covered with tire tracks. Although there was obviously a fair bit of traffic around here, I couldn't see any cars.

Three masked and hooded Kindred emerged from the trees behind us. Hackman nodded at them and instructed us to turn away. I faced the opposite direction along with the rest of my team, to avoid interfering with whatever they were about to do.

The ground rumbled, and birds shrieked, disturbed by grinding that rang out across the clearing. A minute later, the noise stopped, and we turned around. A car sat atop one of the patches of disturbed soil.

Rachel laughed at my surprise. "Cool, hey? Two guys make the dirt heavier; the other makes the car lighter. It'll need a wash once we get it back, but it's pretty hard to find sitting six feet under."

"World's weirdest parking garage," I said. But it made sense. They didn't want a build-up of abandoned cars near a secret entrance. The dirt piles were reasonably inconspicuous, and as long as rangers didn't come up here too often, nobody would think twice about them. It was pretty clever, although it seemed like a lot of work; the hooded Kindred were panting like they'd just run a marathon. Fortunately for them, the other teams had already deployed, so ours was the last car they had to lift. They headed back up the stairs, disappearing into the scrub.

The big, black, dusty van was our transport. The sun was setting now, and the windows reflected the deep red framed by the trees above.

Hackman opened the back door for us. There was a bench along either side of the van, no seatbelts, and no windows. Hackman drove, so Rachel, James, Vicki, and I sat in the back. The drive out of the clearing was seriously bumpy, and I started to feel sick.

The drive would be about an hour, so I took the opportunity to get to know the team a bit better. Plus, talking gave me something to think about other than the nerves and nausea.

It turned out James did remember me from primary school; he recalled my two-toned eyes. Kids tend to remember stuff like that. He, like Rachel, had discovered tuning on his own, but he hadn't used it to break into shops. He'd tried to be the town superhero over at Cawley but failed when he tried to stop a robbery. He mistuned and burned down the shop he was trying to save. The Kindred had heard about a strange fire and a caped crusader running around Cawley and connected the dots, approaching him soon after to give him the chance at a more structured use of his abilities.

I couldn't resist asking what his superhero name had been. He sighed, knowing how lame it was. He called himself *J-Man*. We all burst out laughing for a good minute, and Vicki teased him that using your real initials wasn't the best way to keep your identity a secret.

Vicki was quiet for most of the trip but opened up when I asked about the tattoo on her shoulder. I'd seen it a few times now, although I couldn't right now because of the jumpsuit. It was a snake wrapped around a staff, a religious symbol, she explained. In the Bible, Moses made a staff with a brass snake on it, and if someone got bitten by a snake, they looked at the staff and were healed. Anyway, when she was sixteen, she was bitten by a snake on a bushwalk and almost died in hospital. Her family had taken her to this visiting minister to be prayed for, and overnight, she got better. She'd gotten the tattoo as a kind of faith symbol, and although she didn't really follow it now, it still meant a lot to her. This seemed like news to James as well, which confirmed what I had suspected—they probably spent a lot less time talking than doing the other things new couples often did. I got embarrassed thinking about it, so I tried to talk to Hackman instead.

He said he liked to keep his "real-world history" to himself. I thought the expression was strange, considering his so-called real life was a cover for this one. The world of the Kindred felt real enough to me. He did reveal that the Kindred would transfer him into hotspots to smooth things over. He was the fixer, the guy you sent in to repair what the last guy broke. He'd been all over the country and was transferred here because of the increased Unseen activity. The Mother had also tasked him to make sure I assimilated well. He changed the subject to the drought as we passed a dead wheat field.

The conversation left me uneasy. A guy who ranked that highly looking after a rookie like me? Too much was connecting. I was marked by the Shadow and targeted by the Unseen before I even knew I had abilities. The thing in the chapel had reached out to me, and it seemed the whole Kindred were watching my every step. It was like everyone knew some big secret about me, but nobody had bothered to let me know what it was.

We pulled up on the opposite side of the cornfield we would use as cover, having driven the last twenty minutes or so without lights on. It was safer to approach in the dark, and tonight, clouds muffled the moon, which helped make us harder to spot.

Hackman led us into the cornfield, and we spread out from there. He, Rachel, and I would take a direct approach to the house. James and Vicki would flank on each side and hang back near the road to signal the support teams in case there was trouble. The support teams were already in place and had been for some time; they could be at the farmhouse in less than a minute, although I had no clue where they were actually positioned.

Cornfields have always creeped me out, and this night was no exception. The constant rustling as we moved through the stalks made it impossible to be silent, and the corn grew above our heads so I couldn't see very far. Someone could sneak up and take me down before I even knew they were there, and even though as a child I'd always imagined that happening to give myself a thrill, tonight it was a very real possibility. We moved through the field quickly, and as a result, Rachel and I tripped on a few fallen stalks we didn't see coming. Hackman didn't break his pace once.

We slowed as we neared the edge of the field, moving at a crawl through the last few rows, corn leaves lapping at our heads. We finally stopped one row from the road.

The night was pitch-black and eerily quiet, like someone had sucked all the light and sound up with a vacuum cleaner. I'd seen some televangelist once on TV talking about his trip to hell. He said when he woke up in hell there was no sound and no sight and no feeling. I didn't know if I believed him—I'd always thought hell was more like Mrs. Walkley's math class last lesson on a Friday—but this was as close to his description as I'd ever seen. Even the moon was swallowed by a suffocating layer of clouds.

Hackman stopped one row from the road and held his hand up to signal we should freeze. He was in front, at the very edge of the field, and wanted us to be ready to cross the asphalt road ahead. James and Vicki took up positions on either side of us, ducking down behind fence posts and weedy shrubs to wait for our return. A three-wire fence strode the edge of the field, and Hackman stood on the bottom two wires so we could duck through quickly. The road was horribly exposed, with a direct line of sight to one side of the house, but the chicken-wire fence on the property was topped with barbed wire and only had one clear point of entry.

I stepped onto the tarmac, and time slowed as I waited for retaliation, for a shout that meant they'd seen us, for a flare to explode in my lungs. It was four seconds of death waiting on a tarmac graveyard.

Nothing happened.

We reached the other side without incident. If they had seen us, they didn't make it known. We would find out for sure as we approached the house.

Once through the gap in the fence, we flattened ourselves completely. The ground was dry and cracked, and my face scraped it as I stayed low. Dusty red dirt kicked into my mouth from Hackman scrambling in front of me, but I didn't complain. This was about staying alive, not being comfortable.

We were headed for the tree line to secure our cover when something changed. Something that could get us all killed.

TWENTY-SIX

A line of light raced towards us—the moon was coming out from behind the clouds, its glow dazzling after the oppressive darkness. Anyone left in the moonlight would be seen for sure. Someone would spot us from inside the house, and before we could scream, our lungs would be fried inside our bodies.

Hackman saw it the same time I did and began a frantic scramble along the grass to the first tree. I followed, but Rachel was taking a closer look at the silos and didn't see the moonlight about to betray us. I hissed her name, and she looked, her face wide with fear. The light was halfway between the house and her position, and she had less than three seconds before it reached her. She was too far away, and she knew it.

I reached the cover of the first tree with a moment to spare, but Rachel was caught completely in the light. It might as well have been daytime, and if anyone was inside the house watching, it was over.

She cut her losses and jumped to her feet, half-rolling, half-diving into the cover of darkness. I was glad the owners had planted a big, dark pine here. We were safe in the shaded circle beneath it, dark in comparison to the moonlight around us.

I readied myself for a firefight. We had made so much noise scrambling for cover, and Rachel had been exposed for so long they had to know we were here. We hid around the back of the tree, on edge, listening for the crumple of feet on the dry, crackling lawn, the creak of a floorboard, the click of a latch, anything that would give us warning of Unseen retaliation.

My lungs burned. I was holding my breath. I slowly exhaled, trying to be as quiet as I could. It felt like we were frozen there for days, waiting for a sign, waiting for our deaths. In reality, it was probably ten minutes, but when you think you're about to die, time slows. I'd learned that a few times over by now. It's like your body tries to soak up every moment of living, and your mind puts your senses into overdrive so you can drain every last possible second out of existence, savouring every scrap of time you have left.

Hackman moved first, confident we were still undetected. The tree line was thick at this end, a whole row of pines that created an unbroken line of cover. The bottom branches were so close to the ground we had to stay flat to change position. I moved along the back of the row, keeping the trunks between me and the house. Rachel kept far closer than before, not wanting to be left out in the open again.

About halfway between the fence and the house, we were close enough to get a better look. The farmhouse had a corrugated tin roof, rusted in parts, and guttering that flaked blue paint onto the dead grass below. The broken window was obvious now; it led into what could've been a bedroom.

Breaking a window at the front of the house to gain entry was sloppy. It would have made more sense to break one that faced away from the road. Maybe they were in a hurry, or maybe it wasn't them at all, just some ratty local kids with too much time and not enough to do. Three sets of windows faced us, and a screen door hung slightly off its hinges into a veranda that leaned a fraction to one side. The whole place looked unstable. It hadn't been maintained in a long time.

A sad-looking garden ran along the front of the veranda on either side of the steps. It was filled with spindly, dead plants, the remains of whatever the owners had planted before the drought. The driveway was on my right and ran around to the back of the house from the road. There was a broken-down play set out front, one of those hollow plastic ones with a tiny slide, but the joints had split and, at some point, filled with murky mould and rainwater. That was all dried up now, but the watermarks remained.

There was a creak from inside the house. Then a second one. A third. Footsteps.

The front screen door wailed, opening slowly out into the veranda. A figure stepped out onto the grey, weathered boards. He let the door close behind him and walked to the top of the steps. He looked in my direction. I tensed, ready to run. A glow lit up his face. A phone. He was on a call. I exhaled and tried to listen in.

"Have you heard anything else?" A pause. "No. It's strange for an operative to go dark this long ... Yes, I know it's deep cover. But everything's quiet, right across the board. The Kindred are never this silent. If we haven't heard from our eyes inside ... I'm just saying, what's the use of having an agent in the Kindred if they don't tell us anything?"

I almost gasped but managed to swallow it. Hackman's eyes went wide, and Rachel's face dropped. The Unseen had someone inside the Kindred. We had a traitor.

The phone call ended, and the figure stepped off the porch into the grass. We were almost level with the house, and he was far too close for comfort. Stepping slowly across the lawn, he walked our way. I wanted to run, but the others stayed still, so I did my best to follow their lead.

He was close now, breathing only a few steps away, thick deodorant wafting through the air. He stopped at the tree next to ours. We were made for sure.

There was a zip and then the sound of dirt splattering, like someone emptying a bucket of water a few drops at a time.

"Got to get the plumbing going in this God-forsaken house," he muttered as he relieved himself on the tree trunk. I almost laughed. Thankfully, he hadn't chosen the tree we were hiding under. Either he would have seen us, or we would have stayed hidden and had a pretty disturbing new experience. He zipped his pants up and wandered back into the house. Rachel stifled a laugh, and I joined her, snorting quietly. Hackman glared at us. We settled, with some effort, and waited for a long half hour, until we were certain the house was still again.

Then, on Hackman's order, we crept forward. Every time a twig cracked, I panicked, sure it would give us away. I tripped on an exposed tree root and made way too much noise as I regained my balance. But the house remained silent.

Finally, we were level with the house, and one by one, we scurried across the moonlit gap to press ourselves square up against the wall. The whole house was raised to avoid flooding, the same as many farmhouses around the area. The floor was even with my waist, and the windowsill sat way above my head. We would be safely out of view as long as we stayed close to the wall. We were on the opposite side to the driveway and flanked by trees, so even though this was the closest we were to danger, I felt the safest since we'd left the cornfield.

Hackman had brought a periscope, a tiny mirror on a stick like the ones spies in movies use to see around corners. We were to go from window to window to get an idea of numbers, learn the layout of the house, and confirm my family's presence. That would give the following night's assault a far better chance of success.

We wouldn't be able to check the front, as the veranda was far too creaky for us to stay hidden, but the front rooms hopefully shared windows with the side of the house so we could check them from there.

There were three windows on this side of the house. One was small and made of the speckled glass used for bathroom windows, so we couldn't check it, but the rooms on either side were bedrooms. We couldn't see into the first due to thick blinds, but the second had a hole in the curtain, and Hackman signalled that there were two Unseen inside.

We slid around the corner to the back of the house, which was level with the ground on this side. The land sloped up slightly so we had to crouch as we stepped onto the paved back entrance. We were in a small yard with a few dead flowers and a shed, and beyond that were fields as far as I could see. The windows back here were big, covering nearly the entire back wall of the house. Most likely the living room and kitchen were here, but they looked empty. As Hackman looked inside with his mirror, I edged forward and ducked from one side of the screen door to the other.

A light went on like a gunshot, and I dove to the ground. The whole yard lit up, and a shadow covered the shed. It was someone inside the house, standing in front of the light. The shadow began to shrink. Whoever it was, they were coming to the door.

I pressed flat against the wall and ground, trying to disappear into the corner where the weatherboards met the earth. Light blazed through the screen door across the paving, cutting me off from the others. I couldn't go back, and the others couldn't come forward. I was on my own.

The shadow moved from the window and entered the light of the doorframe. Hackman and Rachel crawled for cover, and I backed away as fast as I could, unable to turn around for fear of being seen. The door hissed open as I turned the corner. Footsteps came my way. Keeping low, I crouched and ran, hoping Hackman and Rachel would meet me around the front.

This side had four more windows, and the one in the middle was barred. I didn't have long, but I had to make the most of this. I leaped up to the barred window as I ran and caught a glimpse of a figure asleep in bed. She was facing away from me, but I could tell she was older. And her hair was red.

Mum.

I couldn't stop. The footsteps were not yet around the corner behind me, but they were coming fast. There was no cover on this side of the house except for a rusted truck a short sprint away. My feet slid on the driveway stones, and I ran for it, diving into the truck's bed. I lay flat and tried to keep my breathing quiet.

A torch switched on, lighting up the top of the trees. It was pointing away from me, so I dared to lift my head to glance over the side of the truck. A man was walking toward the pine trees with purpose. He was heading for the others.

I found a small rock next to me in the truck bed, and threw it as hard as I could towards the entrance of the drive. The clatter got the man's attention, and he walked away from the trees, towards the front fence. Dark blobs crept under the trees. Rachel and Hackman. I'd saved them. For now.

The torch arced back my way, and I ducked again.

"Hello?" the man called.

I was caught. There was only one way out of this.

The field of corn had looked dry. Maybe it was just dry enough. I prayed the team were already running. They would be in a moment, regardless.

I looked through the truck's windscreen towards the field we'd used as cover, tuning in to a stalk of corn. It was challenging—the organic matter had a howling resonance that hurt my head. I raised the tuning fast, and smoke rose from the base of the stalk. I was far away, but a small glow flickered alive. The field belonged to the next farm. Hopefully, they were insured.

The glow caught the figure's eye, and he ran towards it. If I stopped now, he would know the Kindred were here, and they'd evacuate the safe house. I had a few more things to do before then.

I slipped out of the truck and cracked the door open. No one ever locked their cars around here. I took the handbrake off, put it in neutral, and pushed it in reverse as fast as I could. It hurtled down a small slope towards the silos before smashing into the base of the largest one.

Time to complete the ruse. I grabbed a rock and hurled it through the window, yelling and laughing and swearing as loud as I could. Lights went on inside the house.

"Did you see that?" I screamed to my imaginary gang of friends and then swore at the house. "Get out of here, damn squatters! Get your own home!"

I ran hard, legs windmilling as I got away as fast as possible. They wouldn't follow a gang of teens vandalising an abandoned house, and they definitely wouldn't do it while the field was on fire. They would have to scramble to hide evidence and clean up before the fire brigade arrived. Hopefully, they wouldn't evacuate the house altogether. I ran for the silos on the opposite side of the driveway.

As I rounded the corner, hands grabbed me. I fought them off.

"Stop it!" Hackman whispered. "Follow me."

We scrambled through the field, keeping the silos between us and the house. By the time we reached the road, I was wheezing, the air thick with smoke. Red lights flickered next to the field. The firefighters had arrived to get the blaze under control.

The Kindred van pulled up beside us, driven by Vicki. "Get in!"

It took me a moment to catch my breath as we sped away. "They're in there." I panted. "We found my family."

TWENTY-SEVEN

The ceiling had seven pipes. Three electrical, two water, and two I wasn't sure about. The light was out, but the residual light from the hallway cast deep shadows across the rough stone surface of the ceiling. In the corner, the camera glared at me with its little red light.

I rolled over. Since we'd returned, I hadn't slept, too amped from adrenaline but even more so from the hope that soon my family and I would be reunited. When we'd gotten back, Hackman had gone straight to meet with someone important, probably the Mother, and we all shuffled off to our rooms to stare at the ceiling. The others might've been asleep, but I was far from it. I should have been exhausted, as it was nearly dawn and my body was aching. My eyes burned, but my mind was buzzing.

I gave up on sleep and went for a walk. Fresh air felt suddenly essential. If I was quick, I could probably catch the sunrise from out on the secret ledge. Rachel was probably still sleeping, so I went by myself.

I snuck out of my room towards the training ground. The patrols were drowsy and didn't notice me cross the Apex, and I found the hidden entrance and made it through the passage with no trouble.

As I neared the end, the light bouncing in was brighter than usual, a deep blue rather than the milky white of moonlight. The sun was about to rise.

Just before the end of the tunnel, I came to a dead stop. Ahead, a black figure stood against purple sky, silhouetted in the mouth of the cave. I panicked for a moment, but the shape was human, not Shadow.

"Hello?" It was Rachel.

I opened my mouth to answer her, but she spoke again. She wasn't talking to me.

"They've identified the safe house, and the attack is tomorrow night, just before dawn. There'll be three units, two on either side of the property and one through the front." She was on some sort of phone, but it was big and bulky, not like the phones in shops. "I'm sorry I couldn't warn you earlier. There was no opportunity."

A pause. My heart thumped in my ears, and I felt sick.

"No. You can't relocate, not yet. Get the target out by midnight; the others will have to stay and fight. They overheard Jacobs talking; they know there's a mole. Only a handful of Kindred know about this operation, and if the place is evacuated too early, they'll suspect me. I don't feel like dying today. By the way, tell Jacobs to watch his mouth."

A longer pause.

"Ari? She doesn't know. I'm not sure she's ready. If she's as important as you say, we've got to get our timing right. Her family are alive, but if it's up to the boss, they're not going to stay that way."

I wanted to shove her off the cliff and be done with it. The girl I trusted, my only friend in here besides Josh, had been working behind my back from the beginning. For all I knew, she was responsible for the attack on my house. Hell, she might have killed Noah.

How many more times would my trust be betrayed? Nathan from the hospital, Rachel, even Noah had lied. Who else would it be? The Unseen had taken the best parts of my life away, and they were taking my faith in people with them. Bile burned my throat, but I swallowed hard. As much as I now hated Rachel and everything about her, I had to play this smart. If I did something drastic now, we wouldn't be able to use her. Hackman would know what to do.

Her call ended, and she moved to come inside. I slipped back into the tunnels, praying I could stay far enough ahead that she wouldn't hear me. If she caught me farther in the tunnel, I could pretend I was coming out, but this close to the entrance she would know I'd overheard. She would probably kill me to protect her secret. I had to be alive to make sure she paid for this, even if I had to kill her myself.

I made it to the training ground and hid behind a cubicle. I watched her leave, calmly walking around the outside of the cavern as if nothing had happened, as if she hadn't just sold out me and my family. As if she wasn't a poisonous, backstabbing bitch. She closed the door to the Apex, and I waited long enough for her to make it to her room.

Retreating to my room to figure out my next move, I glanced in Rachel's window before I went in. She had gone straight to sleep. She looked so peaceful that for a moment I forgot how evil she really was. It was all suddenly very hard to believe. Had I misheard her conversation? Was I missing something important? I wanted to believe so. Still, no matter how many laps I did of my room, how much I paced, how many times I ran her words over in my mind, the truth was undeniable.

Now what? I had to act quickly, before the Unseen moved my family. A part of me was torn. Should I confront Rachel directly, give her a chance to explain herself? I desperately wanted to believe I'd heard her wrong, that there was something else going on. Of course, if I did confront her and she really was Unseen, she might kill me on the spot—burn me from the inside out and throw my body off the cliff.

Others began to wake and move about the corridors, casting shadows across my wall. It was time to act.

I made my way to Hackman's door and knocked. He was bleary eyed and had obviously been asleep. "Ari, you're shaking. Is everything all right?"

I was shivering, rippling with adrenaline. There are moments in our lives that define us, moments that change everything. After these moments, nothing is ever quite the same. Part of me knew this was one of them, and my body was reacting.

"Last night, when we heard about the traitor." I stopped.

He sat down on the edge of his bed and leaned forward, his hands on his knees. "Yes?"

I told him what I'd overheard. When I finished, his eyes glared bullets.

"How sure are you?"

"I know what I heard, but I could be wrong about what it means. I thought you'd know what to do."

"I see. Thank you for coming to me with this. Stay here and lock the door. I'll be back soon." He strode out of the room, and I followed his instructions, a sick fog in my stomach. I sat down on a metal chair in the corner of the room and stared at the wall, not sure what to do or even think. My eyes were heavy, and I fell asleep in the chair.

A knock shocked me awake, and I jumped to my feet. I creaked open the door. Hackman stood at the entrance, eyes dark.

"We confronted Rachel, but she's not talking despite our best interrogation. It's clear she's guilty, but we have nothing so far. We would like you to speak to Rachel directly. Talk to her, tell her what you heard. Once confronted with the reality that we have proof, she may be more willing to open up."

I followed him out of his room and across the Apex, into the west wing. We went to the end of the corridor and down another flight of stairs, descending into a basement level. This floor was horrible. Dark, cold, padded rooms crawled past as we marched steadily along. Cameras covered every corner of every room, creating enough interference to prevent just about anyone from using their abilities. One door was closed and bolted from the outside, but someone was making noise moving about in there. The windows were shuttered and locked, so I couldn't see in.

We entered the room at the very end of the corridor, and I felt sick. The room was dark, except for one hanging light that cast deep shadows on the walls—and over Rachel. She was slumped in a chair, cable ties cutting deep into her wrists. Red poured out of a cut over one eye, and her cheek was swollen and purple-black. Her lips were split, and her neck had dark finger marks on it. She'd been choked at some point, but she was still breathing.

It looked like two of her fingers were broken, and her pants were covered with sticky blood, hopefully just from her eye. There was an IV drip in her arm. A bag of clear liquid trickled slowly through the drip.

A man stood behind her, bright red spray covering his jeans, shirt, and fists. I had seen him around before. His name was Dominic.

I looked at Hackman, horrified. He returned my gaze, steady and unflinching. "Talk to her."

I stepped slowly forward. She raised her head, eyes barely able to open.

"Rachel?" I said.

You have no idea what you've done," she said, her words slurring.

"What *I've* done? I heard you, Rachel. I heard you call them. I heard you tell them to move my family."

She spat, clearing the blood from her mouth. "You have no idea what you've done!" Her voice rose to a screech.

"Where are they?" I yelled. "Why are you doing this?"

She grinned, a dark smile spreading across her face, exposing teeth that swam in bloodied gums. "You've clearly chosen your team," she said, her voice cold, "and I chose mine. We both have to live with that now."

"Answer her question!" Dominic barked, punching her hard in the back. Something cracked, and she arched her back, screaming.

I staggered into the hallway for air, my head swimming from the violence and the sick smell of blood. What kind of hell was this war? Despite her betrayal, somehow, I still felt Rachel was my friend. It made no sense—feelings almost never do—but I still cared about her. I wanted justice, not torture. If the Kindred were the good guys, just how bad must the Unseen be?

Hackman joined me, putting his arm around my shoulders. It was the first genuine act of compassion I'd seen from him, and it felt awkward and uncomfortable, like watching a dog walk on its hind legs. "Are you all right?" he asked.

"No."

He pulled his arm away and sat against the wall. I joined him, and he spoke softly. "This war. This fight. It's more important than any of us."

"I know."

"It's about the whole of history, the whole planet. So many people have fought, so many have died for our cause."

"I know! But I can't be as detached and cold as you can. It's my family we're talking about. There's no way you could understand what I'm going through!"

He lowered his head, and I apologised. That was too far.

"It's all right," he replied. "Losing Noah was ... Most nights I can't sleep. It's like a part of me has been ripped out, like something in my soul has died. Thinking that maybe it was all for a purpose, that maybe his death will serve the greater good—it's the only way I don't break down completely. I have to be detached, for the sake of everyone." He put his hand on mine. "For you."

I shifted under his stare. He was grieving, I understood that. But it was weird seeing him so vulnerable. I wasn't sure I liked it, and I was tense until he pulled his hand away.

He pointed to Rachel's cell. "That is the only way we're going to get answers. It's the only way to make good come from Noah's death, and the only way to protect our cause. It's certainly the only way we're going to get your family back."

He was right, as much as I didn't want him to be. If I was being truly honest, a tiny part of me enjoyed watching Rachel suffer for her crimes. To punctuate my thought, a scream shot out from the holding room. Then another. And a third. There was nothing for a moment, and then a sob. A battle raged in my head and heart between compassion and revenge. If I wanted her to pay, I needed to become the kind of person who was okay with the consequences. I couldn't have one without the other.

More screaming. Way more, animal in its intensity. The kind of scream that has broken through humanity into primal fear. It was horrifying, and it didn't stop.

I covered my ears but couldn't block it out. Finally, I couldn't take any more and got up to leave. As I stood, dead silence filled the hallway. The door creaked open, and Dominic stepped through, blood dripping off his hands. "She wants to see you," he told me. "Alone."

At least that meant she was still alive. I looked at Hackman, and he nodded.

I stepped inside, and the smell was once again overwhelming. Rachel's head was slumped over. She looked dead, apart from her chest slowly moving up and down.

"Rachel?"

She nodded.

"You wanted to see me?" I could barely hear her response, so I crept forward. "I can't hear you."

"I said get down," she croaked.

"I don't understand."

"In about twenty seconds, you will."

My eyes widened. "What have you done?"

"My fail-safe is about to activate," she said, her voice barely a whisper. "It's my insurance policy. If I don't reset it every twenty-four hours, bad things happen. Judging by the time I saw on Dominic's watch, that's about twelve seconds from now. So. Get. Down."

I ran for the door as Rachel counted. "Ten."

I yelled at Hackman to evacuate. He jumped to his feet and gave the order.

Turning back to Rachel, I screamed, "Turn it off!"

"I can't," she said. "Five."

Crossing the room, I slapped her. "Turn it off now!"

"Get down. Two."

I didn't hear her reach one.

TWENTY-EIGHT

The roar was deafening, like being inside a jet engine. Heat blistered my skin. I coughed up smoke and tried to stand, but my leg was pinned under a slab of concrete. It didn't feel broken, but the slab was too heavy to lift. Flames were building, shooting from a gas pipe dislocated by the blast. If it split any more, I was dead.

The cameras watching Rachel were broken, or at least offline. I focused on the concrete slab and raised the resonance as high as I could, shielding my face. The slab split apart, shooting debris and dust in all directions. Time to run before anything else collapsed.

Rachel lay crumpled and unconscious in the corner. I could leave her to die. That would be easy. But she still had answers, and for some reason, she had tried to save my life. I hobbled to her and threw her over my shoulder. Either she was light, or the adrenaline made me stronger.

The corridors were a tornado of flames and concrete and steel. There were no bodies here, which was something. I was disoriented in the swirling smoke but made it out of the basement.

Hackman stood at the top of the stairs. He took Rachel from me, and I collapsed to catch my breath. The ground was wet and the air was clearer here. A burst pipe sprayed water over everything, which kept the flames at bay.

My head felt light, and the world went black again.

"You know, I think you're turning head trauma into a sport."

I blinked and rubbed my eyes. Josh lay on the bed next to mine. I managed a smile. "I'm semi-pro right now. A few more, and I'll qualify for nationals."

He laughed, and so did I. My ribs hurt. He sat up, reached over, and put his hand on my shoulder. "Seriously, though, are you okay?"

"I think so." I sat up slowly and checked myself, coughing smoke out of my lungs. My legs throbbed like they were sunburned, and my knee was pretty sore, but I was remarkably all right, considering.

Josh smirked. "You look like dirt."

"Yeah, thanks." I smiled, punching him in the arm.

He moved and sat next to me, running his fingers through my hair. "I'm sorry about before. Our fight."

"Me too."

"Honestly, I don't want to underestimate you. You're a lot tougher than you look. I heard some guys talking about how you carried Rachel all the way out of the basement. That's crazy."

"Is she all right?"

"They didn't mention it. They said she was the one who set off those bombs. Is that true?"

"Did they say anything else? Is everyone okay?"

Josh shook his head. "This part of the compound didn't get touched, but they put you in here with me 'cause they were running out of space in the medical rooms. About eighty dead. Couple of kids ... The bombs were on a timed delay or something, but you probably know that already. They got the fire under control pretty quickly. I offered to help, and they told me to watch you instead. I do know they're prepping for retaliation. It's gonna be major." He paused. "You didn't answer my question. Was it Rachel who bombed the place?"

I nodded and tears welled in my eyes. "I don't know who to trust anymore. I thought she was my friend. But after her, and Noah, I feel like the whole world is keeping secrets from me. Everyone except you."

He slid his hand into mine. "There's one thing I'm keeping from you. But it's probably the world's worst kept secret. I think it slipped out a while ago, in your kitchen."

I smiled at him.

"Ari, I—"

"Don't say it. Not right now. Not here."

His eyes dropped.

"It's not that," I said quickly. "You're amazing. And sweet, and kind, and you know me better than anyone. It's just that, right now I don't have space in me for anything but hate."

He drew back. "Hate?"

"Hating the Unseen, hating every little part of them with every last part of me ... It's all that's stopping me from melting down completely. I want to feel something else, but I'm scared that if I let in any other feeling, anything else but anger, all the other emotions I'm keeping down will blow up in my brain and I'll become a vegetable."

He nodded. "I get it. And I'm a patient guy. What's it been, two years so far? I can handle a few more days."

"Two years?"

"Ever since you broke your ankle that day at lunch. You were wearing those ridiculous pink socks with butterflies on them. You had a little smudge of dirt on your cheek from the fall, and the tears made your eyes sparkle. Most people look like a sea lion when they cry, but not you. You were beautiful."

I shook my head slowly. "I can't believe you remember all that."

"How could I forget?"

"That was so cheesy," I smiled, "but sweet." He shrugged, and we sat in silence for a while.

There was a knock at the door, and Hackman entered without waiting for a response. I let go of Josh's hand self-consciously.

"Good, you're awake. Follow me." Hackman whirled out of the room into the hall.

"Nice to see you too," I muttered in an imitation of Hackman's voice, and Josh sniggered. I kissed him on the cheek. He smiled, and I left.

TWENTY-NINE

We walked through blackened hallways and crumbling corridors. Most of the mess was cleaned up already. The Kindred were definitely efficient. There was one pile of rubble that hadn't been moved. As we walked past, a melted face stared out at me from between the rocks. Whoever he or she was, they hadn't made it.

Hackman stopped for a moment and gazed at the blackened mess. "This is why we fight." He turned resolutely and marched on. I followed, unable to shake the image of the face.

We stopped outside a briefing room. Hackman looked at me for a moment. "This is it, Ari. Make sure you're ready."

Without any further explanation, he entered the room. There was nothing else for me to do, so I followed.

The others were already there, seated around a table. Frank, Nareem, James, and Vicki were poring over maps and photos, talking in quiet whispers and pointing to different landmarks and roads. There were two other teams as well, eight more in total. Probably the backup units from the previous night.

"We need to strike, and we need to strike now," Hackman began. "Our oversight has approved a full-scale attack against the Unseen. It's time to wipe them out of our region, exterminate them like the vermin they are."

There were nods from around the table.

"Thanks to Ari, we've located the traitor, and we also know they're keeping her family in the farmhouse. An examination of Rachel's previous movements and her satellite phone has led us to several other Unseen facilities. We must wipe them out before they have the chance to run. If they don't already know we've found them, they'll work it out soon. The time is now. This is the final solution." He leaned forward. "I've already briefed the teams who are taking on the other safe houses. This group will attack the farmhouse, as we already know the layout and location. Pay close attention."

The plan was for one of the experienced units to take up positions around the perimeter and create a distraction that would lure the Unseen fighters out of the house. Once they were far enough away, we would enter through the front and back doors and take down any resistance inside. It was short, sharp, and brutal, and had the greatest chance of success. We spent ages studying maps and diagrams with different coloured arrows, circles, and lines that all meant different strategies and defensive positions. James, Vicki, and I would join half the remaining unit through the back door, while Frank, Nareem, and Hackman would join the others at the front. There would be six people entering the house from each side. If something went wrong, we would meet up at an old shearing shed about forty minutes' walk away.

We were due to begin at sundown, which was only an hour away, once the light had completely faded, to ensure adequate cover.

This was all in theory, though, and as I spent the hour waiting, I ran through every possible way this could go wrong. I do that sometimes—run through scenarios in my head and work out all the different outcomes.

Once, I had to confront Caitlyn about her gossiping behind my back after she told everyone at school about how I was crazy jealous of Taylor Sparks when she was dating Isaac Lewis because I had a massive thing for him. I spent the whole weekend stewing over the fight we were going to have on Monday, going through every possible conversation in my head, every response she could have and what I would say, and then what she would say and how I would counter. I got so caught up in my head that when I went to talk to her that morning at school, I was shaking with anger. Turns out, it wasn't even her who started the rumor. We'd been talking in the bathroom, and Jackie Trawler had overheard and told everyone. I'd wasted the whole weekend boiling in my own rage, and it wasn't even her fault in the first place.

Sometimes, it's not the greatest habit to play these things out in your head, but it's not as bad as working out what you would have done after it's all said and done. That's just pointless. But this time, I felt like I *had* to run it through, work out every way I could be cornered, every way we could be caught, every way this tightly stretched plan could snap and whip back into our faces. If it came to the crunch, I had to know what I was going to do. I couldn't let anyone down—not my unit, and certainly not my family.

When the call came to head out, I was still feeling underprepared. We'd had a soldier visit our school on Remembrance Day once, and he said that no amount of training or preparation gets you ready for a real-life battle. I understood that now; I had experienced some nasty things for sure, but I'd never run head first into this kind of fight. Hopefully, I wouldn't freeze, or even worse: crack up under the pressure.

We piled into the van, and I felt really sick. Not just motion sickness from the bumpy drive out of the park, but a churning anxiety in the pit of my stomach. In a very short time, a lot of people were going to die. I stared at the others, trying to take in their faces in case it was the last time I saw them alive.

James was visibly scared, staring at a spot on the wall behind me. He looked how I felt, and I could only imagine what I must have looked like to everyone else. Vicki sat next to him with a calm anger. Her eyes burned, but she was holding James's hand to comfort him, and she leaned her head on his shoulder. Nareem had his eyes closed and brow furrowed, trying to ready himself for the coming fight. I felt sorry for Frank. He looked so defeated and afraid, every scrap of false bravado devoured by terror. He swallowed hard. Hopefully, he wouldn't choke tonight. I couldn't see Hackman—he was up front driving—but he would be wearing his usual weird smile.

The drive felt five times longer than the previous night, partly because I knew what I was heading into and partly because I wanted to absorb every last living moment I had before the battle. They were potentially the last moments Mum and Skye had left as well.

I focused on my hands and tried to count backwards from a thousand to take my mind off things. I was so tired but alert at the same time, like my brain had drunk ten triple-shot lattes but hadn't told the rest of my body about it. I was running on pure adrenaline and had been for a while now. My eyes closed for one second.

I snuffled subconsciously as I woke, and everyone turned to stare at me. The van was slowing down. Somehow, I'd fallen asleep on Nareem's shoulder. How on earth had I managed to sleep knowing what was about to happen? I was more tired than I thought.

Trying not to show my embarrassment, I went to stand as the van stopped, but my foot had fallen asleep and I tumbled back into Nareem, who caught me awkwardly. Winded, I laughed at how uncoordinated I was, and everyone else quietly joined in. It broke the tension, which was nice, although it also slightly hurt my pride.

Hackman glared at us and motioned for us to be quiet. We had stopped a fair way from the cornfield we'd planned to use as our cover like the night before, and there was a big problem.

The sun was almost down, casting thin light over a now blackened field. Where the corn had been, there was nothing but smouldering ash and charcoal, wisps of smoke rising from the burned-out crops. The fire I started had blazed way out of control. Our cover was gone.

"This complicates matters," Hackman said. "Our reconnaissance teams would normally pick this up in advance, but after Rachel's attack …"

"They're still in the house," Nareem said, looking through binoculars. "I can see them moving through the windows. So they're alert, but I don't think they've seen us. It looks like they're packing, getting ready to run."

"We have little time, then." Hackman turned to me. "You said Rachel advised them to leave before midnight. They're moving faster than they should, which means they likely know we're coming. We don't have much time."

"We don't have a safe approach," Vicki jumped in. "They'll see us the moment we try to move closer."

Everyone in the van went silent. My face burned; this was my fault. In my escape the previous night, I'd ruined our plan. I hunted for a solution, wanting to redeem myself. I looked at the fields, deep furrows running in a grid along the edges.

Suddenly, the solution was obvious. "Irrigation channels," I murmured.

"Excellent idea," Frank chirped, which came as a shock. It was the first time he'd said something positive about anyone but himself.

"What do you mean?" James asked. He'd been a townie too long.

"The irrigation channels are deep trenches dug through a paddock to get water to the crops. They won't go the whole way to the house, but they'll get us pretty close. I noticed some on the way in last night. They're deep enough to crawl through without being seen if we can find where they meet the road. They'll probably be fed from the old dam nearby — we drove past it yesterday. It's only a few minutes back."

"Find the dam, find the trench, crawl to the house, and we're on them before they know what's coming," James mused.

"Done," Hackman said. He reversed as quickly and quietly as he could, turning around at a junction and heading back towards the creek crossing. We pulled in underneath a weeping willow, its long branches hiding the van from the house.

Hackman handed out fighting masks to hide our identities from any Unseen who might escape. Of course, the plan was to kill them all rather than let that happen.

I paused for a moment, taking in our surroundings while the others piled out of the van. I hadn't seen the other units yet, the ones creating the distraction and joining us in the house. The air was spinning with flies, so I didn't breathe in deeply in case I swallowed one, but the night was alive with smells clamouring for attention. There was the sweetness of the weeping willow, musty wet mud under my feet, the sting of smoke from the burned field, and a hint of rotten flesh from a dead fox filled with maggots on the other side of the road.

The paddock we were next to was enormous, and the farmhouse was smaller than my thumbnail from this distance. It was going to be a long crawl. I climbed into the bowl formed by the old dam. The earth was so dry it had cracked into plates, like a miniature earthquake had caused fault lines running all the way along the basin. They crunched under my feet as I stepped across the dam. The ground felt like rock, except up one end, where the irrigation channel sat. Some water was seeping through from the almost dry creek, making this end a touch muddy. Once, this whole thing would have been filled with water; now, it was just a reminder of lost prosperity.

It was almost completely dark now, and I strained to make out how far the irrigation channel went. Maybe it connected all the way to the paddocks on the other side of the farmhouse, but there was no way to know for sure.

At the edge of my vision, something moved. A brambly patch of shrubs shifted, and I froze as a masked face emerged from the tangled thorns.

Hackman turned. "Stanley. Good to see you. I was wondering when you'd show up."

"We're all here," said the man called Stanley. "Saw the field burned out and assumed we might meet up this end. Sorry we couldn't call, no reception out here, and we were told to keep radio silence."

Five other faces emerged from the bushes, and Hackman told them our approach. Stanley said the other unit was in position for their distraction, waiting for our signal.

We got down on our hands and knees, keeping our heads under the lip of the channel. It wasn't a deep one, so we were pressed pretty low. I kept scraping my knees on rocks and sticks that coated the ground or stuck up out of the mud. A few minutes in, my hand pushed down on the pointy end of a barbed wire offcut, drawing blood. I bit my lip to stifle the groan. Hackman was in front with Stanley and two others from his unit. I followed, then James, Nareem, Frank, and Vicki, with the remainder of Stanley's unit bringing up the rear.

The pace was frantic. I scrambled through the ditch like I was being chased by wildcats, which was almost true with Vicki crawling at the back of the line. From what I could hear, she kept shoving Frank forward as he slowed. It was causing some tension. I stopped for a second and looked back. Frank was sweating like a roast chicken and didn't look well. I felt kind of sorry for him, but there were more important things at hand, so I turned around and got back to it.

Hackman slowed the pace as we neared the house. We were almost there but still out of earshot. He went through the plan once more. By this time, I had it memorised practically word for word. James, Vicki, and I would go through the back with Stanley and two of his team, while the rest breached the front of the house, with Hackman on point. Once we were in position, Hackman would set a small stump alight near the back of the property, which could be seen from where we were now but was so far away it would take a lot of skill to tune. The hidden unit would see the signal and create a series of explosions behind the silos before engaging the Unseen fighters that came to investigate.

That was the plan, at least.

We split up. Hackman's unit stayed where they were, to edge their way around to the front. They only had to head to the tree line, which was simple, considering how dense the trees were between them and the house. Our move was a bit harder. We continued towards the back of the property, but we were still a fair distance from the house, so the next part was risky. We had to make it out of the irrigation channel all the way to the scrub without being seen.

I peeked over the edge of the ditch to scope the route. The scrub grew thick close to the backyard but was cleared a long way between there and our current position. We'd have to run for it, leaving ourselves visible from the kitchen window for at least ten seconds.

My hands sank deep into the mud, and I grimaced. Hopefully it wasn't septic runoff. Mum used to tell me horror stories from when she was a toddler and lived on the farm with her parents. Their septic system would break all the time and leak into the soil, and my grandparents would come out and find her paddling around in mud created by their own refuse. Life on a farm isn't as romantic as it's cracked up to be. I shuddered at the thought and refocused on the mission at hand.

Hackman had given us five minutes to get into position before he gave the signal, and our time was nearly up.

"We need to move," Stanley whispered.

I nodded. Time to go.

One by one, we scrambled over the top of the ditch and sprinted for the bushes. Stanley first, then his two team members. Vicki moved, and my turn came. My feet skidded on the dirt as I climbed over the edge, and I lost my footing, slamming hard into the cracked earth. I was winded but didn't have time to stop. I was exposed, and every second out in the open was a second closer to being seen, a second closer to death.

Launching back to my feet, I ran, with James close behind. We were halfway to cover when the ground lit up, freezing us on the spot like the world's scariest game of Red Light/Green Light. Someone had turned on the kitchen lights, which were shining blue-green out over the yard. We were completely in the open.

A figure moved around inside. It walked to the cupboard. James and I stayed still, breathing heavily.

The others' eyes gleamed, wide and motionless, from the bush in front of me. My legs were paralysed. I couldn't feel them at all.

The figure inside drew a knife out of a drawer. We were so close to the house I could hear the cutlery crash together as he closed it. He walked to the window and looked out. My mind screamed *Run!* but my body wouldn't listen.

I held my breath.

The figure walked back out of the kitchen, and the light went out. My whole body came to life, sprinting as hard as I could. I dove for the scrub, but James didn't move. He was still frozen with fear. I whispered his name, but he didn't respond. Vicki dashed out of her hiding place and grabbed his arm. When she touched him, it broke the spell, and he followed her to cover. As he reached us, he collapsed, exhausted.

"Rookies," muttered one of Stanley's teammates. Vicki glared at him, and he looked away.

James started to apologise, but Stanley stopped him. "No time for that. Look."

I followed his gaze to the back corner of the farm. A lone tree stump lit up with flames, like a lantern in the night. Hackman's signal. The attack was ready.

THIRTY

A ripple ran under my feet and out across the paddock. Then searing heat, my face burning to the point of pain, and a blast of air that punched me to the ground.

It was a huge explosion behind the silos to my left, probably a fuel storage tank. While I was on the ground, a second, blinding plume of fire rose next to the first. The unit had done their job, and it didn't take long for the distraction to be effective. I counted eleven people running out of the house, six from the back door and five sprinting across the driveway from the front of the house. There might have been more; it was hard to tell in the dark.

Once the Unseen were halfway to the silos, Hackman's voice took command from the radio on Stanley's hip. "Go!" Radio silence was over.

I pushed through the thicket, ignoring the thorns ripping up my skin. I flicked a branch into Vicki by accident, but she didn't say anything. It didn't matter now. Nothing mattered but the mission.

A few steps later, we found freedom, breaking out of the bushes and running across the lawn. The explosions had died down, and the bright light with them, replaced by a crackling amber from the flames now building behind the largest silo. Stanley flew past me, his much longer legs giving him an advantage. The back door was left open, but we didn't dare run in blind. Stanley, James, and I took up positions on the right side of the door, crouched underneath the window. The others joined Vicki on the left. My long training sessions were paying off. It was all down to instinct now.

Stanley poked his head around the corner. Screams melted the air from the silos. The unit had engaged. They were outnumbered two to one, but it seemed they were holding their own. Stanley clicked the button on his radio twice, and two bursts of static came back. Hackman's group were in position at the front door. Counting to three, we moved in through the back.

The house was pitch-black, but I could see right through to the front door. It creaked open, and the others moved in, silhouettes against the dark sky. It was so black it would be hard to tell who was friend or foe in here. We entered a second living room. A small TV sat on a low bench, possibly left here by the previous occupants. Six mattresses filled the floor, stripped of linen. Five half-packed suitcases lay against the window.

There was a small bathroom to my right, and I split off to check it out. The flames and yelling at the silos covered my footsteps. The house itself was quiet but oppressive, like a blanket lay over the place. This house felt heavy.

I stepped through the door to the bathroom. Mouldy tiles festered under the toilet, thriving in water pooled by a leaky waste pipe under the pedestal sink. Colours were muted in the darkness, but the sink and bath were pink, with green tiles trimming the fixtures. It was gross. And it was empty.

As I moved to leave, the shower curtain rippled. I tried to run, but huge arms grabbed me from behind, one across my front and the other over my mouth. A sharp sting at my neck stopped my struggle. He had a blade pressed against my throat.

A trickle of blood ran down my front from where the knife cut in. His breath was heavy on the back of my neck, warm and musty. His skin was oily, and hairy arms scratched against my shoulders. I could feel his stomach pressed against my back. I couldn't run. If he flicked his wrist, the mouldy tiles would be sprayed with my blood. The flames died down and the screaming dimmed to a background hum, in my mind, at least. He asked me a question, but I didn't hear it.

I took a deep breath and tried the only thing I could. "I'm a friend of Rachel's," I mumbled through his hand.

It was enough. He was surprised by the mention of her name and relaxed his grip on the knife, dropping it slightly from my neck. It was low enough to be out of his view, so I tuned in to the cold steel. It was a one-piece knife, the blade and handle all made from the same metal which rang a high, clear note as I locked in to its resonance. I raised the note, and the knife burned glowing hot.

The man swore and dropped it on the tiles. I ducked to escape his grip, but he tightened his arm around my neck to choke me. I bit hard into his arm, and his blood filled my mouth. He yelled and let go of my neck, giving me enough leverage to reach for the knife despite his other arm still firm around my waist. I picked up the knife, and it was still burning hot. Pain shot through my hand. I stabbed blindly behind me, hoping to connect with something that would force him to loosen his other arm still wrapped around my waist. The blade glanced off bone. He swore again but didn't let go, the other arm coming up to try and regain control.

I slashed behind me again, and this time the impact was far softer. When I let go of the knife, it stayed in the air next to my head. His arm dropped—both did—and he tumbled limply into the bath. I didn't want to look, didn't want to see what I had done, but I could feel a wet spot near the back of my head where his blood had soaked into my hair. I turned slowly. The knife protruded from his eye, gory mess dribbling down his cheek and into the bath drain. The blade was long enough that it had passed all the way into his brain. He groaned. My head swam, and I crouched so I wouldn't pass out.

Vicki barrelled around the corner, having heard the noise. She stopped, taking in the dying, bloodied body in the bath. "You okay?"

I nodded. I wouldn't be later, but I could hold it together for now.

The rest of the house had sprung to life. Shouting came from somewhere near the front. I had to get up there. I had to find my family.

Vicki and I ran toward the living room at the front of the house. James and two of Stan's unit came out of the kitchen, signalling that it was clear. There was no sign of Mum or Skye yet. If they were here, they'd be in one of the front rooms.

The closest bedroom had two doors, one that opened out onto the dining room and the other into the hall around the corner. James crept towards the hall door while Vicki and I took the other, closer one. The rest of Stanley's unit were quiet, probably either dead or fighting elsewhere, but there was yelling from the front lawn. James reached his position, and we flung open both doors at once.

The room was empty save for mattresses on the floor. There was no one in here. A door opened behind James across the hall, and I shouted for him to turn around.

Too late.

There was a sizzling sound, and smoke rose from his chest. He grabbed at his throat, gasping, but it was useless. Smoke poured out of his mouth and nose too, like a demon leaving his body. The flare had torn apart his lungs, burning him from the inside out. In my mind, he became Noah, eyes glazed, dead before he hit the floor, but of course he wasn't. This was James, the little boy who wanted to be a superhero. He fell slowly, and I had a memory from primary school. Mum once had a meeting with my teacher after school, and James was there. I'd been feeling sick, so he played with Skye on the playground for probably an hour, taking care of her for me. He was an only child and must have loved the chance to have a little sister for an afternoon. I'd forgotten about that until now. It had been a beautiful moment, in a life that must have been filled with beautiful moments.

Now they were gone.

Vicki took action faster than me. She was so angry, she didn't even try to use her abilities, just ran at the man in the doorway at full speed. She almost made it to James's body before the figure got her. Her back exploded as the silhouette repeated the deadly flare. She staggered and fell to her knees, letting out a sob before slumping over James. The man turned to me.

THIRTY-ONE

I ran, throwing furniture and slamming doors behind me to block the man's line of sight. I burst out the back door and onto the grass. There was no way I could take on someone of that skill and focus. Not directly. I had never seen someone that strong, except perhaps Hackman. My eyes hadn't left him, but he had broken through the interference and slaughtered James and Vicki in seconds. My only choice was to hide.

I ran toward the back of the yard, letting out a cry. It was primal, nothing in it but animal terror. But before I reached the bushes, something else took over.

My legs locked up and wouldn't let me run any farther, like I was tethered to my family back inside the house with rope.

They were still in there. I had to finish this. I had to get them back or die trying.

The garden shed was close, and I ducked behind it, cutting my arm on the rusted tin. The man who'd killed James and Vicki burst out the back door, slowed by the obstacles I'd put in his way. I stayed hidden in the dark behind the shed. I couldn't take him directly, and I couldn't let him see me. But I wasn't good enough to flare from this distance. To win this, I had to be smart and deadly.

The garden path was made of pebbles, and he sank slightly as he stepped onto them. A plan formed in my mind, but was it possible to execute?

I tried to focus, to tune in to a whole section of the path at once. A million tiny stones swirled in my head, each a different resonance, pitch, and texture. My mind wanted to explode, and the pain made me lose tuning. I refocused and tried again. I had to tune every single pebble at once and then the dirt underneath. I could hear earthworms and beetles and cockroaches in the layers of soil beneath his feet. They would have to move if they wanted to survive this.

My nails bit into my palms as I pushed through the pain, raising the resonance of a large chunk of earth under his feet. I tuned it higher and higher, past the point of integrity, right up to where I had vaporised the mug so many weeks before. At the last moment, he saw what I was doing. The dirt and rocks and worms and roaches vaporised, splitting into their basic elements, most likely hydrogen, oxygen, and carbon gas. A void opened under his feet. He leapt for safety but missed and tripped backwards into the huge hole I'd created beneath him. There was a loud snap as he disappeared from view.

I lost focus, and my mind shattered. My vision blurred and went dark for a moment, and I dropped to the ground to avoid fainting. My ears were wet, and I put my hands up to them. My fingers came away red with blood.

It took me a minute to recover enough to stand. The house was silent, although I could still hear a battle near the silos. I crawled to the side of the hole. My pursuer lay upside down, his neck twisted at a horrible angle. It'd broken when he fell. If he hadn't tried to leap for safety, he would probably just have broken a leg. Ironic.

Hackman, Nareem, and Frank made their way out of the house with Stanley. The rest of the house was quiet. It looked like these guys were all that was left of our team. Stanley swore as he saw the hole I'd made. Hackman looked at me and then back at him. "Told you she was special."

"I've never seen anyone ... not this soon," Stanley mumbled.

"Later." Hackman motioned for him to be silent. "Ari, I'm sorry. We've cleared the house, and there's no one inside but the Unseen. Dead Unseen, that is. Your family isn't here."

"But the person I saw through the window ..." my voice cracked.

"The level of security in this house is far too high for them to be holding such low-value hostages." Hackman saw the look in my eyes and stuttered, "I-I mean from a-a purely strategic standpoint. Whoever they were holding here is far more valuable to them than your family. I don't know if your mother or sister were ever here. Whatever target they *were* holding is gone. We're coming from this empty-handed, but at least we killed a few of them in the process. Including the simultaneous attacks on the other safe houses, we've dealt the Unseen a very serious blow tonight. We must celebrate any victories we can."

I was too empty from the violence and death to be shocked, or sad, or even angry. I nodded and sank to the ground.

A voice came over Hackman's radio, asking for assistance. Four of the original six in the distraction unit were still alive, holed up behind the silos in a standoff with seven remaining Unseen. Hackman raised an eyebrow at Stanley.

Stanley nodded. "We can take them."

237

"Let's clean this up then," Hackman replied. He looked at me. "You look like you need a few minutes, but we need to move now. Will you be all right if we go on ahead? You can stay here and join us when you've caught your breath. This area's clear, so you'll be safe."

I agreed, and they left to assist the others. My head was ringing, like I had just come home from a massive concert. I started to feel dizzy again, so I put my head down between my legs to recover. I wasn't sure if that was a good idea with my ears still bleeding, but it seemed to help.

After a minute, the ringing began to clear, and I tried to stand to go help the others. There were fireworks behind my eyes, and I sank back down again before I passed out. Tuning always had a slight mental cost, but this was too much. Vaporising such a large chunk of earth, especially with the complicated organic bits, had almost broken me. I couldn't have done any more. I felt if I had pushed much further, tried to make the hole bigger, I could have died, my brain turned to soup in my head or something. No one had explained that in training.

More yelling came from the silos. Hackman's cavalry were on the scene. A few pebbles fell into the hole, clattering down the sides.

I felt like the hole was watching me, judging me. I had taken two lives in as many minutes and hadn't even thought about it, hadn't stopped to wonder if it was okay. Maybe the men I killed had families, or friends, or lives outside of this ridiculous secret world I was caught up in. What gave me the right to decide my life was more important than theirs? Nothing, really. But nothing had given them the right to decide mine was less valuable than theirs, either. They'd tried to kill me, and the dead body lying broken in the hole next to me had made two corpses inside, as well.

Who was going to bury them? It was an absurd thought, given the situation. At least the guy down the hole was halfway there. That made me smirk, but I caught myself for smiling. I couldn't allow myself to be okay with what I had done, and I sure couldn't start finding it funny. If I did that, the darkness would take over for sure. It had already become such a constant that I was used to its presence. Somehow it belonged, it felt right at home. That scared me more than anything. I put my hand to the inky black splotch on my stomach. It felt colder and wetter than before, and I withdrew my hand.

I tried to stand up again. I was more successful this time and made it totally upright. The few steps I attempted were all right but still unstable; I wasn't in fighting condition just yet. Even so, the hole was creeping me out and I wanted to move away, so I stumbled towards the house. Hackman said Skye and Mum were never here, but I wasn't ready to give up on their trail just yet. I had to check it out. I might find something the others had missed, and besides, sitting still while the others were risking their lives at the silos was driving me crazy.

The back door still hung open, and as I stepped inside, the house smelled like someone had cooked steak. I gagged when I realised what it was. Burned flesh.

The back room looked the same as when I'd first entered—no battles had been fought here. I steered well clear of the bathroom; I didn't want to see my handiwork in there. Gingerly, trying not to make the floorboards creak, I crept to the hallway entrance at the left of the double-doored bedroom where James and Vicki had died. They were still there, and as I came level with the door, I jumped. James's eyes were staring at me, still open. He almost looked alive, but as I came closer, I saw they had already glazed, and my hope of a miraculous recovery was shot to pieces. Death always looks so peaceful on TV. Even when someone dies in an action show, they just grunt a bit, close their eyes, and fall forwards. It's not like that in real life. Not even a little bit. I really wished his eyes were closed, but I didn't want to touch him. That was too scary, especially because his mouth was still open, lips blackened from the smoke inside.

Vicki's hand lay on his cheek. If it weren't real, it would have been beautiful, like *Romeo and Juliet* or something, but no romantic music played, no credits rolled, and no one stood up after the director yelled cut. Death isn't like the movies. It's far more final.

I turned away, not able to look any longer, but my cheeks were wet. Weird, as I felt nothing. I was numb from everything that had happened, but it was good knowing some part of me was still able to cry. I wasn't totally broken just yet.

Across the hall was the room their attacker had come from. I pushed the door open. Inside were three mattresses and a corresponding number of suitcases, which I unzipped to rifle through in case they gave me information. The first two were mostly full of socks, shirts, and some very questionable underwear. The third was a bit more interesting. Half the clothing inside was formal, as if the owner was a businessman in real life. Suit pants, dress shoes, that kind of thing. There was also an organiser, which I opened to its last bookmark. Four days ago. That probably meant he'd been here at the house since then. Flicking through, I tried to get a picture of who the owner of the suitcase was. The page with tomorrow's date was marked

Andrea's 8th birthday. As I was putting the organiser down, a photo fell out, and everything clicked horribly into place. It was a family photo. Dad, Mum, two kids—one boy, one girl. The girl, Andrea, I recognised from the park near our house; sometimes she and Skye had played together. And her father was Elijah Crawford, our real estate agent.

I ran outside as fast as I could without making my head spin, tearing off my mask and hood to clear my vision. The hole hadn't moved, and neither had the body, but from this angle, I got a good look at his face for the first time. It was Elijah. Andrea's dad.

My stomach twisted into knots. I had killed a father. A loving father, judging by the moments I had seen at the park. As hard as it was to reconcile Elijah's actions that night with his identity as a businessman and dad, those kids would grow up without him. I don't know how long I sat staring at the picture still in my hand, but I didn't ever think I could move again.

Not even when I saw a glimmer of movement out of the corner of my eye.

Not even when a voice called my name from the dark shadows to my left.

Not even when a boy stepped out into the soft glow of the fires still raging beyond the silos.

Not even when his eyes met mine like they had across the quad at school so many weeks before.

Noah.

THIRTY-TWO

Neither of us moved for a moment. My mouth hung open as I took him in. His hair was short now, cropped in a military style. He was wearing the same long, dark shirt and pants as the rest of the Unseen. Above his left eyebrow was a fresh scar, and his cheek was bleeding. His eyes were the only thing that felt the same, although they seemed wilder than before, like two horses chafing at the bit.

He stepped towards me, and I scrambled back. This didn't make sense.

"Ari, it's okay. It's me."

"You—I saw—"

"You saw me dying, but you didn't see me dead. Everything they've told you is a lie."

"You're with the Unseen." It was an accusation, not a question.

He nodded. "It's not what you think."

"I don't know what I think."

"Right now, all you need to do is trust me."

I frowned. He sighed and looked over my shoulder towards the silos. "The Kindred are coming back. We need to move."

I hesitated, and he crouched so that his eyes met mine. "Ari, I know where Skye is. And your mum. If you want them back, we need to run."

That was enough. I didn't trust him, not at all, but he was my only lead. If he was lying, I'd find out soon enough. I took his outstretched hand and got to my feet. I was feeling a bit better, but he still wrapped one arm around me for support.

He led me across the yard and around the scrub at the back. We moved fast, which was difficult, as the field was still furrowed from an unfinished ploughing. I stumbled every few steps at first but soon got the hang of it. The farther we went, the faster I could go. After a few minutes, we hit a slow jog, although I still needed Noah for support. We were in total darkness now, the light from the fires a distant glow. Figures moved near the house, and Hackman yelled my name. The air was still warm with smoke, but it didn't have the sweet smell of bushfires; it was acrid and toxic from the fuel and plastic burning behind the silos.

We moved in silence except for our breathing and our feet on the soil. Behind us, several torches switched on, turning like lighthouses as the Kindred searched the fields. We were too far ahead for the light to reach us, and as long as we kept moving, we would stay undiscovered. As we neared the back of the property, the search party turned around, probably recalled by Hackman.

I still didn't know what to think. Was Noah leading me to safety or an Unseen trap? I was committed now either way, and loyalty to my family took precedence over loyalty to the Kindred. It had to.

"How are you alive?" I whispered.

Noah shushed me. "I have no idea if something's following us, but if they have the farm under surveillance, someone could still be tracking us. I'll explain everything when I know it's safe, but right now you need to trust me."

I went to speak again, but Noah cut me off.

"I'm serious. Either trust me, or don't, but if you keep talking you might get us both killed."

Nodding, I decided to trust him, for now at least, and kept my mouth shut. We walked forever in silence, crossing farm after farm, road after road. There was no way Hackman or the others could find us now. It was the advantage of a country as big as ours, although it also meant help was a long way away if needed. Noah's watch said it was after three in the morning.

We passed the edge of farmland and into part of the national park. This part of the park was a long way from the Kindred complex. Trees formed a dense canopy overhead, but the path still glowed slightly from the stars so it was easy enough to follow. It sloped gradually uphill, and my calves burned from the slow climb.

It was hard to believe Noah was alive, but I couldn't deny he was here. I'd grieved for him, cried for him, laid flowers at his funeral. None of this made any sense, although, over the past few weeks, my definition of sense had been surgically removed.

If my life had been a bad teen movie, Noah would be a zombie, or a vampire, or a ghost brought back from the dead by his everlasting love for me or something, but he was none of those. Noah was alive, warm, and didn't even slightly sparkle in the moonlight.

I kept waiting to wake up back at the farmhouse, but if this were actually a dream and I had any choice at all, I'd choose to wake up back at home the day before the truck blew up, when my family was home and the laws of physics made sense and nobody at all was even a little bit dead. Although, if this were all a dream, I'd never have met Noah. I'd never have looked into those eyes. I'd never have felt him hold me. Pain and Noah was a package deal. After tonight, I'd know if it was worth the trade-off.

Several times I went to speak, but Noah signalled for my silence. We weren't safe yet, although my feet scraping on the rocky path were so loud I could have woken a graveyard.

He was limping, and there was dressing on his leg. I was surprised he was walking at all considering how bad his injuries had been the night we were attacked. Somehow, he managed, and after an hour inside the national park we stopped at a clearing where a river fed into a small pool before continuing its way downstream. The moon was up and just visible over the huge trees surrounding us. I slumped down onto a big flat rock, and Noah sat next to me. Before he had a chance to speak, I made my demands.

"Tell me what's going on. Don't be mysterious, or sugarcoat it, or leave out any details. I've had enough of that. I want the truth. If I decide I can't trust you, or if I think you're lying to me, you're dead." I was tired—not just physically—and I didn't care if he thought I was harsh. "I've learned how to do a flare inside lungs just like the one that nearly killed you at the Boulders," I lied, "and I don't think you'll survive a second one."

Noah grinned. "Rachel said you learned how to flare. Impressive. But please, try to avoid setting me on fire. At least until I've finished my story. Telling you my experience is the easiest way to explain what's happened."

"Fine, but make it quick. I'm not in the mood for a bedtime story."

"Five years ago, I found out what my father really did for a living. We had always moved around a lot, and I was sick of it. We'd moved six times in five years. Mum was sick of it too—she left when I was eight—but Dad never stopped moving. I hated him for that.

"When I was twelve, after he'd been stationed in Port Haigh for two years, I got the feeling we would be moving again, so I snuck into Dad's office late one night to see if I could find out where we were moving or maybe how to stop it from happening. Dad came in, and I hid under the desk so I wouldn't get in trouble. He sat down and started talking to some guy on the phone about the Kindred and their global agenda. He wanted to meet up somewhere to talk in person."

Noah absently skimmed a rock across the water. It reached the other side of the pool and clattered on the bank. Something ran away through the undergrowth. Probably a possum.

"He left the house to go jump in the car. It was after midnight, so he must have thought I was asleep. I hid around the side of the house and climbed in the boot when he unlocked the car. We stopped at an old winery outside town. He went in through a huge oak door, and I followed him inside, staying way back so he wouldn't catch me. It was a Kindred complex, smaller than the one here, so it had less security. There were only a few people around, so it was easy to sneak down the hallway he used and hide outside the door of the meeting. Inside were a whole bunch of guys discussing how to accelerate the Kindred's plan. My dad wasn't just a cop. He was a high-level member of a secret organisation.

"While I was listening, this huge guy grabbed me—came up behind me while I was listening so intently. I freaked and tried to run, yelling as loud as I could. Dad ran out of the meeting and saw me. He sighed, then smiled, then started to laugh. He said he was wondering when to bring me in on this, but I had made the decision for him.

"He told me I had abilities, that somehow he had known this for a while, although I had never used them or even known about them myself. But he'd been waiting for the right time to recruit me to the Kindred. I was brought in, trained, and grew my ability faster than the other guys my age. I moved fast through the ranks, even got sent out on missions. When I was fifteen, I got promoted to Brother, which is a supervisor over younger Kindred members.

"Every family has secrets, and the Kindred is no exception. The higher you go and the more you're promoted, the more you find out. I heard rumours of what they call the Agenda. It's the reason the Kindred exist, the cause they fight for. They don't tell you what it is when you join. That, you have to earn.

"When I was promoted to Brother, they said the Agenda was the 'advancement of all mankind towards the final day,' which sounded kind of honourable. But Dad told me more. He wasn't supposed to, but he figured I could keep the secret. I think he was trying to bond. Turns out the 'final day' was the destruction of humanity, the purging of the world so the Kindred could rebuild it again to their design.

I shook my head. This was way too much to take in, and so different from everything I had been told up till now.

"I traced their history through Kindred records. They helped build Babylon. They invented gunpowder in China. They fuelled the Crusades and the Spanish Inquisition. They created the Black Plague. They owned the East India Company. They started both World Wars. They funded

Hitler. They ran the Manhattan Project. They have been positioning themselves for years in key positions across the planet, readying themselves for the Agenda to be fulfilled. Ever wonder how prime ministers and presidents get elected when they're always so unpopular? Our last twelve have been Kindred. There are cells all over the world, with hundreds of thousands, maybe millions of members trained in resonance, infiltrating every level of power in every country, preparing the way for destruction.

"There are rumours the founders of each side are still alive, and that they've been here all along, even before the Kindred or Unseen existed, fighting it out with kingdoms and wars and civilisations, using them like pieces in the world's longest game of chess." He paused. "But that's just hearsay."

I frowned. "Rachel said the Unseen were the ones doing this, the ones trying to destroy us all."

"Rachel didn't think you were ready for the truth. She wanted to tell you, right back at the start, but didn't feel she could without blowing her cover. She was going to tell you that night on the ledge, but then you said you had an encounter with a Shadow, and she didn't know if you would be on our side or theirs. She didn't trust you."

"She talked to you?"

"She was keeping me updated until we lost contact with her early yesterday morning."

I stood, taking a few steps away. I kicked a rock into the water, and it sank to the bottom, leaving ripples that spread out across the pond. "I don't know what to think. You're telling me I've been working for the bad guys. That the Kindred are evil and the Unseen are good."

"I wouldn't use words that black and white, but if you'd like to simplify things ..."

"None of this makes sense!" I yelled into the clearing. My words returned, dulled by the trees in a quiet echo.

"It will once I've finished."

I took the correction, and shrugged. "Go on then."

"The Unseen have been around for almost as long as the Kindred, started by defectors from the Kindred who opposed the Agenda. Once I found out the Kindred's true agenda, I got in touch with the Unseen. They weren't that hard to locate once they got wind I was willing to switch sides. We may be badly resourced and way outnumbered, but we've always managed to keep the Kindred in check. We operate in secret, like the Kindred, and espionage is our greatest asset."

"Hence the name." I placed my head in my hands. I was so tired, and this was all so much to take in.

"Right. The Unseen took me in without hesitation. They figured I could be a double agent, working inside the Kindred and passing information back to the Unseen." He shifted uncomfortably, seeming a little guilty even though he was doing the right thing. "My father's high rank gave me access to information normally reserved for higher orders. And then there was a truck accident in a little town called Ettney, and the Kindred moved my father here after they got word of an unusually powerful civilian. A teenage girl."

My eyes widened. "Me.

THIRTY-THREE

Noah stood and joined me next to the pond. "I was meant to befriend you and recruit you to the Kindred. I went along with it, to maintain my cover, but then I met you and knew I didn't want you to be part of this world. It's so dark and full of pain and violence and death. I tried to save you. That night at the Boulders, that cavern I took you to, it's an Unseen meeting place. I arranged for the Unseen to meet us there and take you into protective care. When they didn't show up, I knew something was wrong. The Kindred had tailed us, followed us into the park and found the Unseen contingent coming to meet us. They killed them all and knew for sure I was a traitor. That's when we were attacked."

"Those figures, the ones that nearly killed you ... they were Kindred?"

He nodded. "They were about to kill you too, except Rachel got herself assigned to follow the Kindred ambush team. She knocked you out and convinced the Kindred to recruit you instead. She managed to dampen the flare in my lungs just enough that it didn't kill me, saving both our lives. She told the Kindred I was dead but got a message to the Unseen. They found me several hours later. I was in an induced coma for a week. Thank goodness the Unseen have the same medical capabilities as the Kindred. My father still thinks I'm dead, killed at the Boulders and burned beyond recognition. The Unseen made sure no one could identify the bodies."

I frowned. "Your dad faked a car accident. I get that he wanted to cover up the truth for the rest of the town, but why pretend to me? If he was going to bring me in, why the charade? He could have skipped all that and brought me into the Kindred straight away."

"Rachel stalled for time, told my father he should wait a few weeks, until you'd dealt with my death properly. She was trying to get an Unseen contingent to come pick you up, but after the slaughter at the Boulders, they were hesitant to approach directly. She ran out of time. My father came up with the attack plan, to fake an assault on your house, blame it on the Unseen, and swoop in to save the day. He figured it would be the fastest way to earn your trust. At least, that's what Rachel told us. She couldn't stop it. I don't know why they took your family too, but they're being held in the Kindred complex. They've been there all along. He's been playing you, Ari, although I still don't know why."

No. *No.* I was such an idiot. I'd fallen for the whole thing! The whole time, Hackman had been lying to my face, telling me he was on my side. He probably had my family as leverage in case I wanted to leave. They were the only reason I'd stayed, and the search for them was what kept me tethered to the Kindred. Hackman was smart. He knew exactly what would make me tick. He probably even faked the attack on the Kindred school, knowing it would tip me over the edge to join them. The last few weeks had been a giant chess match, except he had all the pieces. It was all some kind of sick game.

One thing didn't make sense, though. "Why attack the farm tonight? They knew my family wouldn't be there, so why send me out knowing I wouldn't find them?"

"I'm guessing they told you your family was there to give you hope and keep you controlled. They were holding a carrot out to keep you compliant. Once they attacked, they could pretend your family had been moved and keep the carrot out a little longer. I know how my father thinks, and that's the most likely explanation. He wasn't counting on my appearance, though. He knew the farm was holding a high-value target, but he didn't know it was *me*. I was being kept there for my own protection, until the heat died down and I recovered enough to be able to fight for myself. When you attacked, they sent me to the basement, accessed through a hatch in the front bedroom. Once the battle cleared, I climbed out. That's when I saw you."

I shook my head. "I don't believe you. There's no way."

Noah pulled a plastic bag out of his pocket, opened it, and pulled out a huge phone like the one Rachel had. He brought a photo up on the tiny screen and held it out to me. In it, Mum and Skye were being marched into a room by two armed guards that looked like Kindred. The walls were shiny and metal, and the door read *Confinement*. It was the west wing, the very doors I'd walked past on my way out of the complex. My family were in there the whole time. They were so close.

"Rachel took this the night you were brought in," he said.

"Why didn't she tell me that first night?"

"She wanted to, but the Unseen heads didn't want to rock the boat. They ordered her to stay quiet for the time being and let things play out. You were too valuable an asset to risk destabilising too early."

"I'm not an asset!" I screamed into the night.

Noah put the phone back in his pocket and took my hand. He held it for a moment. "I know. I fought for you, but they didn't listen. They were formulating an extraction plan when Rachel went dark."

Some part of me had known the whole time, deep down. There was something off about Hackman and the Kindred, about their speeches and their rituals. I'd once read an article online about the way cults work. They target the vulnerable, make people feel special, give them a common enemy … How could I not have seen it happening right in front of me? *To* me?

The way they'd treated Rachel was horrible. And it was all my fault. She'd been on my side the whole time, and I ratted her out. She was tortured because of me. If she was still alive, they were probably torturing her right now. I felt sick. "I've been working for the enemy."

"You didn't know."

"You didn't tell me," I shot back.

"That's not fair. I was kind of dead."

I gave him a weak smile. "I know; I'm sorry. I just don't know if I can trust you."

That was a lie. In my heart, I knew I could trust him, and even if I hadn't, the photo would be proof enough. He was telling the truth. It was in his eyes, his voice. Sitting here next to him, the night seemed brighter. I felt so guilty, knowing Josh was stuck back there with the Kindred. What would they do to him? If we got him back, I would have to explain about Noah.

But I couldn't think about that now. There was too much going on in my head to fit anything else. The only reason I'd joined the Kindred was fear. They provided a safe place, or so I'd thought. I had fought for them. Killed for them. Tears threatened, and I blinked them back. Andrea's dad, Elijah. I snapped his neck. And he was a *good* guy. That meant I was a *bad* guy. I was fighting on the wrong side of this war. Noah had put his life on the line for me, and I'd failed him. Rachel had tried to help me, and I'd failed her too. I had failed everyone.

Water trickled quietly into the pool, reflecting a billion points of light from the stars and moon overhead.

"You risked your life for me," I whispered.

"Technically, I died. Really."

"For how long?"

"Two minutes. Then I came back."

"No one's ever done that for me before," I said.

"Died?"

"Lived."

"Well, I've never had anyone worth living for. Not until now." His gaze was so intense I had to look away, choosing instead to stare at an owl watching us from her perch in a tree.

I hugged my legs close and sighed. "I don't know what I'm meant to do with everything you've told me."

"There's nothing you need to do. Just keep yourself alive."

I shook my head. "I'm tired. I haven't slept for two days, and I can't think clearly. Especially not when you're around."

He smiled and brushed my hair away from my face. "Get some rest. You should be able to get an hour's sleep before the sun comes up. I'll keep watch. You're safe here."

I leaned into his arm and slept.

The sun was still below the horizon when I woke, stirred by a gaggle of nesting birds. My head rested in Noah's lap, and as I moved, he ran his hand through my hair. It caught on some dried blood, and I winced.

"Sorry," he said.

"It's not your fault." For the first time, I was aware of how awful I must have looked. I had dirt and mud and blood all over me, starting to crack as it dried. "I need to clean up. Can you turn around for a bit?"

He did, and I stripped down and waded into the water. It was warm and clear, and light shimmered over my feet as they stepped over the rocks at the bottom. The water was only waist deep, and I crouched down to wash the blood off my neck and shoulders. To his credit, Noah stayed facing firmly away from me.

I took a deep breath and sank under the water to get my hair wet. I opened my eyes underneath, and my view was framed by my black curls floating around me. Moonlight scattered across the surface and down through the water. Red fog seeped around my head and off my body as it was washed clean. The red slowly floated downstream in the current, and I closed my eyes, allowing myself to float with it. The creek was a cocoon around me, wrapping me up and carrying me away. I was safe here. Nothing could touch me. Maybe this was what babies felt like before they were born. Warm, dark, safe, the only sound a dull throbbing in your ears, although mine was caused by the river's motion rather than a mother's heartbeat.

When I came up, my mind felt cleaner, thoughts as crystal as the water running down my skin. The sun was just starting to rise, and the sky had a beautiful purple glow that signalled the beginning of a new day. I waded back to shore, made sure Noah still wasn't looking, and stood there for a moment, drying in the air, mist rising off my body like it rose from the surface of the river. Then I got dressed. My pants were fine, but my shirt was ripped and caked with blood. I should have thought to wash it, but that wouldn't have done much for the rips, anyway.

I said that part aloud, and without hesitation, Noah took off his long-sleeved shirt and handed it to me, keeping his eyes still firmly fixed on a tree in the distance. Gratefully, I put it on. It was warm and smelled like him. "All good, thanks," I said.

Noah turned around. He still had a singlet on, and it showed off his arms. I stared at them for a moment.

"Hey, my eyes are up here," he laughed.

My face went hot. "Sorry."

"I'm just kidding. Besides, who could blame you, really?" Noah teased.

"Shut up!" I laughed, and pushed him gently. He playfully pushed me back, but I lost my balance and fell into the water, managing to stay on my feet but soaking my pants completely.

"Oh no! Sorry," he said, stepping to the edge of the rock, offering his hand to help me up. I grabbed it, but instead of getting out, I pulled hard, and he fell forwards into the pond, completely submerged. He stood up, laughing, and looked at me with a mischievous grin.

"No, no way," I protested.

"You'll pay for that." He leaped forward, chasing me farther into the water. I squealed like a little girl until he dove and tackled me, dunking me underwater. I came up and tried to pull him down with me, but he was too strong. Instead, I ended up with my arms around his neck and legs round his waist, hanging off him as my dunk attempt failed. He stood up, and I didn't let go.

Slowly, he wrapped one arm around my waist, holding me in the air, while the other moved my wet hair from my eyes. He moved to kiss me as the sun hit the trees overhead, and I let him.

For a moment. Before I realised what was happening.

"I can't," I said, stopping him. "Not right now."

He swallowed. "It's okay. You've been through a lot."

"I don't know what to feel." And I still had feelings for Josh. I didn't say this, but Noah could see something in my eyes. He looked hurt for a moment, before slowly setting me down back in the water.

"I'm sorry," he said.

"Don't be." I took his hand, and we walked back to the edge of the pool, where we lay back on the rock to dry as the sun crept up to warm us both.

I closed my eyes, eyelids glowing as the sun shone through them. I could think about my confusing love life later. For now, it was a new day, and I had to save my family.

THIRTY-FOUR

"Sorry, guys, there's no one left," the voice on the other end of the line told us.

Noah groaned. "No one?"

"The Kindred attacked all our safe houses at once. Nearly everyone in our entire cell was killed. You're lucky there's anyone left here to answer the phone."

This was bad news. Noah and I had spent the morning dreaming up a plan to recover my family from the Kindred compound, but it relied on decent support from the rest of the Unseen. Luckily, Noah kept his satellite phone in a ziplock bag per Unseen protocol, so it had survived me tackling him into the river. But he had spent close to an hour trying to get someone from the Unseen on the line, and by now, the battery was almost dead. Unfortunately, it was a new guy, Hud, who finally picked up. Noah explained our predicament, but he'd recruited Hud just a few weeks before my accident, so the guy didn't know much.

"Can you try to muster up some support from one of the other cells?" Noah asked.

"I can try, but they're more than a day away. You're not going to like this, but … we heard some noise this morning about an upcoming execution in the Kindred complex. They've worked out that your girlfriend has defected, and they want to send a signal that betrayal is not an option, especially considering she's not the first to do so recently. They're going to kill the hostages—Rachel and the other three."

I grabbed the phone. "This is my family we're talking about, and one of your own! They've suffered enough in this stupid war. You have to do something! Plus, I'm not his girlfriend!" That last part was petty, but I thought it was important.

"Look," Hud said, "the only guy who'd have the authority to get anyone here in time is Elijah, but I haven't been able to get in touch with him."

"Elijah's dead," Noah said coldly.

There was a pause. "Things are even worse than I thought."

Noah glanced at me to see if I was all right. I couldn't meet his gaze.

"All of our key members, our entire leadership team is dead," Hud continued. "The only reason I survived is because three bodies fell on top of me during the assault. We can't even do a proper head count, because the Kindred took all the dead and torched the place to keep things quiet. I got out just in time. Still smell like smoke. It's chaos out here."

"Any news on Bek?" Noah asked, concerned. I didn't know who he was talking about, but it seemed important.

"Safe for now," Hud said. "They moved her out of area a few days ago, so she wasn't in our region when it all hit the fan."

"How is she, though?"

"The same," Hud sighed. "Still unresponsive and still that weird colour."

Noah shook his head. "I'm so sorry."

259

"It's not your fault. You got us out of there, remember? You're the only reason we're still alive."

Their conversation was lost on me, but I had other priorities right now. I took the phone. "Is there any way at all you can help us?"

"I'll do my best," Hud said. "I honestly wish I could do more, but we don't have the resources or leadership to mount a full frontal attack on the Kindred compound. Even if we did, the place is so heavily guarded we wouldn't get past the front door. The execution is set for sundown. That's about eight hours from now. I'm sorry, but if you want them back, I think you're probably on your own."

"What about the—" Noah began, but the battery indicator blinked and his phone died. He smashed it on a rock, storming a few paces away.

I came up behind him and put a hand on his shoulder. "This is all my fault."

"Don't talk like that."

"It is. I killed Elijah. I turned in Rachel. The whole attack was because of me. They're going to kill her, and Josh, and my family, because I didn't know better."

He didn't answer. He couldn't. He knew I was right.

I sat down on the ground and hugged my knees to my chest. Noah crouched behind me, putting his arm around my shoulders. He was warm. We sat silently for a while.

And that's when it came to me.

I looked up, smiling. "There is a way in! It's been in front of me the whole time."

Noah sat up. "What do you mean?"

"Rachel showed me, and now I think I know why. She knew something was going to happen, or at least suspected.

There's a hidden entrance, unguarded. I don't think anyone knows about it. It leads directly to the training ground."

Noah thought for a moment. "If we could get there, we'd be right inside the compound. They won't be on high alert. They'll be overconfident, thinking they've crippled the Unseen permanently."

"Which they have."

"Maybe, but they didn't count on one thing."

"What's that?"

"Us." He grinned, and I smiled back. This would probably be a suicide mission, a one-way trip into the heart of the Kindred, but we had to try. There was no other choice.

"If we're going to find the complex, we need to get our bearings, find higher ground."

"I think there's a hill over there." Noah pointed behind me. "I got a glimpse of it through the trees last night as we came in. I can't be sure, though; it was so dark."

We set off in that direction. An educated guess was better than nothing, and we had eight hours until sunset. Eight hours until my family were either rescued or dead. The second option was far more likely.

It got filthy hot, the kind of sticky heat that feels like you're swimming through the air rather than walking. Pretty soon, the clean feeling I had from washing in the pool was gone, crusted over by sweat and the dust kicked up from my shoes. Noah was in front, as he had a better sense of direction than I did out here. I didn't mind; it was nice to sit back and let him lead for a while. It gave me a chance to look at him, too.

Somehow, it still didn't feel real that he was alive. I'd known him as dead longer than I'd known him alive, and the memory of his death had been played so many times in my head that it had become more real than most of my other memories. Just goes to show you can't really trust your memories. You could live your whole life believing something is true, believing some version of reality that never really happened. Your whole life could be defined, understood, rewritten by a lie. Mine had been. Memory is a powerful thing. And it can't trusted.

I'd had so many defining moments over the past month, moments that had seemed so true. I'd pledged my allegiance to the Kindred and felt so safe, when all the while they were plotting to take away everyone I cared about. My anger at the Unseen had been so strong I could taste it, but it was really the Kindred I needed to hate. I'd trusted Hackman and known beyond all doubt that my family were in the farmhouse. I was sure I'd seen Mum through the window, when it was really just some random Unseen. I had murdered that guy in the bathroom and still didn't know his name. We'd both tried to kill each other, even though, in principle, we were on the same side. I'd been so angry when James and Vicki were killed... Did they know they were actually my enemies?

How many in the Kindred knew the truth about their agenda? Noah said the new recruits knew nothing much about anything, but once you got promoted you began to learn the truth. Hackman was an Elder Brother, which meant he knew for sure. As the heads of each complex, the Arch Elders would know everything. Nareem and Vicki were a Brother and Sister ranking, but did they know enough to be aware of the evil lurking around them? If Vicki knew, did she tell James the truth? They'd gotten as close as two people could, at least in the physical sense, and from her reaction when he died, she'd genuinely loved him. But if she'd told him the truth about the Kindred and why she was really there, he might have pulled away. Maybe it was better for him that he probably never found out.

It was hard to believe there weren't more defectors, more people leaving the Kindred once they learned the truth. Guys like Nareem, Vicki, even Nathan from the hospital—they felt like good people. What would make someone stay after they discovered the evil at the heart of the Kindred?

The Kindred seemed so well connected, so integrated into society and positions of power that when they made whatever move they were planning, the world would be caught off guard. Their plan felt close to fulfilment, and I was afraid that when the Kindred entered the final stage of the Agenda, nothing would be the same. No one would be able to stop them. The end was coming and the world had no idea.

THIRTY-FIVE

Reaching the hill, we began a slow ascent. It was steeper than it appeared, and the ground was covered with gravel and rocks that slipped under our feet, making it impossible to get a firm footing. It was easier to crouch low, because I could grab a handhold if I slipped. It also meant there wasn't far to fall. I had a few slides, but Noah had more, at least until he saw what I was doing and copied.

The sun was baking me inside my skin; I felt like a jacket potato shoved into a microwave. Noah was raspy, struggling to breathe; his lung capacity was low because of his injuries. I tried to take his mind off it. "So, for everything that's happened to us, everything we've done together, I still don't really feel like I know you."

"Want to know your fellow kamikaze pilot, huh?" He grinned.

"Something like that, but not quite as depressing."

"Sorry." He stopped walking to catch his breath. "What do you want to know?"

"I don't know … What are your hopes, fears, dreams, stuff like that?" It sounded so lame considering our situation, but I had to take his mind off things. Plus, I genuinely wanted to know.

"I hope to destroy the Kindred. I'm afraid of failing. Dreams? I haven't thought much past the next twelve hours."

"Permission to treat the witness as hostile?"

He started climbing again. "Sorry again. It's been so long since I've thought about that kind of question." We walked in silence for a moment. "For a long time, I wanted to be a cop, like my dad, but then when I found out what he did, I wanted to be a Kindred Elder. Then I found out what *that* really meant, and I spent months and months just kind of drifting. I mean, aside from wanting to take the Kindred down, I really hadn't thought further than that. That was everything I thought about, everything I wanted. It gave me so much purpose but at the same time was so ..."

"Empty?"

"Yeah. I don't want the whole purpose of my life to be about destruction. I want to build, create. When I met you, I don't know, I guess I started wondering what could be." He looked back at me, and I raised my eyebrows. He continued. "I always thought that where you've been defines you, like where you are and the actions you've taken and the situations you've been a part of, those are what shape your future. But then meeting you and talking to you and even seeing you last night ... You've been through so much, you've carried so much pain, but you keep going. You stay strong." I didn't feel strong, but my cheeks flushed as he looked at me. Was that really how he saw me?

"The past happened, there's no changing that," he said. "The past affects your future, there's no changing that either. But I can choose *how* it changes things. We all can. I can dwell on the past, live in the mess and the lies and the death and everything else, or I can use it. I can harness it, use it as fuel to change the future."

There was a blaze in his eyes as he talked.

"When I was recovering, just lying in bed in the farmhouse, with nowhere to go, I had a lot of time to think. I'm not the only kid who's left the Kindred; there are so many others like me. When you leave, you lose everything. If you join the Unseen, you have a place to fight but not a place to belong. It's not that kind of environment. I've seen a few young kids, twelve, thirteen years old, leaving the Kindred with nowhere to go. They come into the Unseen for a while, but it's not the kind of place a child should live. The Unseen don't send kids into the firing line, and there's nothing else for them to do. Most of the time, they drift and then quit. When they leave, they have no family, no friends, no place. They end up on the streets, using their abilities to scrounge or steal to survive.

"I was in the city a few months ago, and I saw this girl, ten, maybe eleven years old. Her parents had left the Kindred and were murdered as they fled. I recognised her from my time there; she was only about six when I knew her. Brown hair, brown eyes, she had such a cheeky smile. But now that was gone, and she was so skinny and small it was obvious she hadn't been eating or anything. I tried to help her, tried to get close, but she used her abilities to bring down a chunk of awning, got me square in the head. When I woke up, she was gone.

"It's dangerous for people like us out there, but even more for these kids. If enough of them out there got together … They're angry, they're tired, they're alone … Who knows what they could do? I couldn't even imagine the consequences if they became known to the Kindred."

He teared up a bit talking about these kids, especially the little girl. He was really scared for them, really moved. I found myself moved too. Hopefully, the girl was okay; hopefully, she was still alive.

"I want to start a place for them," Noah said.

"What, like a kids' home or something?"

"I guess. I wouldn't even know what to call it. But after—I mean, *if* we take down the Kindred, there's gonna be a lot of kids without parents running around. Even more than there already are. That's the aftermath of war. Always has been."

I'd never really thought about that too much, and I especially didn't want to now, after killing Elijah. But there was no doubt many of the Unseen killed in the assault were parents. Not only that—so many of the killed Kindred had children, innocent bystanders who would never know why or how their parents died or what they were involved in. If by some miracle the Kindred collapsed, the world would be flooded with a new wave of orphans, some with abilities like mine. I had been so focused on destroying my enemies, I hadn't stopped to think too hard about the consequences. The realization blunted my determination to fight. I couldn't be responsible for that kind of death, that kind of suffering.

"I want to help you start it," I said. "Your home. Orphanage. Whatever you call it."

"I wouldn't even know where to begin. It's just a hazy kind of dream right now."

"Doesn't matter. I'll be there. It's been hard enough losing Mum and Skye, even though they're still alive. I can't imagine what I'd do if they died. These kids have lost everything, and they won't be the only ones. So I'm there. Let's do it."

We reached the top of the hill, and it was time to get our bearings. Noah had spent more time with the Kindred, so he had a better idea of where we were. We could see most of the landscape from here; the hill was rocky and mostly bare, and the trees lower down only just got in the way at the bottom of our view. There was a series of cliffs that stuck out like pineapple on a pizza, huge lumps rising from the bush. In places, they joined up and formed ranges cutting their way across the horizon. Noah pointed to the largest one, which covered about a third of our view. That was our goal. That was the top of the Kindred complex.

"I'd say that's about six hours from here," he said, "if we keep up our speed."

I thought he was being optimistic but needed all the hope I could get. We tried to spot the easiest path through, which is normally a riverbed. If we followed the river up, it might turn into the creek that ran right near the hidden entrance and past the arena.

Noah found the river glimmering through some trees to our right, not too far away, and we set off towards it. He was still breathing heavily, but that was probably from the hard slog up the hill. The way down the other side was easier and gave us both time to catch our breath.

We tracked the river for ages, sometimes having to step into the water to avoid huge tangled bushes that blocked our progress on the bank. The river was never more than waist deep at the centre, so walking upstream was easy enough, aside from our feet slipping on the rocks. The cold water was nice anyway, as the sun was really starting to cook. The shirt I borrowed from Noah had long sleeves and was turning my top half into a pressure oven. At least it stopped me from burning. Noah's shoulders were bare in his singlet, and the sun had coloured them bright red. That was going to hurt later.

We reached a bend, and the water blazed bright orange, alive with a colony of algae that streaked across the rocks and through the water. It happened sometimes, especially in summer, and I'd seen it in the creek near our house a few times as a kid. I'd always thought it was pollution, but up here everything was crystal clear, untouched by humans. For all my angst, all the worry and pain and stress and chaos happening all around me, it was like this part of the world hadn't even noticed. For these trees, these rocks and birds and spiders, none of this battle mattered. We could win, we could lose, but they would continue, oblivious to the fate of the two intruders currently crashing their way through the water. We would go, and they would forget.

As we walked, even the water forgot us. It sloshed around as our legs cut a path through the surface, rippled off the bank, and then moments later returned to its normal rhythm. It was strangely comforting, knowing the world would continue just fine without me. It was also a little sad.

The orange streaks continued, and so did we. Until a hard edge caught my eye. Out in the bush, it's all curves and soft edges; nature doesn't like straight lines. It was off to the right, through some stringy paperbark trees. Noah had seen it, too, and was shading his eyes trying to get a better look.

"It looks like sandstone," I said.

"It's man-made for sure. A big sandstone wall. How would you even build something like that out here?"

"Sometimes hikers or rangers set up shelters with emergency supplies in case bushwalkers get lost."

"Let's see if there's anything we can use. I could do with some lunch even if it is from a can."

"I'd love a burger." My stomach growled.

"Burger in a can? Sounds delicious."

"That's not what I meant," I laughed.

Noah clambered over the side of the bank and gave me a hand up. As we drew closer, I got a better look at the structure. This was not a hiker's shelter. It was too well built and about the size of a carport. The walls were made from flat sandstone blocks that must have been dragged here from somewhere else. There was no natural sandstone around that I could see.

We walked around to the front, and I stopped dead.

The entrance was incredible, with carved stone columns that looked almost Roman. They weren't that tall, only a few heads higher than Noah, but they were impressive. Two statues stood motionless on either side of the entrance, dressed in robes, hands over their eyes, mouths curled in identical snarls. Neither was armed, but they were definitely guarding this place. The entrance itself had no door, just a threshold of worn timber embedded in the dirt floor. Wind whipped through it and whirled around inside, moaning as it tried to escape back out into the open air. The whole place felt cold. Dark. It looked different, but it was the same building for sure.

In the daylight, it was just as terrifying as it had been the night I passed my test with the Kindred.

The chapel.

I turned to Noah. "We need to go. Now."

The sun dipped behind a cloud, and I shivered from the wind that scattered angrily across fallen leaves and twigs.

"What is this place?" Noah murmured. There was a fear in his voice I hadn't heard since the first night we were attacked.

Something was calling. I could feel it reaching out to me, to the darkness in my stomach. A whisper swirled around my mind, behind my eyes, and into my heart. There was no figure this time, no melting, awful ghost, but I knew it was calling. The whisper coalesced into my name.

Ari.

"I don't know why, but I feel like we shouldn't be here," Noah said.

I nodded, but whether it was the wind at my back or the calling in my gut, I was propelled forward, legs pulling me over the threshold.

Inside, the air was damp and dark, the only light fighting its way in through tiny cracks in the stone joints. The ground was dust, and the atmosphere ancient. It was an aberration, a place that shouldn't be. I'd thought the first time that maybe it wasn't real, but here I was, inside it. The last time, an awful figure had grabbed my arm and held me tight. This time, there was nothing holding me … and yet I couldn't run. The building itself had taken hold. I couldn't have left even if I'd wanted to.

"Ari? What are you doing?"

I barely heard him.

I was looking at the bodies.

THIRTY-SIX

They stood watching me. Six figures propped up by rope and twigs and wire, arranged in a half-circle along the back wall. They'd been there for a long time, decades at least, because most of the skin was gone, along with the flesh. They were mostly just bone, but not the white, glistening kind of bones you see on TV. These were brown, worn, with stuff still hanging onto them like someone had toilet-papered a house before a rainstorm. Dark stains on the floor showed where most of the remains had fallen, and small paw prints indicated anything that had fallen there was cleaned up by scavengers.

Was it an altar? Some kind of sacrifice? Perhaps it was a warning.

There was one feature of these figures that I found even more disturbing than their cold, eyeless sockets. The robes. These once were Kindred.

I should have been thrilled that someone killed these Kindred. I should have been excited that whoever it was could be on our side. But this was so gruesome, so utterly, intentionally dark, that whoever had done this to the Kindred had the potential to be even worse than them.

"Look at this," Noah said behind me.

I turned and followed his gaze. On the wall, above the door, were words written in a language I didn't understand. It looked a bit like Latin, which I'd seen in history class a few times at school, but the shapes were all wrong, square, and angular. They were carved into the wall as a banner.

PEAH CWALU SUNIS CONSUMPTEI

"I know this," Noah said darkly.

"What do you mean? You can read this?"

"It's the traditional language used by the Kindred."

"Latin?"

"Almost. It's a modified version, not too hard to interpret if you know Latin. Not that I do. The Kindred adopted it as their written language when Rome did, but it morphed over time and across continents to become its own version of the script. Some of it is taken from Anglo-Saxon English, the oldest form of the language, spoken more than fifteen hundred years ago. They call it the First Language. The higher you go in the Kindred, the more of this you learn. The Eldership all know and speak the First Language in their closed meetings."

"Can you read it?"

"I think so. The promises you made on entry into the Kindred were just the first creed. As you move up in the Kindred, you learn the creeds in the First Language instead. A lot of these words were in my creed to become Brother, although they weren't in this order. I had to memorise it by heart."

He paused for a moment, carefully studying the text. When he turned, his eyes were narrowed. "This is a loose translation, but I don't like what it says."

I raised an eyebrow.

"It means 'Through death we are consumed.'"

Goosebumps rose on my neck. "That's creepy."

He frowned. "I get the feeling these guys died on purpose."

"They sacrificed themselves?"

"Or let someone sacrifice them. *Cwalu* doesn't just mean death. It means violent death."

I started to shiver, half from this revelation and half from the cold wind seeping through my clothes, which were still wet from the river.

There was a screech from outside, the sound of something dying. Then another, and a third.

"Something's out there," I whispered.

"I'll take a look," Noah said. "Will you be okay to stay here?"

"Better the devil you know," I said, trying to sound brave. "I'll see if there's anything here we can defend ourselves with." I nodded at the bodies. "They might have something useful on them."

"Don't come outside until I'm back."

I nodded and turned to face the bodies as his feet crunched outside through the leaves.

"So," I said to the bodies strung up before me, "let's see if you've got anything useful on you." It was weird talking to a row of corpses, but it helped me ignore the dread creeping up my spine. I walked slowly towards the figure on the left, trying not to look him in what remained of his eyes. I wasn't even sure it was a him, as the bodies were so badly decomposed it was hard to make out gender. At least the smell had faded a long time ago; although, the wind stirring around the room occasionally brought a pungent pang of death.

The robes were remarkably intact, and there were pockets stitched onto the outside of each. I grimaced and looked inside the first, not wanting to simply stick my hand down there in case a spider or something worse had moved in. The first corpse's pockets were empty, and the second. The third and fourth had a few scraps of cloth, and the fifth a small pocket knife, which I stuffed in the back of my jeans. That could come in handy.

The sixth body, the one on the far right, was just as decomposed as the others. The robe was different, though, a lighter colour. The body seemed fresher somehow, as if it was newer. It wasn't gooey, but it had more skin on it than the others. I could almost make out its face, but I tried not to. I was spooking myself too much.

There was screech outside, followed by a howl, but it was far away, so it couldn't be Noah.

The left pocket of this body was empty, but the right held a small, folded scrap of paper. It was yellow, browning around the edges, and nearly fell apart as I tried to unfold it.

"What have you got?" I said aloud. The storm outside was building, and the atmosphere felt charged. I couldn't make out the writing on the paper in the half-light, and wind scattered dust into the air. There was a tiny shaft of light glowing through a crack in the wall to my right, so I turned towards it, holding the paper up. The writing was in English but really old. It could have been from medieval times, but that was impossible. Europeans had only been in this country for a few hundred years. I read aloud:

"Light will die,
and the bones of the fallen
fuel the fire of resurrection.
We stand eternal."

Something caught my eye as leaves blew through the door, and I turned around, expecting to see Noah. He wasn't there. I was. It was me. The sixth corpse had become me.

Its rotting eyes were mine—one blue, one brown, both dead. It had my mouth, grey, and my hair, caked with blood. It was my body, tied limply to a frame of twigs, cold and lifeless and decomposing like all the others. I couldn't move and couldn't look away.

I reached toward my own dead face. The wind whispered my name with one voice, then two, then a hundred, thousand calling me.

Ari.

They rose in crescendo as I touched her cheek. *My* cheek. It was deathly cold and tight like wax. It felt real, but it couldn't be.

Her eyes clicked towards me, and her mouth dropped open. I screamed and tripped backwards. Hands grabbed me from behind, grasping at my waist. I couldn't break free.

THIRTY-SEVEN

"Ari! Ari, it's me." They were Noah's hands. I stopped struggling. "What's wrong?"

I looked up at the figure. It was no longer me. It was back to being a cold, dead corpse. I couldn't tell him what I'd seen, not until I knew what it meant; I didn't want him going uber-protector like Josh had. "Spider. Big spider. It's gone now."

He chuckled and rolled his eyes before holding out his hand and pulling me to my feet. "There was nothing outside. Probably just animals fighting."

"There was a knife in one of the pockets," I said, trying to sound calm.

"That's something. Good work."

"We're running out of time."

Noah nodded. "There's nothing else for us here. We should go."

"Gladly." I refused to look back at the body as we went outside, even though I could feel it watching.

The sun remained behind clouds, which helped ease the heat, although Noah said he could still feel his shoulders burning. The river split into creeks as we moved upstream, and we headed right. We were only ankle deep in the water, but my pants were still wet from before and the wind hadn't stopped. I was so cold I was shivering, and Noah put his arm around me, holding me close as we walked. It worked a little, and I stopped shaking, although it slowed us down a lot. He noticed, too, and now that I was warm he broke away so we could pick up the pace. It made sense, but I still missed him a little.

It was mid-afternoon when we saw a huge rocky outcrop rising over the trees. There was nothing to suggest it was anything but a natural cliff, ridged along the edge of the mountain range beyond, but now I knew what was inside. Now that I knew what lay beneath the surface, it seemed darker. Every edge was dangerous, every shadow a figure; even the clouds above were ghostly apparitions, spirits reaching for us. I felt like any moment a hand would reach out of the ground and drag me down to the caverns below.

The creek forked, and we went left, following our line of sight. The walk became harder as we rapidly rose towards the base of the cliff. We were only a few minutes away, so we stopped to catch our breath and plan our next move. We'd talked strategy for the last few hours, but on seeing the cliffs, we went silent, our voices stolen by their shadow.

"Have you seen the ledge yet?" Noah asked.

"I think so. There's a bit of a walk to go, but it sticks out from the cliff. I think I saw it farther around."

"You think?"

"Yes," I replied, too uncertain to be sure.

"This whole plan relies on finding that ledge."

"And being able to climb up there." I sat down to rest for a moment, and Noah joined me.

"We can use our abilities to help." He wiped his forehead with his singlet.

"After last night, I'm pretty wrecked. I hope I've got enough strength to use them."

"Me too. It's been hard for me to tune at all since we were attacked."

"We'll need to be quiet from here on up. I saw the Shadow hanging around here once. It might come back."

"I've never even seen one," Noah said.

"A Shadow was there during the night the Kindred attacked my house, so the Shadows must be connected to the Kindred somehow, right? How haven't you seen one?"

"I only heard about them through rumour. They emerge at critical points in Kindred history. I don't know what they are, not many Kindred do. We just know they show up when needed."

I looked around, half expecting it to be coming towards us through the trees. It felt like we shouldn't even say its name here, like that could summon it somehow. That was probably ridiculous, but after everything, I wasn't taking any chances.

Having sorted out our basic approach, we stepped onto the bank. The ground cover here was sparse so we could stay out of the water. It would at least give us time to dry off a bit, which I was thankful for now that the sun dipped ever closer to the horizon. We stayed low, keeping to the trees. I wasn't sure if anyone had found the entrance up above, or if Rachel had revealed it as they tortured her, but if someone was up there, they'd spot us for sure. The trees were just thick enough to lower visibility, but not thick enough to hide us from anyone or anything wandering around out here. It made me nervous. As we walked, my head darted around so fast I felt like it was going to fall off, looking for movement, shadows, anything that hinted at an ambush.

Noah stopped, but I was looking the other way and nearly ran into him from behind. I didn't say anything, in case he'd stopped for a reason. "I know what we heard before," he said.

He stepped out of the way.

We were at the entrance to a clearing, a space in the trees that wasn't natural. Bodies littered the ground. Birds, snakes, possums, even a cow that must have gotten lost and made its way out here. At the centre was a pile, at least as tall as me, where most of them had been stacked unceremoniously after they'd been ... What *had* been done to them? They were dried, emaciated, empty. Leathery skin stretched taught over bones that remained somehow intact. Black eyes rotted in their sockets, and the stench was awful.

I gagged and covered my nose. There were at least thirty bodies here, of all shapes and sizes. Several were human.

Noah broke the silence with a whisper. "The skin doesn't look broken on any of them. They weren't eaten. Not exactly. I haven't seen this before, but I'm willing to bet I know what happened. You said the Shadow was wandering around here one night?"

"Rachel said it was hunting."

He gestured to the carnage. "Dinner, anyone?"

"But they haven't been eaten."

"Not in the traditional sense," Noah said wryly. "They've been ..."

"Consumed," I finished. "What the hell are we up against?"

"I wish I knew. But even the Elders are scared of them. I sure am."

I took another step, and tripped over a body. A human one, with skin dried out, eyes shriveled but open, mouth frozen in a scream. My stomach turned.

We had to move, or that would be us too.

THIRTY-EIGHT

"Let's go. Now," I urged Noah. We picked our way across the clearing, trying not to step on any of the bodies. I stumbled at one moment, and there was a sickening crunch as my foot went through the rib cage of a decaying parrot. Thank goodness I'd put my shoes on when we left the river. This was the second collection of bodies I'd seen today, and that was two more than I was okay with.

"On the bright side"— I grimaced —"at least we know we're close to the entrance. If this is where I saw the Shadow hunting, we're right underneath it."

I turned right and stepped farther uphill, out of the tree line and towards the base of the cliff. Far above my head was the outline of the ledge. This was the entrance.

"Now what?" Noah asked.

"I can't see any hand holds, can you?"

"No, and any edges are too thin to stand on. It's what, two storeys up?"

"Three at least."

"Not a height I want to fall from."

"Me neither."

We stood for a moment, thinking. I got an idea and explained it to Noah. He thought it was good, though risky. If we started a fire up here, we were dead. The forest floor was dry and covered in kindling; any fire would go up in a second and spread through the mountains in no time. But we didn't have any other options.

We stepped back and picked the tallest tree we could find. It wasn't too far from the base, and if we got the angle right we'd be fine. Timing was everything. I had to lower the tuning of the top front section of the tree while Noah shattered the base. If he could control the size of the shatter and I could make the top heavier at the same time, the tree would fall away from us and end up leaning against the cliff, like a ladder. That was the theory, anyway.

Pausing for a moment to catch our breath from the climb uphill, we held hands—the signal for me to tune was when Noah squeezed. He had far more experience than me, so he was in charge of timing. His hand was warm but dry. My hands were freezing cold. It was good to get some blood flow back into them.

I closed my eyes and began to tune in to the tree. It was a huge tree, old and full of sound. I felt bad we were about to end its life, but in the grand scheme of things, I'd rather have my family than a tree.

Concentrating on the top, I waited for Noah's signal. His hand squeezed, and I lowered the tree's resonance as much I could without breaking it. Noah blasted the front part of the trunk into oblivion, right at the base. The tree stood for a moment in shock and then slowly fell forwards, against the cliff. It hit hard, the top cracking into the cliff as leaves sprayed down around us. A bird screeched, flapping wildly away, woken from his bed inside the trunk. Noah had gotten his tuning right, so the tree had shattered rather than caught fire. That was a relief.

But the tree slid against the cliff face, away from the ledge. The trunk overbalanced and slid the other way. Noah yelled for me to duck. I did, and the base of the trunk flew over my head as the tree smacked hard into the earth. That was close.

We stood, staring for a moment at our dismal failure of a plan.

"If at first you don't succeed," said Noah dryly.

We picked a second tree. It was a little shorter but also at a better angle to the ledge. If we got it to fall straight at the ledge it would land more securely than the last one. We tuned again, and the tree fell. No birds this time, but a wisp of smoke rose from the base as the tree toppled. It slammed against the ledge, dislodging a few rocks, but stayed in place. The plan had worked.

The smoke at the base grew bigger, and flames burst from the stump. Noah had created too much heat when he shattered the base. I ran forward, and Noah followed, trying to put out the small fire before it became a big problem. But the ground was covered with leaves, and the dirt was too hard to dig, so I had nothing to smother the flames.

"Can you put fire out by tuning?" I yelled at Noah.

"It's possible, but I've never tried. You?"

I shook my head. "No time for practice. We have to get this out now, before it spreads."

The river was still close. There was only one option.

"Take off your singlet!" I yelled at Noah. He took a moment to work out what I was thinking.

"Any excuse, huh?" he joked. He ran to the water and soaked his singlet, then ran back and wrung it out to douse the flames. It wasn't enough.

"I need help!" he called, but I was already down at the river.

"Don't you dare turn around!"

My khaki pants were thick, and they would soak up the biggest amount of water. I took them off quickly and dunked them, then sprinted back to the trunk and threw them on the flames. The trunk sizzled, and my pants steamed like crazy, but after a few seconds, the crackling reduced to a quiet hiss.

I had stepped right in front of Noah. He was dutifully staring directly at my eyes, trying not to glance down.

He mumbled something and went bright red. So did I.

"Just turn around," I said and grabbed my pants off the trunk. They were burned through in a few places, but just on the legs. On the bright side, the fire had mostly dried them, although they smelled like smoke and were still steaming a bit.

Noah's singlet was a little worse for wear, with a huge hole through the front and back. Once I was dressed, I threw it to him. He was still facing away, and it landed around his neck, smearing his skin with charcoal. He put it on, even with the hole burned all the way through.

"Nice pants." He smirked, looking at the patchwork of holes seared into them. They did look ridiculous. I grinned, doing a spin as if I were in a fashion show. As I turned, one of the holes got caught in a fallen branch, and I tripped. Noah doubled over with laughter.

"Shut up!" I laughed with him. I couldn't have that happening halfway up our tree-ladder; I'd plunge to my death. Using the knife from the chapel, I cut both pant legs into shorts. It was cold, but at least I'd be safe. I used a scrap from them to tie my hair in a ponytail. Noah looked at me with a shy smile.

"What?" I asked.

"Nothing," he replied. "It just ... suits you."

My face went hot again and I changed the subject. "Light's almost gone. We need to get moving."

"Who first?"

"You. I'm not having you staring at my butt the whole way up."

"Wouldn't dream of it." He smirked, and I gave him a gentle shove.

He began the climb. The trunk was on an angle towards the cliff, a pretty steep one. The tree was bare for the first storey, which made it difficult to get a handhold. Noah tried to walk up it like a gymnast on a balance beam, but his shoes didn't have enough grip and he slid back down twice, sending pieces of bark flying off the trunk. The only way was to shimmy along, arms and legs wrapped around the tree. The trunk wasn't that thick, but his arms still only made it about halfway around. Stability would be an issue for me as I was shorter than him.

After Noah made it to the first branch, I began to shimmy up the trunk, same as he had. It was hard to keep my weight centred. I climbed a few body lengths but overbalanced, slipping to the side. I tried to grab the trunk, but there was nothing to hold on to, and my arms flew into the air as I dropped off the trunk. I hit the ground hard on my back, and my lungs emptied. Noah noticed from his position near the top and called out, starting to move back down the tree to help me. "Ari! Are you all right?"

I nodded, gasping for air, and gave him the thumbs up, waving him away so he wouldn't come back down. I was just winded. I'd heard somewhere that if you breathe out as you hit the ground you won't be as winded. That would have been helpful to remember *before* I fell.

I staggered to my feet, doubled over and sucking in oxygen. After a minute or so, my breath returned, and I tried the climb again. This time, I was far more careful and made it to the first set of branches with ease, aside from the bruising emerging around my ribs where I'd landed. It was easy moving from branch to branch after that, stepping up and along like a staircase. It would have been fun, except I was heading ever closer to the Kindred.

Towards the top, the branches grew thin, and my movements slowed. I picked my footholds carefully, hearing cracks as I placed my weight on them. Noah's hand appeared in front of me. He was standing on the ledge above. I grabbed his hand, and he pulled me onto the ledge where I'd once stood with Rachel. It was clear to me now. She'd brought me here so I would have a way in when the time came. She knew. Somehow, she knew I would need this place.

The sun was nearly gone behind the mountains. The clouds that had blocked it out now formed a canvas on which it could paint, tracing orange, red, and purple waves as far as I could see. But there was no time to admire the artwork; the moment it set, my family were scheduled to die. Strange that something so beautiful could trigger something so ugly.

"Ready?" Noah asked.

I took a deep breath. "Ready."

THIRTY-NINE

The entrance was how I'd left it, covered with moss, vines, and climbers trailing down, dripping with water that came from who knows where. The creek was barely visible far below, and looking over the edge was dizzying. A thin wisp of smoke still rose from the fire we extinguished. Hopefully, no one came to investigate. If the Shadow returned to its hunting ground, it would see the tree against the ledge and work things out pretty fast, assuming it was intelligent enough to do so. But we couldn't just push the tree over to hide our plan; it was our only way out for the time being. Hopefully we'd be gone before anyone saw it.

I'd walked the passage enough times now that it was easy to make our way through. I held Noah's hand to help him in the dark. It was a nice change, taking the lead.

The closer we got to the end of the tunnel, the faster my heart went. It started as a dull thump, like a bomb blast on the horizon, and by the time I could see light in the distance, it had become a crack ripping through my body like an earthquake. I had to get it under control, or I wouldn't even hear the enemy coming. Slowing my breathing helped a bit, and by the time we reached the training ground, my heart had settled.

"Looks empty," I whispered.

"They're probably still cleaning up after the bombs. No time for training." He didn't voice the other possibility—they could already be gathered for the execution.

Despite the stillness, we stayed well out of sight, keeping to the walls and shadows. I cracked open the door and peeked out into the Apex. There were fewer guards than I'd expected, only two directly below on the floor and another two guarding the east wing. Rachel's bomb must have seriously crippled security. Plus, they were probably feeling confident after the attacks on the safe houses. There weren't enough Unseen left to pose a serious threat.

The door creaked as it opened further, and I froze. The guards were directly below, several storeys down, the top of their heads just visible through the grilled slats on the floor. If they looked up, we were both dead.

They continued to watch the ground floor, so I stepped softly out onto the metal landing. The metal pinged, creaking in protest as my weight fell on it. I stood still, blood pounding in my ears.

Nothing happened. There was no shout of discovery. After a minute, the thudding in my head settled enough for me to hear again. Noah stepped out onto the landing beside me, but I had already primed the metal with my weight and it didn't creak again.

There were footsteps below, slapping against the stone floor. One guard walked across the Apex towards the west wing. The last step echoed through the cavern as he stopped at the door. If he turned around now, that was it. Game over.

My breath was a freight train rattling from my lungs, so I held it in. A clunk in a lock, jingling keys, and a metallic whine as the door opened on its hinges. He moved to step through.

"Hey!" came a shout from directly below me.

A swear word plastered itself in huge letters across my mind, but fortunately, nothing came out.

"Grab me some water too, will you?" the guard below us called to his friend.

"Sure thing," the other replied, before going through the door without turning around.

Noah's eyes were as wide as mine. We were using up our luck far too quickly. We had to move.

We snuck across the gangways as fast as we could. One flight up, we reached a storeroom Noah remembered. He turned the handle, and ducking inside, we let the door close behind us. I let my breath out, panting as I slumped against the wall. Noah rifled through the shelves, looking for the next stage of our plan. Grinning, he pulled out two sets of robes and two masks. I slipped mine on. It was scratchy, especially the mask, and limited my movements a bit. They made it hard to see, and I wished we could have worn the ones the trainers did, all tight and form-fitting, but we had to try and blend in as much as possible. I should have kept the one from the farmhouse.

Noah did a twirl and put a hand on his hip. "Does my bum look big in this?" he whispered.

I giggled, then snorted, then died a little inside that I'd made that sound in front of him.

He chuckled quietly and looked at me, eyes smiling through the mask. "You're cute."

My face flushed on cue, but he couldn't see it underneath my mask. We composed ourselves for a moment, then Noah creaked open the door. We could move more freely now, although I still felt like I had a flashing red sign on my head that screamed *Enemy agent!*

We moved down to the ground floor and towards the west wing. The basement torture room had been destroyed in the explosion, so Rachel would probably be held in the confinement cells I'd passed on my way to the arena. My family were probably there too, but we needed all the help we could get to retrieve them. The west wing was also where the live-ins stayed, which significantly increased our chances of being caught.

The guards ignored us, assuming we were live-ins heading for our quarters, and the door was unlocked. This was easier than expected. Noah had worked out a whole script in case we were challenged, but he didn't need to use it.

These halls I had only seen a few times before, but Noah knew them better. He hadn't spent much time in this particular complex before he left, but the layout was similar to the last one his dad was in charge of.

It had all been put back to normal after the bombs. Row after row of doors led into identically furnished rooms. Two beds, two chairs, one desk, coat rack. Same look, same plan. You could almost hear the precision, the snap of the shoes laid in right angles on the floor. These guys meant business. Compared to the chaotic and overcrowded farmhouse where the Unseen were hiding, it was a wonder the rebels had survived at all against such a well-resourced and organised enemy.

We turned left into another corridor, then right, then left again at the next junction. Every hallway looked the same.

Aside from the faint smell of smoke, there was almost no sign of the bomb blast that had ripped through this section of the building, at least until we turned the fifth corner.

This corridor was black, the doors half melted. A light fitting swung precariously by one wire, bulbs cracked and blackened. The power was off in this part of the complex, which was good considering the bare wires hanging from the roof like streamers from a huge burned party popper. The floor was swept of debris, but repairs hadn't started yet. This whole section seemed empty, which was encouraging, although it also meant my family might not be here.

Reminders of the violence were burned into the floor like crime scene outlines. The bodies were gone, but the floor beneath, where they'd died, was untouched by flame. On several, red stains smeared across their middles made the floor look like a life-size rock painting.

Six outlines. Six people had died here, burned to death by Rachel's sabotage.

No one really wins in war.

"Where are you taking us?" A voice came up the corridor, scattered fragments of conversation. "Get your hands off her, you son of a—"

The male voice was cut short by a brutal crunch. A little girl began to cry. It was them!

The voice belonged to Josh, fighting against his captors, and the girl had to be Skye. I hadn't heard Mum, but she must be with them! I was a second away from running to them, the urge to see them overriding my survival instincts. But Noah grabbed my hand.

A moment later, they rounded the corner. There were no doors near us, not any that could open, and nowhere for us to hide. Noah dropped to his knees and pulled me with him.

I copied what he did. Head in one arm, he stroked the blackened outline of a body with his other hand. He pretended to cry, and I followed suit. No one would challenge two people mourning the loss of a loved one.

There was silence now, no more talking, just the shuffle of feet and the clink of handcuffs. I tried not to look so I wouldn't draw attention to myself, but I couldn't hold it any longer. I glanced up, trying to keep my eyes empty of any recognition the guards would notice. There were two guards at the front and two at the back, both wearing combat hoods and masks like the trainers, ready for battle. My stomach dropped. One of them was Nathan, a patch covering his left eye. He'd been hiding out here the whole time, probably in the restricted area. I should've looked away—he might recognise me—but I couldn't.

In the front of the line was Mum, her red hair hacked short like she'd been in a concentration camp. Her face was bruised and swollen, and she was thinner than she should have been after only a few weeks in captivity. Her eyes were dead, like she'd already checked out of existence. There was a cast on her wrist, and she held it close to her body with her other arm. What had they done to her?

I nearly cried when I saw Skye, but I swallowed to keep it in. Her hair had been hacked to pieces, too. It had been so long, so beautiful, but now it stuck out in chunks, like the back of a hedgehog. She wasn't bruised, thank goodness, at least not that I could see. Her eyes were red and watery, and tears quietly ran off her face onto her shirt. I wanted to run to her, hold her, and keep her safe from the world forever, and she was only an arm's length away. Noah's hand on my shoulder kept me grounded. If I tried anything now, we were all dead.

Last was Josh, and he was by far the worst. He had a nasty cut on his forehead, a bloodied mouth, his arm in a sling, and he walked with a limp. His shirt was soaked with blood running from his ear, and his eyes were swollen. They were eyes I'd looked into so many times before, but they were almost unrecognisable now, as they burned with hate. As he went past, he spat on me. "Sorry for your loss," he mocked. "Burn in hell."

The guard behind him smacked his neck with a baton, and he fell. He was right in front of me, on his knees. The convoy stopped, and the guard kicked him in the back to force him to stand. Josh looked at me for a moment, right into my eyes, and there was recognition. His eyes opened wide and his jaw dropped, and then he was back on his feet being forced down the corridor.

"They're being taken to the Apex," Noah whispered. "That's where the executions take place."

I panicked. "What do we do?" We couldn't have come this far to miss our opportunity by a few minutes.

An ominous bell rang from somewhere deep inside the complex.

"That's to call the Kindred to assemble," Noah explained. "Once they're in the Apex, the prisoners will be readied for the ceremony. The whole thing takes about half an hour. There are rites, last words, the whole bit. It's all very civilised, in a sick kind of way. I've seen two in my time with the Kindred, so I'll know when they're getting close to ... completion."

He began a coughing fit that lasted several seconds. The last one was raspy, from deep inside his chest. "I don't think we could take out the guards escorting them, not directly," he went on. "Those guys are high levels, Elder Brothers at least. I'm not exactly in top physical condition."

"Me neither," I said. "I'm still pretty shot from last night. The tree was about as much as I could handle."

"So our original plan is gone. We can't grab them and get out quietly. Not now. This has to be big." Noah stood, and I joined him.

"How big?"

"As big as we can get it without killing ourselves or your family."

"We definitely need Rachel."

Noah frowned. "She wasn't with them. They must be holding her to get more information, or maybe as a bargaining chip against the Unseen. The other possibility …"

He didn't need to finish his sentence; I knew what he meant. We could only hope she was still alive.

After a few tense minutes, we had a plan. I snapped at Noah a few times, but he knew it wasn't about him. This was the most stressed I'd been in my entire life. My shoulders felt like they were clamped in a desk vice, and my forehead ached from frowning. My whole body was twitching with fear and tension and adrenaline. Heroes always look so calm in the movies, but maybe they're just good at faking it.

Noah seemed a lot less panicked than I did. Maybe he was just faking it too, but it helped knowing that at least one of us had his head on straight. This whole plan banked on Rachel and an incredible long shot.

One way or another, in less than thirty minutes, we would know if it had worked.

FORTY

We picked our way through wrecked hallways to a
section of the west wing that remained untouched by the
bombs. A few groups of Kindred passed us on their way
towards the Apex, and we tried to look like we were going
there too. Each time we walked by them, my heart threw up
in my chest, sure we would be discovered. In spite of my
fear, we passed unchallenged. None of the security cameras
had lights on, either, so they were still offline after the blast.

These confinement rooms were similar to the basement
ones Rachel had destroyed. She knew my family were held
here, so she must have disarmed the bombs in this section
or not put them here in the first place. Our plan relied on
the first option.

Every door was wide open, except one.

She must be in there.

Two Elder Brothers guarded the door, one standing at
attention on each side. Security had relaxed but obviously
not as much as we'd hoped. They blocked our path. "What
do you want?"

I launched into our prepared routine, keeping my eyes lowered so they wouldn't recognise the distinctive colours. "The Elders sent us to question the prisoner."

The outspoken guard frowned. "Regarding?"

"What is your circle?" I asked him.

He shifted uncomfortably. "Elder Brother."

"This knowledge requires an Arch Elder circle," Noah cut in, "but I think you can be trusted. We suspect further explosives are still hidden inside the complex. Our time is limited. We've been sent by the Fathers."

The name-dropping had an immediate effect.

The guard's eyes widened, and he dropped his gaze. "I'm sorry, Brother. I didn't mean any disrespect. Your robes aren't normally worn by the Fathers' emissaries."

"It's all right," Noah replied benevolently, "we are keeping a low profile. With all the chaos of the last few days, the Fathers felt it best to keep things clandestine. We don't want to cause unnecessary panic."

"I understand fully, and thank you for your forgiveness." The guard was so deeply repentant it was almost funny. I felt like making him grovel and getting him to clean my shoes or something but didn't want to push our luck.

"I trust you will keep this information controlled for the time being?" I said, grinning under my mask.

"Of course," the guard replied.

"Excellent."

The other, silent guard unlocked the door. His eyes were suspicious, but he didn't want to get himself in unnecessary trouble by challenging us. Noah met his gaze, staring him down. The guard looked away at a tiny black bug crawling across the floor.

As the door swung open, I gagged. The room was dark, but I could smell what had happened here. Blood gave off a metallic tang, and there was the overwhelming stench of rotting meat. The rest of the air was filled with a cross between gym sweat and bodily fluids. The room didn't have a toilet, and Rachel obviously hadn't been allowed out.

My eyes slowly adjusted to the dark, and as they did, I only felt sicker. Rachel, or what was left of her, was still tied to the chair. She faced away from us, so I could see the cable ties had cut into her wrists and rubbed them raw. She was stained deep red from the blood that soaked her clothes. There was a pool of it on the floor, as well as small pieces of skin ripped out of her back by some kind of whip. It was still in the corner, little pieces of glass tied to leather straps around a handle. Just looking at it made my skin crawl.

Her head was slumped forward, and the only indication she was still alive was her slow, shallow breathing. The IV was still in her arm, pumping some sort of drug into her system. The security camera in here looked offline too. I stepped towards her, my feet sticking to the blood on the floor. Noah came around the other side.

"Rachel?" I whispered.

No response.

"Rachel?" This time I prodded her gently on her shoulder, one of the only uninjured parts of her I could see.

She snapped her head up and looked at me, her right arm grabbing mine, having somehow worked itself free from the restraints. She dug her nails into my skin, and I tried not to scream, not just from the pain but from her appearance.

She was unrecognisable. Her face was swollen and raw, different shades of purple, blue, brown, and black. Her right eye couldn't even open. There wasn't a patch of intact skin visible anywhere. She snarled at me, an awful, primal growl, like a dog tormented by its master. She was barely human, that had been beaten out of her by Dominic and the others. She was pure instinct and rage.

"Rachel, it's me, Ari, and Noah's here too." I used my free arm to remove my mask, and her features softened. "We're here to get you out."

"Real?" she slurred, with so much hope I nearly cried.

"Yes, yes. We're real. I'm sorry. I'm so, so sorry."

"Drug." She looked at the drip in her arm.

"Are you sure?" Noah asked. "The bag says morphine. It dulls our abilities, but it's the only thing keeping your pain at bay right now."

She nodded. "Drug."

I reached over and turned the wheel so the dripping stopped.

Noah turned to me. "There'll be a lag period where it doesn't hurt. I have no idea how long it'll last. After that ..."

Shock was a big deal; they'd told us that in the first aid class I did at school. If the injuries didn't kill her, the pain could. I took out my knife and cut her other hand free, then her legs. Noah gently pulled out the huge needle. I tried not to watch.

We helped her out of the chair. She was unsteady on her feet, staggering across the room to the shower in the corner. We had to wash her down; we wouldn't be able to stay unnoticed if she was leaving bloodied footprints on the floor, not to mention the smell. Noah helped her in, and we both undressed her and washed her quickly. There was no time for modesty right now. She grimaced when the water hit her back. Aside from the gouges in her back and a cut on her head, she didn't have any other open wounds. That was something.

There was a small locked cupboard in the opposite corner, and Noah popped it open with the leg of the chair Rachel had been tied to. There were a few sets of robes and masks inside, and a couple of very nasty devices that must have formed part of Dominic's toolbox. I would make him pay if I ever saw him again.

We dressed Rachel in the robes, and she winced as the fabric scraped down her wounds. How long would these painkillers last? The mask we gave her was extra large and helped hide her face. If I looked carefully, I could see the bruising around her eyes, but if she kept her head down, we would be able to move unnoticed.

Noah checked his watch. "Twenty minutes."

We had to move.

Rachel was in worse condition than we expected. She could barely walk, let alone fight, and the guards at the door were going to be a problem. We couldn't pretend we were moving her—the silent one was already suspicious. I stared at the instruments of torture arranged neatly on hooks in the cupboard. There were two huge batons with handles, like baseball bats but shorter. They would do.

Noah and I grabbed one each and stood on either side of the door. Both guards were visible through the window, dutifully staring off down the hallway. With a tied-up prisoner, their job was to keep people out, not in, and as far as they knew, Rachel was still restrained. They didn't expect the door to swing quietly open.

There was a synchronised crunch as Noah and I each smacked one in the back of the head. Noah took the gullible one, and he went down straight away, but I didn't hit the suspicious guard hard enough. He staggered for a moment and turned to face us. He tried to flare but was too dizzy to focus. I panicked and brought the bat straight down on his face. His cheek bones cracked, and he hit the ground. It felt good. And that scared me.

As we walked, Noah explained our plan to Rachel in hushed whispers. She'd already guessed and was leading us exactly where we needed to be. A few corridors over, she pointed to a small air vent in the ceiling. Noah gave me a boost, and I popped it open. I felt around inside, and my hand made contact with our hidden treasure.

It was small, metal, and round, with wires coming off it in all directions. There was no big timer to count down—that stuff only happens in movies—but it was definitely what we were after. Rachel had placed bombs all over the complex at first but, like I thought, had disarmed the ones in this wing when my family were moved here.

We only needed one; we didn't want to bring the whole complex down on our heads. Thank goodness the Kindred hadn't found it yet.

Rachel grabbed the bomb from my hand. "How long?" she croaked.

"Ten minutes," Noah said.

This was it.

FORTY-ONE

I perched on a third-storey stairwell above the south wing entrance, blending in with the rest of the crowd gathered on different levels around the Apex. Noah had taken a lower position on the opposite side, and Rachel was on the ground floor with the bomb.

From here, I could see Mum, Josh, and Skye standing in a line on a raised platform in the centre of the room, each arm held by some huge Elder. Josh had stopped struggling now, Skye was still crying, and Mum just looked absent; she was there, but nobody was inside.

The same three figures who had presided over my induction ceremony were running this show. The long-winded one who knew a lot about history was rambling through some sort of rite. The woman was there, too—the Mother. She stood like a pope overseeing the proceedings. Hackman stood behind her, with his usual self-satisfied grin. I wanted to punch it right off his stupid face.

The entire Apex was full from top to bottom. There was almost no floor space, except a small circle around the platform. Every staircase, every landing was filled with Kindred members. There had to be nearly a thousand of them here, far more than I thought there would be. We didn't stand a chance. I checked my thinking, trying to stay positive, but it was hard, considering the odds.

Rachel would set the bomb off on a timer on the ground floor, away from my family. She assured me it was smaller than the other one, and my family would be untouched by the blast. In the ensuing chaos, Noah would grab my family while I covered him from up here. I still didn't know how I was going to do that. There were so many people here, no one would be able to tune. As soon as we could, we would meet up in the training ground and get out through the tunnel to the ledge. I didn't have a watch, so the only signal would be the bomb itself.

They were getting to the end of the ceremony. We had to move soon.

The Mother stepped forward. She spoke, and her words spread like tendrils through the room. "It is a sacred bond, a hallowed oath one takes when one becomes bonded to the Kindred. This oath is thicker than blood, truer than love, and more real than death."

Skye started to sob when she heard that last part. It was all I could do not to join her.

"Yet, still some choose to betray us, all of us, by joining with the very enemies we are sworn to destroy. For thousands of years, the Kindred have survived in our many forms, moving the world towards the Final Day. So many have lived, so many have fought, so many have died for this most noble cause. These traitors spit on their graves. They spit on the name of the Kindred. They spit on you."

She grabbed Mum's hair and dragged her to the front of the podium.

"So, let the deaths of these be our vengeance. Let this sacrifice be swift justice to the traitor, and let their blood be a warning to all who would dare betray their brothers and sisters of the Kindred. Let it be so!"

"Let it be so!" the crowd answered with one voice.

Come on, Rachel. Come on.

The Mother continued, "It has been more than a century since the Sanctuary was opened for an execution, but this is a special case. These prisoners will receive a unique honour indeed."

Noah looked up at me from the floor and shook his head. He didn't know what was happening any more than I did.

Hackman stepped forward. "Open the Sanctuary!"

The entire crowd dropped to their knees except the Mother and the guards holding my family and Josh. I followed suit so as not to stand out. Far below me, through the grill in the landing, the huge carved doors to the south wing swung silently open. I had never seen them open before. From his position across the Apex, Noah made eye contact again, shaking his head subtly to stop me from moving. The whole Apex stopped breathing, frozen with anticipation, reverence, and fear. A damp stench drifted from inside the Sanctuary, sucking the warmth out of the air. My stomach chilled.

A huge Shadow entered. The top of it nearly brushed the first-floor landing. The crowd had cleared a path to the platform, and it moved silently through the crowd, heading towards my family.

This Shadow was different from the others I had seen. It looked like the one that had perched on the ceiling of my bedroom, although several times that size. Its body was ghostly, almost transparent, but huge tendrils like intestines spread out from its body, twelve in all. I had seen a cow slaughtered once, and this Shadow looked like what was left at the end.

It walked on each tendril, and they shivered and pulsed and propelled it forward. At the end of each tendril was an open space, like a wound, about the size of a fist, so black inside it felt like they were rips in space, gateways to oblivion. Every few seconds, its body became solid for a moment, and I could have sworn a face emerged, pushing out from inside the crusted skin. It reached the platform and began to ascend. There were only four steps, and it didn't take long.

Skye screamed—it was the only sound in the room. The Shadow was going to feed, suck them dry until they were nothing but dead shells like the bodies in the clearing. I tried to tune, but the interference was overwhelming. A thousand people all staring at the same place—there was no chance I could use my abilities here.

The Shadow moved towards Skye first, drawn to her scream. I couldn't wait any longer. I stood and ran for the stairs, shoving my way through kneeling figures. There was no way I could make it in time, but I didn't care. Skye rose in the air, suspended by three tendrils. It had her. It began to feed. Skye stopped moving.

The floor lifted. The whole world twisted and skewed and rose to meet me. I tumbled over the side of the railing towards the ground floor, hitting two Kindred, who sprawled flat. They broke my fall, but the wind was knocked out of me. Feet running, robes everywhere, blood and fire and chaos and death. I couldn't stand, so I twisted my head towards the platform. Rachel's bomb had worked. The Shadow was no longer on the platform, but my family weren't there either.

I looked back, up to the third-storey gangway I'd fallen from. It was peeling away from the wall, sending Kindred tumbling over the edge to break their skulls open on the Apex floor. One hit the stairwell railing as he dropped, snapping his spine in half. He screamed for a moment then went still, folded backwards at a horrible angle. The mask slipped off his head and clattered to the floor. It was Frank. I looked away.

I was lucky to have hit the Kindred standing on the floor; they had accidentally saved me. Neither of them were moving.

Rocks broke loose from the ceiling and walls, dislodged by the stairs as they ripped from their footings. The whole Apex was weakened by the blast. It was falling apart. Several large cracks ran up the blackened wall where Rachel had set the bomb. I couldn't see her anywhere. Hopefully she was okay.

There was someone yelling, a voice over the screams. I tried to move myself and see them, but my right wrist was broken and wouldn't support my weight. My other arm seemed fine, and I used it to roll over. The screams came from one of the Kindred, held in the grip of the Shadow. He struggled, pled, screamed, and then his skin drained of life and colour, wasting away to the dull texture of a corpse. His lips peeled back into a permanent snarl, and his eyes sunk in their sockets. He screamed once more, but the noise was cut short as the Shadow took the last of his breath. The body fell to the floor, crumpling in a heap, and the Shadow grabbed another man unlucky enough to be nearby. It was angry and feeding indiscriminately, making its way through life after life until it found the traitor. I had to move before it reached me.

I pushed up with my good arm and staggered to my feet. The world shivered for a moment, then settled as my head adjusted to the height change. The door to the training ground was wide open, and I made a direct line for it, stepping over blood and bodies as best I could. The Shadow took another life behind me, and a woman screamed for help but I didn't dare look back. My hood slipped over my eyes, and I ripped it off; if I tripped, I wasn't sure I could get back up again, and no one seemed to be watching anything but their own skin. Camouflage was pointless now.

I was almost at the training ground doors when a crack ripped through the air. The stairs were tearing away from the wall right up the side of the Apex, like they'd been scraped away by an apple peeler. I paused for a second to watch, and that second saved my life. The stairs crashed down in front of the training ground doors a few steps ahead of me, pulling down rocks and debris that completely blocked the entrance. The east and west wing doors were locked, guarded from the inside to keep the Shadow out, although from what I knew of their ability to move, a little steel door was a pointless barricade.

A woman bashed on the west wing door, pleading to be let in. Of course. The doors weren't to keep the Shadow out—they were to keep its food from running. If it could satiate itself with the bodies in the Apex, it wouldn't go hunting for the ones who'd escaped. The woman was a sacrificial lamb. The Shadow moved to her, lifted her, and she stopped screaming.

There were only a few people left alive in the Apex, and I didn't want to be the last one standing. There was only one way I would make it out of here alive. The south wing. The Sanctuary. The doors were still wide open, and I ran straight for them, stumbling as my foot kicked a limp arm laying on the floor. It wasn't attached to a body.

The Shadow was preoccupied by a rather large man near the east wing entrance and didn't see me as I ducked inside.

The first thing I noticed was the size. I couldn't see far, as only a few steps in front of me were lit by the light leaking in from the Apex, but I could feel I was in a cavern far bigger than the training ground. The echoes from my footsteps took a long time to come back, reflected off a thousand different surfaces. The floor was flat and scuffed under my feet, kicking up dust that filled my nose. I snuffled quietly and tried not to sneeze.

I stopped for a moment, and my eyes adjusted to the light. Columns reached from the floor to a huge arcing roof above. There were at least ten columns running in two straight lines, framing a plinth at the far side of the cavern. The floor was patterned with drawings, huge murals. They were moments in the Kindred's history: a man with a wreath on his head playing a violin in front of a burning city; a warlord holding a gun as hundreds were buried in a mass grave; a gas chamber filled with figures who bore numbers on their arms. The darkest moments of human history were shown here, frozen in time and celebrated like a cathedral of death. In each picture was a Shadow, lurking in the corner or hiding behind a wall. During each of those moments they had been there, watching. Approving. The lead figures in each scene bore the same mark as on the Apex floor and the Kindred uniforms. The Kindred had played a part in each of these moments. They were so much more than a bunch of bad guys with powers. They orchestrated and celebrated the darkest things in this world.

I walked towards the plinth at the other end of the columns, and the murals became more and more recent. They were arranged in chronological order, from the past to the present. Slaves forced aboard a tall ship. A mushroom cloud above a burning city. Women and children slaughtered in a jungle village. Two towers burning high above a metropolitan skyline. Gunmen storming a concert hall. It was all horribly familiar.

The final drawing was of a city, burned out and empty, and every street was covered with the dead, every window and door filled with figures screaming and hiding. The sun was black, and the sky was filled with shadows. This, I didn't recognise. It hadn't happened. Not yet. This drawing was of the future; this was the final day, the end spoken about in the Agenda, the purging of the world in blood and darkness. It was coming.

My eyes adjusted even further to the gloom, and I could make out the edges of the cavern. Around the walls were huge carved figures, like the ones that guarded the entrance to the chapel. These were several storeys high, hewn from the rock itself, each facing towards the plinth. Each one held its hands over its eyes, not daring to look at whatever it was facing. There were thirteen in all. They felt like altars. Idols, maybe.

I neared the plinth, keeping as quiet as I could. Screams still echoed through the open door to the Apex, but they were fading and there were fewer voices crying out in protest. The Shadow was nearly done. I had to find a way out before it came back here.

The plinth was at least as tall as me, with the same letters from the chapel. The same message in the first language:

Through death we are consumed.

The last scream from the Apex stopped, and the air fell silent, drained of sound and life. The doors were a tiny square of light on the other side of the cave, and they framed a huge black figure. The Shadow was returning, and I was trapped.

FORTY-TWO

I ran to the side of the plinth. It was offset from the wall far enough for me to hide behind it. I ducked around it, sticking my head out a little to keep an eye on the Shadow's movements. It slid slowly to the middle of the room, seeming sluggish after its meal. It stopped for a moment and stretched out its tendrils wide. I had to move, but there was nowhere to go.

Black smoke poured from the eyes of the huge statues in the wall. More Shadows.

Twelve more, emerging from their idols, trickling onto the floor like sand through an hourglass. Each statue gave birth to a Shadow. Except for one: the thirteenth statue stayed dormant. Its Shadow was already in the middle of the room.

It lolled in the centre, waiting for its brethren, huge and fat like a swollen cancer. The twelve circled around it and reached out towards its tendrils. It began to pulse, to shift and rotate and change, and the other twelve tilted back in ecstasy. They were feeding from it. It was like a mother bird regurgitating meals for its children.

With thirteen Shadows here, I had nowhere to go. My best chance was to wait it out and hope they didn't see me. I moved right back behind the plinth, feeling the wall behind me so I wouldn't trip and give myself away. My wrist was throbbing now; it felt like it was going to explode at the slightest movement, and I held it close to my body so it wouldn't be bumped.

The wall disappeared under my hand, and I was reaching into space. A faint breeze came from behind me in the dark. An opening. There was an opening. I turned and groped blindly in the blackness, and no wall came up to stop me.

The tunnel was cramped, but it didn't take long to reach the other side. It opened out into forest, leaves, and sky. Stars flushed thick overhead, and lightning flickered over the mountains beyond. I was on the opposite side to the training ground. This was the tunnel the Shadows used to head out for their hunting sessions.

Maybe my family had made it out through our planned exit and were around here somewhere, although I wasn't sure how Rachel would have made it down the tree ladder in her condition. My best bet was to follow the creek around the base of the cliffs and pray it met up with the other one. There was trickling to my right, and I walked towards the sound. Dry leaves crunched underneath my feet like paper, but the night was eerily still, which was strange considering the chaos I had left. The earth forgets violence so fast.

I hit the creek and followed the bank as best I could, sticking to the shadows to stay hidden. Unfamiliar voices shouted in the distance. A search party, but it was coming from far away, most likely the west wing entrance. That was a good sign; they wouldn't look for anyone near the training ground, as they didn't know that entrance existed. And no one would dare come through the Sanctuary. With any luck, they'd keep searching in the wrong direction.

Everything felt so far away as I trudged along the bank. Aside from a few shouts that rippled across the mountain it was almost possible to forget where I was and why I was here. I didn't, not completely, but for a moment I imagined what it would be like to forget all of this. Forget what it felt like to be covered in someone else's blood, blood I myself had taken. Forget Skye being held up by the Shadow. Forget the dead look in my mother's eyes, the bodies tossed aside like empty bottles drained of life. Forget the way Elijah's neck was twisted in the hole I made. Forget Adam's eyes as we lay broken in the darkness of the café a lifetime ago.

I wanted to disappear, to be absorbed into the water and the trees and the sky. When I tuned, I could touch them for a moment, hear them, feel them. If I stayed there long enough, maybe it would feel like forever.

My mother's voice entered my mind, and a memory long forgotten chose now to rear its head.

I was twelve, and Mum was pouring herself another glass of red, tipping the bottle right up so the last little bits of amnesia dripped out.

"Why do I drink? Why do you think I drink?" she slurred.

"Because of Dad?"

"Yes. And the world."

"What's wrong with the world?"

"What's right with it?" She took me under her arm, wine-perfumed breath blowing over me like cigarette smoke. Even the fumes were enough to lighten my head. "Ari, everyone wants to forget. Everyone. You remember Mrs. Bantam? The lady I took you to see when Michael left?" She never called him *dad* any more. "You know why she's a counsellor? Her son died, that's why, and she helps others because it helps her forget. She pretends it's for some noble reason, but it makes her feel needed. It's a narcotic, my darling. Just like everyone else needs.

"You know how Caitlyn always chases the boys? It's 'cause when she was eight, her dad said she was ugly, her mum told me, and so she runs to boys to help her forget. Mr. Sandson, the police officer? He's a cop 'cause when he was in high school his sister was murdered right in front of his eyes in a home invasion, and so he punishes others to help him forget. Everyone tries to forget, my darling, and we all try to forget in our own way, the whole damn planet. Some people read, others watch movies, others take drugs, others get violent, others make money, and still more jump from relationship to relationship, meaningless physical moments that just for one moment help them take their eyes off how completely miserable and empty and pointless they really are. Me? I drink. To forget Michael, and me, and you, and Skye, and everyone. I love you, my darling, but you would be better off forgotten."

Then she stumbled to the living room and switched on a soap opera. I went to my room numb. My mother was devastatingly eloquent when she was drunk. I lay on my bed, staring at the ceiling, making patterns in the light from the lampshade and wondering if she was right. I determined several hours later that she wasn't, and that the world was okay, even if my little part of it wasn't exactly a dream come true. I would be strong, and I would remember for Skye and me and even Mum. Sometimes I felt more like the parent than the child, but I would remember.

Now, wandering through the bush with my wrist on fire, I had to wonder if she was right. Were we really all just running from reality, standing with a spray bottle, trying to douse the flames of our existence? That was why people joined the Kindred. It gave them a way to forget. Even with the evil and the Shadows and the pain and the death, they felt a part of something. I had, even amongst the chaos. I'd been given purpose.

Was it easier to forget? Maybe. But it wasn't right, and neither was Mum all those years ago. No, there was good in the world. I had seen it. I saw it in Skye, and in Josh, and in Rachel, and in Noah. I saw a tiny little bit even in myself. I had to hold on to that. I had to keep that scrap of hope alive. I strengthened my resolve, steadied my step, and scanned the river ahead for signs of the people I loved. I wouldn't forget. I couldn't. At the end of everything, hope remains.

Around a turn in the river, there they were. My family. My reason for remembering. Josh, who had now become a kind of family, confusing as our relationship was, sat cross-legged on the ground, leaning against a stump. Skye huddled on his lap to keep warm, clearly shaken but alive. Mum stood next to them, staring blankly into space as was her new default. Noah stood, scanning the trees like a guardian angel. Rachel sat on a log next to him, hugging herself to drown out the pain that had probably begun to creep around the edges of the morphine.

Noah and Rachel were whispering to each other but stopped when they saw me. So did Josh, and Skye, and Mum, all at once. They called out and they cried and they ran towards me and I was covered in hugs and tears and joy for a moment.

Just for a moment.

Mum stopped. Breathed smoke from her nostrils. Fell.

Her eyes glazed over, and she whispered my name.

She was gone, and Skye was crying and Josh was running at the man who had taken her life.

The man whose tiny and misplaced smile had irritated me for so very long had been hiding in the undergrowth, watching, waiting for an opportunity. Noah froze as he saw his father for the first time in a month. Josh reached Hackman, hands out, but Hackman sidestepped and grabbed him by the neck, holding a knife to his throat.

A second before everything had been fine, but now Josh was a hostage and Mum was dead. I'd thought the night was over, but it wasn't finished yet.

Tonight, Mum wouldn't be the last to die.

FORTY-THREE

"Everyone stop," Hackman said.

We already had. Everyone was frozen except Skye, who had run to Mum and was holding her tightly. I wanted to join her, to fall apart and scream and cry and rip open the earth and hide inside it, but there would be time for that later. Right now, I had to keep Josh alive.

The wind picked up again.

Hackman's knife was pressed into Josh's throat, not enough to draw blood, but if any of us tried to take Hackman out, Josh would be dead in seconds. I once heard a story of an old shearer who tripped into some barbed wire and pierced the big artery in his neck. It was a tiny puncture, but he was alone and died in a few minutes. If Hackman flicked his wrist, we would have no time to get Josh help before he bled out. There was no sound, save Skye's muffled sobbing.

"Dad, let him go."

"Noah, shut up. This doesn't concern you, and I'll kill you if I have to."

"You'd kill your own son?"

"You're a filthy traitor and a coward. You betrayed the Kindred and betrayed me. As far as I'm concerned, you died the night of the attack."

Hackman had dropped his smile. Finally. I'd always felt like his pleasant, patient demeanour was put on for effect, like someone wearing way too much makeup. There was something horribly fake about him, and now I saw who he really was. I couldn't believe I had ever listened to him. Worked with him. The man who'd just murdered my mother had put his arm around me when I cried. I wanted to take a knife and cut out the skin he had touched, sandpaper my shoulders down to bone to remove all microscopic traces of his contact.

"If any of you move," he continued, "I'll kill Josh here and now. If I get even a hint you're trying to flare he'll be dead in seconds."

It wouldn't be much good anyway. I never really nailed flaring, and Rachel was still too drugged to focus. Noah was the only one with enough ability to pull it off, and there was no way he would murder his own father, even after all the awful things he had done. I didn't want him to have to do that, either. There had to be another way.

"Noah, sit over there with the others," Hackman said.

Noah stood defiant, and Josh cried out as the blade sank a little into his throat.

"Sit. Down."

Consenting, Noah joined Rachel, Skye, and Mum's body on the forest floor.

"Now turn around. If any of you even move your heads as I leave, Josh is dead. Not you, Ari. You'll follow me."

"No way!" Noah and Josh protested in unison, although Josh's protest was cut short by another gasp as Hackman pressed his blade deeper.

Noah's eyes were blazing.

"Noah, it's all right," I said. "I'll be okay."

"Ari ..."

I walked towards him, wrapped my arms around his neck, and kissed him. It was long, and slow, and sent tingles running up and down the whole length of my body and out through my arms like I had been sleeping on them too long. I tried to stay focused on my mission, though, and whispered my plan into his ear as I pulled away.

As I turned to follow Hackman, the look on Josh's face nearly knocked me out. The kiss had hurt him far more than the knife had. There was no time to dwell on that, though. I could explain later.

There were too many thoughts in my head all fighting for attention, too many emotions trying to drill their way out of my chest. It was all I could do to put one foot in front of the other as Hackman walked slowly backwards, watching me as he dragged Josh with him. The night had been so clear and so full of promise just a few minutes ago, but now it held nothing but death. They say it's always darkest before the dawn, but we were nowhere near sunrise. There was still so much that could go wrong.

After the others had disappeared into the distance I tried to keep Hackman talking, to fill the silence as well as keep him distracted. "How did you find us?"

"That was simple." He wasn't even puffing as he dragged Josh along the leaf litter that was whipped up by the wind now tearing through the trees. He still had a cop's fitness after all. "I saw them go through the training ground doors and followed at a distance. I could have taken them all earlier, but the only way to keep my leverage over you was to leave them alive for now."

"So it's me you're after."

"Of course, Ari. It's always been you." There was a sweetness in his voice that made me gag.

"Why me?"

"I've told you, my dear. You're special. Your abilities, they are unique. Very few have had the kind of power that you have so early in their training."

"Noah said you knew about me before the hospital."

"I knew about you even before the accident. The accident was a way to confirm our suspicions."

My heart dropped. "You caused the accident."

His voice dripped with sarcasm. "Very clever. You finally got it. I first heard about you from an Unseen spy that had the misfortune of trying to smuggle information out of the complex. He took some convincing but eventually let slip that there was some stirring in their ranks about a girl they had noticed. A girl whose reverb was extraordinary."

"I've heard that word before. In the café."

"Reverb? It's the amount your ability echoes off the world around you. Someone with the latent ability to tune causes micro-shimmers in the objects they look at, touch, love ... Very few people are trained enough to recognise these shimmers, and they normally only appear during periods of intense emotion, but you cause the whole world around you to shimmer if someone knows what they're looking for. You cause it all the time. You have a kind of gravity."

That wasn't the first time I had heard that word used to describe me. "So the Unseen saw me, knew I was powerful, and you caused the accident because ..."

"We wanted to know for sure. You survived, and you shouldn't have. You should have died that day, but you didn't. That café barricade should have killed you on impact, but your natural reverb slowed it down. As it flew towards you, your subconscious mind deflected some of the energy."

"So if I didn't have this ability, I'd be dead?"

"Yes. Oh, don't give me that face. It may seem a cruel way to discover if someone has abilities, but it's remarkably effective. More people have been discovered and recruited through accidents and tragedy than almost any other means. We don't always cause them, but when there's a miracle survival, someone who should have died but didn't ... That's as good an indication as any that they have a natural reverb."

All those people were dead because I had an ability the Kindred wanted to find. The shimmer around me had caused their death. Hackman was responsible, sure, but if I hadn't been there everyone would still be alive. They said I had gravity. No kidding. Everyone around me was sucked spiralling to their deaths just because I was alive.

"So what now?" I asked bitterly. "You know I'm not going to join you. You're not that stupid."

"I think you'll do whatever it takes to protect the people you love." He knew me well, and I hated him for it. I had to call his bluff. Maybe the only way to save Josh was to pretend I didn't care.

I sat down on a tree stump. "I won't join you. No matter what you do. Kill him if you want, I don't care."

Josh's eyes were hurt for a moment, then softened as he realised what I was trying to do. Hackman grinned, spun Josh around, held his hand against a tree, and brought the knife down hard. Josh screamed, a bloody stump where his right index finger had been.

I wanted to run at Hackman, to knock him down and bash his head against the ground until his skull snapped and his brain bled, and I wanted to watch him burn, and scream, and die a thousand times over for everything he had done to me and the people I loved. Instead, I stood, quietly and continued following as Josh clutched his hand, blood spilling down his front and onto the leaves below. He was back in the headlock, knife at his throat. My bluff had failed, and Josh had paid for it.

"Didn't think so," Hackman said dryly. "Don't play games again. There's only so many fingers and toes Josh has left before I have to get more creative."

There was one small victory though: deep within the scrub to my left, a tiny spark began to smoulder through layers of dead leaves and twigs. It had taken all my focus in the split second Hackman was distracted, but in these conditions, if the wind held up, it wouldn't be long before fire raced through the mountains. Hopefully, Noah would see the flames and pick up our trail. It was dangerous, and crazy, but it might work. There was a hint of smoke in the air, but Hackman didn't notice.

The chapel appeared in the distance through the trees, a monolith glowing in the moonlight against the deep black of the trunks and undergrowth.

"I *thought* we were coming here," I said.

Hackman stopped. "You've been here before?"

"We came through this afternoon. It's not the first time I've seen it, either. I call it the chapel."

He looked puzzled and then deeply satisfied. "The Chapel? It's never had a name before, but I like it. I'm surprised the Chapel let you find it. It's rare that anyone but an Elder is permitted to see this place."

He spoke about it as if it was alive.

"It's kind of hard to miss," I replied.

"Only if it wants to be found. What did it show you?"

"What do you mean?"

"I mean what did you see? If the Chapel let you find it, you must have seen something. A vision, a dream, a picture. What did it show you?"

I didn't want to tell him I saw my own dead body strung up on a pillar. I didn't want to mention the first time, either—the melting body reaching out for me. "I didn't see anything. Just a few bodies and some creepy writing."

Josh gave me a look. He always knew when I was lying. He had the sense to stay quiet, though, or was busy trying to manage the pain in his hand.

"Don't want to tell me?" Hackman said. "Never mind. What the Chapel chooses to show us is a matter between it and the individual it speaks to."

"So why are we going there?" I was fishing, trying to get some advance warning, to work out if I could get an advantage in the next few minutes before the fire burned out of control. Hopefully Noah was heading our way. We were upwind of it right now, so Hackman still had no idea what I had done. He didn't answer.

We reached the Chapel only a few moments later. It was bigger than I remembered, but that wasn't possible. Was it? Hackman had acted like it was alive. It wasn't just an ordinary building, I knew that much.

Nothing had changed inside, although it was definitely larger. Six bodies, dirt floor, creepy inscription, but a lot more free space around them, like someone had done an upgrade.

"What now?" I asked.

"We wait."

We sat in silence for several minutes, Josh breathing heavily to get his pain under control. Hopefully he wouldn't pass out. We would need to run pretty soon if my plan worked.

I broke the silence. "So, what did the Chapel show *you*?"

"Many years ago, I was brought here, upon my initiation into Elder. All new Elders come here to reveal their destiny, and I saw mine. It was my responsibility, my purpose, to discover the child who would hasten the Final Day. She is spoken about in the Agenda, the catalyst for the Great Darkness and everything that comes before. She carries within her the Seed of the Night. Do you know what she is called in the prophecies? The Girl with Dual Sight."

It felt like the floor had opened up. "You think it's me."

"As soon as I saw your eyes in the hospital—those beautiful, two-toned eyes—I knew. You are the child. You will hasten the Final Day. The Arch Elders sought the wisdom of the Chapel, and they too discerned my revelation. They saw it was my destiny to be assigned to you. To train you. To prepare you for the days ahead. To love you as I would love my own daughter."

His words were like a slug crawling down my throat, and I wanted to vomit them out and stamp all over what he'd said. The look in his eyes was worse.

"Your mother's death was a necessary part of the plan. It was spoken about in the prophecies. I am truly, deeply sorry that she had to die, but there was no other way."

"And Josh? What about him? Anything in there about cutting off his finger?" I spoke with as much venom as I could, and the poison spitting out of my mouth was practically visible.

"No, he is not spoken about. But I'm willing to do anything to fulfil my destiny."

"Shut up about destiny! I'm not going to be some part of your Final Grand Plan or your Day of Darkness or whatever the hell you call it! You are never going to change me! I am never going to join you! So take all your prophecies, all your destinies, and shove them into whatever dark cavities you have, because I'm going to kill you, and I'm going to do it soon, and I'm going to enjoy it!"

He stopped, thought, and smiled. "You can feel it, can't you? The Seed. I can sense it; it's been planted deep inside you. The darkness within. It's growing."

I said nothing, but he knew.

"We don't get to choose our destinies, my dear Ari. They choose us."

I closed my eyes, and opened them in a street covered with the dead.

FORTY-FOUR

It was quiet save for the distant echo of thunder and the click of my feet sticking to the blood that soaked the road. I touched my hand to my face to see if I could; I heard somewhere that you can't do that in a dream. But my hand touched my face, and it came away red. I looked down. My whole body was covered in blood. Somehow, I knew none of it was my own.

The city rose around me like a graveyard, and bodies littered the street. Cars, trucks, buses were burned out husks. Whatever had happened here, it happened fast. The buildings smoked, but they had stopped burning a long time ago. Ash fell like snow, drifting in the wind. This was the image carved in the floor, the Final Day, except I was standing in it. Living it.

The sky was dark. I had been under this sky before, in the cafe, after the accident. There was a field of blood, and a Shadow creature, and a face … A face that swallowed the world.

A voice groaned behind me. I turned. Noah lay under a slab of concrete, pinned by a piece of twisted metal that speared through his side.

I ran towards him and knelt in the pool of sticky blood surrounding his body. His eyes widened. "Get away from me!"

"Noah, it's me."

"Get away! Go! You've done enough!" He tried to move but couldn't pull himself off the metal spike. He cried out in pain.

"Noah, what happened? Please tell me what happened!"

He stopped, eyes dark.

"What happened here?" I pleaded again.

"You," he said. "You did."

I felt my body fade and looked down. My legs had turned to shadows; my arms dissolved into black tendrils. I knew what I was. I began to scream and closed my eyes to block out what I had become.

I was in the Chapel sitting against the wall. Limbs made of flesh and blood again. Hackman held his blade to Josh's neck and watched me, expectant. "What did the Chapel show you?"

I felt sick but said nothing.

"You saw your destiny, didn't you? You saw the Final Day."

I didn't meet his gaze.

"No matter. You have seen what you needed to. There is no way to stop the oncoming night." Falling silent, he sniffed the air. He looked at me, eyes widening. Then he grinned. "Clever girl. Started a fire, did we? My son is probably on his way now to come and find you."

He dropped Josh but kept hold of the knife and walked to the door to try and spot the flames. I ran to Josh and put my arms around him. He was cold but sweating. That was a bad sign.

"The wind has changed," Hackman said. "The fire is coming this way. It's time to move. Step away from your friend, Ari. He has served his purpose and will be too slow to run. It is better to bleed to death than burn."

He stepped towards Josh, knife extended. I stood in his way. He wouldn't hurt me, not badly; I was too important to his plans.

"You won't touch him!" I screamed. "You'll have to go through me!"

He dove forward and tried to push me out of the way. I kicked him hard in the stomach, and he aimed the knife away from me as he fell. I was right. He wasn't going to kill me.

He grabbed me around the waist and pulled me down, his knife dropping end-first into the dirt.

I scratched at his eyes, and he yelled, but he flipped me onto my back and sat on my chest, holding my arms against the dirt floor. He grinned, blood pouring from his left eye, which was now half closed from my attack. I kicked hard, trying to knee him in the back. One shot connected, and he arched forward, falling on top of me. I bit his shoulder, and his blood filled my mouth. He rolled off me, picking up the knife and lunging at Josh instead.

In that moment, the world slowed down. I called for him to stop, for Josh to run, but Josh was in too much shock to hear me. I was about to lose him forever, and my stomach turned and my mind broke and a tiny point of light formed between Josh and Hackman, right in front of his face. It grew, and glowed, and points of fire sparked from the ball of flame that was building, and then for the first time in a long time, I really let go.

All the terror, all the fear, all the rage that had been building inside me was channelled into the flare. It felt like an hour but was only a second. Hackman saw it but had no time to run.

The flare expanded and hit his face. His flesh burned, and his eyes blistered over as his hair caught fire and his nose melted closed. His mouth opened, and he screamed as the knife hit the floor instead of Josh, and Hackman, writhing, joined it on the floor soon after.

The flare was still building, and it was going to hit Josh. I had to get it under control before I killed us both. But I couldn't stop it expanding.

Josh yelled at me to stop, but I couldn't. He backed into the corner of the Chapel, as far away from the flames as possible. Still, it grew.

The row of corpses caught fire as the flare grew and grew, driven by my furious heart that was pouring fuel on an already enormous flame. I was out of control. I screamed.

Noah's hands wrapped around my waist, his cheek against my neck. He whispered that I was safe, that everything was going to be all right. It didn't work, so I thought of Skye, and how she would need me now that Mum was dead, and of the life we were going to have to make together, and I cried for Mum and for Rachel and Elijah and Adam and the nameless body in the bath, and the anger and fear subsided and, with it, the flare, shrinking slowly and quietly until there was nothing left but a tiny glow, like a firefly dancing in the night. Then the firefly went too, and everything was still, save the smouldering corpses and the crack of the flames outside.

Josh stared at me like he had at Hackman. He was scared of me.

I looked away and watched Noah instead. He'd seen the smoke as we had planned and followed it here. There was no time to be thankful, though.

"The wind is too strong," he said. "We're going to be caught if we don't move now. We need to run."

I nodded. Noah took Josh's arm, and I held the other to carry him out, letting my broken wrist hang limply.

Outside, the world was chaos. Birds and insects and snakes and bats filled the ground and the air, fleeing the fire raging toward us. Smoke burned my throat, and I gagged. There was no way we could outrun this. We had to get to water. The heat was almost unbearable, and if we didn't get out now, it was over.

We staggered through the bush. The world was bright as day from the flames, so it wasn't hard to find our way, although the smoke stung my eyes and made everything blurry. There was a shout behind me, and I turned. Hackman was standing upright at the door of the Chapel, face burned, eyes empty, but somehow still able to talk.

"Run, Ari! It was my destiny to show you the way, to show you what you're meant to be. No matter what you do, no matter how you feel, you *will* be the Bringer, you will hasten the Final Day, and you will birth the Seed of Night you carry within you!"

Noah had stopped too. "Dad! Come with us! If you stay there, you'll die." He wasn't a hero anymore. In this moment, he was a little boy who wanted his daddy to be all right. "Please!"

Hackman stopped yelling and looked straight at his son through melted eyes. "Son. Stay with her. Keep her safe. She is bigger than the Unseen. Bigger than the Kindred, too. It is your destiny to be with her at the End of Days."

He closed his eyes and smiled, a big, toothy, open-mouthed smile that I'd never seen on him before. He stretched out his arms in surrender and disappeared into the flames.

This, I had seen before. The melting figure in the Chapel. It was him.

The first of my visions had come true.

EPILOGUE

Everything after that is a blur. We ran to the creek where Rachel and Skye were waiting for us and hid in the creek while the fire raged. They'd had to leave Mum where she was and hope the fire didn't burn her body. After the fire burned out, we were found by some Unseen operatives who were sent in to clean up the remainder of the Kindred while they were in chaos. Hud came through for us after all.

The bush was still smouldering around us as they led us to a main road, where we were treated in a converted semi-trailer, the Unseen's moving base of operations. Josh and Rachel were unconscious for almost a full day, but awoke in body, if not in spirit. Skye was physically all right, but not exactly all there, either. We all went through a lot.

The Unseen have told me the Kindred in our town were all but wiped out. So many people died that it was difficult for anyone to cover it up. Turned out nearly a tenth of the town were part of the Kindred, and the powers that be had to invent some story about a suicide cult to keep the truth quiet. Ettney will never be the same after that. Neither will I.

I keep dreaming that my body has turned to shadow and my soul to darkness, and when I close my eyes I see Hackman's face, so certain of his victory, even in death.

Living in the city is taking some adjusting. The people, the crowds, the smell … But with Mum and our house gone, the only place for us to live is Dad's apartment. It's nice enough. Stewie managed to escape the house fire, too. One of the neighbours found him down by the creek, trying to catch beetles, of course. He came with us, although apartment living isn't exactly his style.

Skye wakes at night a lot, screaming at the nightmare figures in her head. Dad thinks Mum died in our house when it burned down. He has no idea what really happened, and it's best things stay that way for now. The less he knows, the safer he'll be. Plus, it's already awkward enough between us; I can't imagine he'd know how to relate to me if he knew what I had been through. So, when Skye wakes up, I try to get there first, and if I don't, I tell him it's trauma from the fire. She's seeing a counsellor; the Unseen provided one who operates out of a local clinic as a cover. It's helped, I think, although sometimes I catch Skye staring at me with this look in her eyes, and I know she thinks all this is my fault. Maybe it is.

The headspace has helped, getting distance from the town and the people and the awful memories. Sometimes, I sneak out at night and just walk, wandering down cold streets, past empty shop windows with their blue security lights, watching the homeless try to sleep, and looking in the windows into another family's world, like I've always done. It's probably not safe being out there at night, but after the danger I've been through, I don't feel so scared any more. I'm not as frightened of dying.

To be honest, I don't feel much right now. I've been seeing the Unseen's counsellor too, and she says it's my way of coping with the new reality, that I'll come out of it eventually. In some ways, I hope I don't. I'm not really sure I want to feel again.

Sometimes, I get caught off guard, though. I'll be looking for this or that and realise it's gone, with the rest of my possessions and memories. Snuggy, my stuffed bear I got when I was four. A letter Caitlyn wrote me in year six about how we'd stay best friends for life. The necklace Josh bought me for my fifteenth. It all sort of hits me, and I break down for a moment and shudder, like a spanner thrown into a gearbox. But then I swallow hard and pull myself together and keep going. I have to.

It's worst when I go to tell Mum something. I'll come home from my new school and call out to her, wanting to debrief about my day, wanting to hear her voice, and after the word *mum* has finished echoing around the empty apartment, I remember that she's gone, and the echoes of her life are all that's left. For all her flaws, for all her problems, she was still my mother, and she still loved me. I loved her too. I wish I'd said that to her before she died.

I haven't found Adam's family yet. Hopefully one day I'll get a chance to see them.

Noah moved to the city as well. He's living in an Unseen safe house a few suburbs over, so we see each other heaps. He gets angry a lot, about really little things, but I think he's mostly angry about his dad. He talked about it once, when we were down at the docks. He hasn't decided what to feel yet, like he's sad and angry and empty and full all at once, and a lot of it is at himself. I held him for a while as he cried, but he hasn't talked about it since. I think he's a bit embarrassed about it.

Josh is here a lot, too. He and Caitlyn hop a train and come visit almost every weekend. Or they used to. Recently, Caitlyn's been here less frequently. I hope she's not going to forget about me. Every time Skye sees Josh, she goes gaga, like she's in love or something. I get a bit jealous at how much attention he gives her, which is ridiculous because I know he's just like a big brother trying to help her forget what she's been through, what they went through together. And, after all, it's my fault she went through it. But it's nice when it's just me and Josh, if a bit confusing. I still don't know how I feel, and after everything he did for me, everything he lost, I'm not sure if what I feel is affection or guilt. He still seems a bit scared of me, but he kissed me the other day, and I let him. I didn't tell Noah. I'm still not sure what to do with that.

I officially joined the Unseen, although I still don't really know what that means. They're far less centralised than the Kindred, so it's harder to communicate. There's meant to be a mission coming up in a few nights' time, and I haven't heard much about it. That makes me nervous. There are rumours the Kindred have increased their activity, that things are heating up right across the country, maybe even the world. Everyone I've talked to says something big is coming. I can feel it, too, lurking somewhere over the horizon.

Trust is hard. I'm on edge all the time, wondering if this person or that person is who they say they are, if this shop owner or girl at school or teacher or busker on the street is secretly part of the Kindred, just waiting for the chance to kill me. From what I've learned, some of them probably are.

 Suspicion might be a lonely way to live, but it might also keep me alive. I trusted far too easily once before, and it won't happen again, not even with the Unseen. On the bright side, we're under the radar at Dad's place for now. Apparently he bought it under a fake name so he could keep the asset hidden from the court in the impending divorce. I should be mad, but it's keeping us safe for now.

I haven't seen Rachel since that night in the mountains. She was moved to some secret Unseen facility, but I heard she had complications from injuries she got during the torture, internal bleeding and things like that. The mental trauma was worse, though, and the guy I talked to said it was going to be a long time before she would be able to live in any kind of normal way. It sounds selfish, but I'm almost glad I haven't seen her. I'm not sure I could cope with it, knowing everything she's been through is my fault. I want to forget that, but another part of me knows I have to remember.

The darkness still lives inside me, but the black mark hasn't changed. I feel like that's a good sign, like maybe I'm keeping it at bay. After Hackman's prophecy, I'm not sure what I'm meant to do. I want to be good. I want to be on the right side, and by joining the Unseen I feel like I am, like I've proved that all his words were just the ranting of a madman and not a prediction of things to come. But a little part of me is scared, terrified actually, that the darkness inside me will take over, that it will win and I'll become the destroyer the prophecy spoke of. That, more than anything else, keeps me up at night.

I'll do my best to prove him wrong. I'll do my best to fight. This war is far from over, and I'm doing everything I can to stay on the right side of the line. The more I see of this secret world, the harder that is, and I have to decide every day to not let it change me. I won't stop. I won't give up. I won't back down. After everything I've been through, all the awful things I've done, I'm going to claw my way back into redemption. I hope that's how it works, anyway.

At least now I'm fighting for the light.

FROM THE AUTHOR

Thank you for reading The Fire Unseen, the first book in the Unseen series. If you enjoyed this, it would mean so much to me if you would leave a review on Amazon or your favourite review site. Reviews are crucial for an author, and even a line or two can make a big difference!

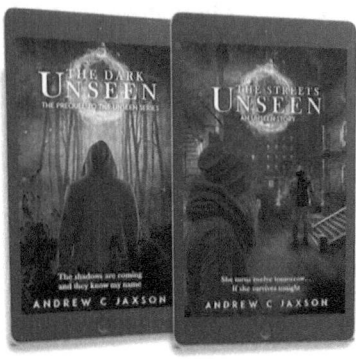

Get your free Unseen starter library today!

Did you know you can get two extra instalments in the Unseen series for free?

The Unseen starter library contains the prequel to the series, *The Dark Unseen*, as well as a short story that bridges the events of The Fire Unseen and the City Unseen. PLUS you'll get further free short stories and novellas in the series as they're released.

You can get the stories with zero cost or obligation by signing up to the Andrew C. Jaxson readers' club here: andrewjaxson.com/free

Ad-blockers may make the sign up form disappear, so be sure to switch it off if the sign up form doesn't show.

ALSO IN

THE DARK UNSEEN
THE PREQUEL TO THE UNSEEN SERIES

The Shadows are coming, and they know my name.

Hud and his friends are camping in the mountains to celebrate finally finishing school. Tonight, he can finally make his move on the girl he's been in love with for four long years. But something lurks in the darkness, something Hud has encountered before and can't quite remember. When tragedy strikes the night turns to chaos, and Hud makes a terrifying and world-shattering discovery. As the teens run for their lives, old memories resurface, and an impossible evil will reveal itself.

"Tense and unnerving. Incredibly eerie." - Sarah Campbell, bookhookednook
"Thanks for the nightmares!" - Shanna
"If you adore on the edge of your seat suspense, you will love this." - Linda
"I am a HUGE Dean Koontz fan and I'm always looking for someone who may do something similar... I'm a fan!" - Christine

Available FREE at andrewjaxson.com

THE CITY UNSEEN
BOOK TWO OF THE UNSEEN

Trust no one. Not even yourself.

There's something terrible coming to the city of Coleton. After six months in hiding, Ari's life might finally be settling down. That all changes when a little girl tries to kill her, and Ari discovers a new and dangerous enemy who has a disturbing effect on her thoughts. Ari's new friend Hud has a strange connection to the Shadows, and he's seen them swarming in the sky above Coleton. But what are the deadly monsters hiding in the old subway? And why are kids going missing from all across the city?

This explosive new instalment in the Unseen series takes the action to new heights, and terror to new depths as the team fights for survival against overwhelming odds. Trust is broken, lives lost, and the group finally learn the true nature of the Shadows.

Get in touch!
Web: andrewjaxson.com
Facebook: facebook.com/andrewcjaxson
Instagram: instagram.com/andrewcjaxson
Tumblr: andrewcjaxson.tumblr.com
Twitter: twitter.com/andrewcjaxson

About the Author

Andrew C. Jaxson writes stories that scare, intrigue and (hopefully) move his readers. He works across genres, although his novels may be best described as Young Adult Contemporary Fantasy Thrillers (phew!). He's worked a litany of jobs, from wedding DJ to teacher to youth worker and even a very brief and horrifying stint as a street salesman. He hates referring to himself in the third person, because it makes him sound pretentious.